Men of Promise

By Chris Fasolino

Author's note: All oceans, navies, islands, and battles in this book are imaginary, despite any seeming familiarity in names or particulars. Some of the people are real; but their first and last names have been changed. In other cases, the names are real, but the people have been changed. For further information, see the poetry of Robert Louis Stevenson, which is quoted on the next page. My thanks to "Bones" Barber, ship's physician, for assistance with this clarification.

First published by Dog Ear Publishing
4011 Vincennes Rd
Indianapolis, IN 46268
www.dogearpublishing.net

ISBN: 978-1-4575-3878-0

This book is printed on acid-free paper.

Printed in the United States of America

Night after night in my sorrow
The stars stood over the sea,
Till lo! I looked in the dusk
And a star had come down to me.

— from *Songs of Travel*

The sun is not a-bed, when I
At night upon my pillow lie
Still round the earth his way he takes
And morning after morning makes.

— from "The Sun's Travels"

*Dedicated to the memory of RLS,
who I hope would have approved of the voyage of the* Promise,
whether as reader or as captain.

Table of Contents

Prologue

It began with the music of a tin whistle. The music reached Admiral Oakes from far off, as if borne on the wind, and he heard it long before he saw the solitary figure standing atop the cliffs. He did not know the song, but it was full of yearning, with a lilting joy for counterpoint. He listened as he made his way up the grassy hillock on the landward side of the cliffs.

Then Oakes saw the figure, but he himself was not seen. The musician was looking out to sea. Oakes continued the climb, feeling as if he was wading through the long grass. As he approached the summit, he saw wildflowers blooming among the grass, violet and yellow and white. And then he saw the face of the cliffs themselves. They were grey and weather-beaten, like great whales beached upon the shore; and at their feet the waves crashed with a music of their own, scattering foam that would soar into the sky to become clouds and then return to the vast ocean.

Oakes called out: "West!" Then the flute was lowered and the figure turned.

The Admiral knew that Captain Bowman West had changed since last he saw him, though he would have been hard put to say how. For an instant, West stood there with the tin whistle poised in his hand, and Oakes looked at him. West wore civilian clothing: cotton slacks and a canvas jacket, with a blue wool scarf that was fluttering in the wind. His figure was slight, and there, perhaps, was one difference; he had once been lean, and now he was simply thin, with an almost frail appearance. His narrow face, with its high cheekbones, was somewhat drawn, making him look like a consumptive poet. The blue-grey eyes that stared from it were full of life. The face was also curiously unlined, despite the silver streaks in the jet-black hair.

The whole impression was somehow completed by the tin whistle that West held. It looked like a child's plaything, but it was a true musical instrument, and Oakes had just heard something of its possibilities.

"Admiral," said West. "It is good to see you again." He stepped forward, and the two men shook hands.

"And you, old friend," said Oakes. "How do you fare? I had heard you were recovering well, and was pleased indeed; for the last time I saw you, you were near death."

"This is a place of restoration, as you can see," said West, with a rather vague gesture. Oakes looked around again; the place looked rather bleak to his eyes, though its beauty was undeniable. But he had the feeling West knew every flower, even every blade of grass, by name.

"So you are well again?"

"I am, yes."

"Well, I am happy to hear it. Because you are my friend, of course; and also on behalf of the Admiralty."

"How so?" West's expression suddenly seemed guarded.

"I am here with news for you, Captain West." The new formality of Oakes' tone was offset by a smile. "A letter would have been more usual, of course, but I wanted to see you for myself, old friend."

"Raising the question, I suppose," West murmured, "as to how you found me here."

"Well, I went to your home first, naturally. Your housekeeper told me you were likely to be here."

"Yes, Martha knows my ways by now."

"In any event," Oakes went on, "I have an appointment to offer you, if you feel you are well enough for service again. How does Commodore Bowman West sound to you?"

West smiled. "You are a good friend, sir, and I thank you. I have thought about going back to sea. But I do not wish to go back to war."

"I do not understand. You said you were well."

West's smile grew more openly melancholic. "It is not so simple as that. I am indeed recovered. But that part of my life is over."

"Captain, no one in the Royal Navy refuses a promotion. You would be a Commodore with a flotilla of at least five ships, making sure the French are stymied in the Mediterranean. It is a reward for a hero— the hero who saved England from the New Spanish Armada, as the press has taken to calling it."

"And it is a reward I wish to forego. If I go to sea again, one ship will be enough. And it will not be to war. Tell me, Admiral. You are kind enough to think of me as a friend, as I think of you. You also call me a hero, though I have my doubts there. Tell me, then: will you give me a mission of exploration? For if I sail again, an explorer I shall be."

Oakes stared at him. "West, the Age of Exploration is over."

"Ah, so they have said; but how can it be, when there are still seas and ships and skies? The Age of Exploration has not ended, and never will."

"Perhaps you are right. Indeed, Captain James Cook may be proving your point for you, even now," Oakes admitted.

West nodded. "I have read of Captain Cook with great interest."

The Admiral continued: "But would you choose such a mission, and a single ship, over an appointment as Commodore? Forgive me, but this does not sound like the do-and-die Captain I have known."

"I imagine not."

"However much you may have changed, though, I know that you have ever been a shrewd man, tin whistle and all. I cannot believe you are simply asking me to give you a ship and send you to the edge of the map." Oakes paused. "If you really are asking for a mission of exploration, you have an idea."

"No, sir. I have three ideas," said West decisively. "Each one could bring as much benefit as the assignment as Commodore that you spoke of. And yes, I knew that some day we would meet again, and I would be able to present these thoughts to you; in the hope that you, as my friend and as a shrewd Admiral, would give them consideration."

"As usual when you want a favour of me, you neglect to mention that you saved my life when you were a Commander," said Oakes.

"Because I know it is not necessary," said West, and this time his smile was one of open camaraderie.

"True. Especially so, since the entire island of Britain is now in your debt. What my fellows at the Admiralty may think of this, I do not know. But name your proposals."

"First, the discovery of the Northwest Passage. I need not describe the benefits to trade. Other such expeditions have been sent out by the Royal Navy."

"And they have all failed."

"Perhaps I will be more fortunate. Second, an exploration of the great forests of South America. There are lands and resources there that may not be fully understood for centuries to come. At least let me make a start of it."

"And the third?"

"The Blue Isles, a small archipelago in the South China Sea. Our knowledge of them is limited because they are surrounded by dangerous coral reefs. However, the archipelago is said to be rich in pearls and jewels; if I can find a way through, a valuable trading relationship might be established."

Oakes was silent for a moment. "So this is what you want to do?" he said at last. "Take a ship, and adventure?"

"Yes."

"Very well. I know of a ship that needs a Captain; a frigate called the *H.M.S. Promise*, in the harbour of Bristol. I can write out the necessary documents in your home to make the commission official. As to your proposed expeditions, I cannot act entirely on my own authority. But if you will trust me, and accept this assignment, I will see to it that you will be given one of these missions of exploration."

West looked at him with what seemed to be an expression of surprise. Then he looked at the land and the sea about him, with uncertainty in his face. Then, at last, he raised his eyes up to the blue horizon, and smiled.

I.
The First Sunrise

$\mathcal{A}$ clouded dawn was breaking when Bowman West saw the *Promise* for the first time. The ship was still in the harbour of Bristol, and West was rowed out to it in a small ferryboat. There was fog upon the waters, and the sky was grey. Here and there, patches of yellow light could be seen, distant and faint.

West stood up in the boat as it approached the *Promise*, not for appearances sake, but because he wished to. He fingered the tin whistle at his belt and smiled to himself. He had been concerned about appearances for most of his life, he realized; but now, he wore a tin whistle beside his sword.

At anchor in the harbour, the *Promise* looked like a caged bird; a thing of beauty, undeniably, but much of the beauty in potential and not actuality. The three masts stood tall, but the white canvas sails were slack. They would be fairer far billowing in a favourable wind— or even an unfavourable one, for that matter. The sleek lines of the bow won West's admiration; but they were designed to move through the waves with fleet grace, and not to wait motionless in Bristol harbour.

Having thus studied the form of the frigate, West could begin to take in those details which pleased the eye but did nothing else. The hull was painted a dark blue, and the bow bore a striking figurehead painted in gold leaf. It was a maiden with flowing garments and wind-blown hair, holding a bouquet of flowers in her hand. The flowers were painted in silver leaf.

West had never seen such an emblem on a ship before. However, he immediately associated it with a literary reference. The Italian poet Andrea Calitri had written of how the Daughter of the Sun, a beautiful and ageless maiden, "bore the immortal amaranthine, with its blossoms of silver and blue." Amaranthine was a mythical flower said to live forever. West also recalled that in the poem, the Daughter of the Sun had golden hair (inevitably); and this too matched the figurehead, for the maiden was all of gold leaf.

The boat came alongside the frigate. West tipped the boatman, and soon he found himself on the deck of his new ship. He wondered what his officers would think of a captain who wore a tin whistle, and found his thoughts oddly echoed by the sound of the pipes welcoming him aboard.

He immediately noted that the decks were sparkling white, although the ship was in port. This was a fine reflection on the first lieutenant, who stood before him, along with the other officers. West looked at them with curiosity and realized that he did not care what they thought of the tin whistle. He felt, as he had in the boat, a kind of freedom in disregarding such matters. He had exerted himself for so long, not simply to *be* an honourable man, but to *appear* to be one; and, even more so, to appear courageous and Stoic in the traditions of the service. Honourable he knew himself to be; courageous he considered debatable, and Stoic simply untrue. As for his officers, they could make what they wished of him.

They were standing at attention, and West matched their formality, aside from the smile that played about his lips. He took the Admiral's letter from his pocket, unfolded it, and read it aloud.

"On behalf of Vice Admiral of the Blue Sir Gervaise Oakes, you, Captain Sir Bowman Balfour West, Knight of the Bath, are hereby requested and required to take command of the frigate H.M.S. *Promise . . .*"

It was read through, and Bowman West thereby assumed command of his new ship. Then he looked up and into the faces of the officers. He stepped forward, shook hands, and accepted introductions.

"Jonathon Kenmare, First Lieutenant."

The First Lieutenant was strikingly aged. His hair was not even grey, but a snowy white. His face was like a walnut; creased with wrinkles, but hard and brown. The eyes were blue, and they alone gave an impression of youth, for they were alive with energy and confidence.

"Pleased to make your acquaintance, Mr. Kenmare. And I compliment you on the condition of the ship."

"Thank you, sir, thank you." The words were simple enough, but Kenmare's voice was lyrical. His accent, and his name, were Irish, and West smiled. There were many Irishmen in the Royal Navy, and as a

Scotsman himself, West welcomed such a variety of backgrounds in the English institution.

The second lieutenant was introduced as Cato Rede (he pronounced the last name "reed"), and he was a marked contrast to his immediate superior. He was young— perhaps about thirty— and his voice and demeanour were clearly British. His hair was black, and his eyes were hazel. His handshake was firm and his presence polished, but he seemed, somehow, not so confident as Kenmare. There was a touch of uncertainty behind Mr. Rede's gentility, and West noted it for reference.

The third lieutenant was also English, but his accent was nonetheless quite different from Rede's. It revealed a lower-class background, probably rural. West was not sufficiently acquainted with the English counties and their variations of speech to be more precise than that; and the man had been at sea for so long that some of the regional peculiarities would have been lost in any case. West could certainly surmise, however, that the third lieutenant started his Naval career on the lower decks. This happened from time to time; West had even heard of captains who had begun before the mast. Since such promotion called for service above and beyond the call, West found the man's speech an indirect recommendation of his ability. His name was Wade Lang, and he looked to be in his early fifties; a big stocky man, with lanky brown hair and brown eyes that looked out from a weather-beaten face. There was a broad scar across his forehead.

The lowest-ranking officer was named Alexander Teal; he was a midshipman who had been named Acting-Lieutenant by West's predecessor. The promotion had been among the old captain's last acts before his retirement. Teal was tall and thin, and his youthful, unlined face was given counterpoint by a sharply hooked nose. At first impression, he seemed eager to please— too much so for West's taste. But the lad was young, and doubtless nervous at meeting his new captain; allowances had to be made.

These were the officers of the *Promise*. With the introductions complete, West decided to ask one of the many questions on his mind. "She's a beautiful ship," he said, truthfully but also by way of transition. "Tell me about the figurehead. What do the flowers signify?"

It was Rede who answered. "The flowers are amaranthine, sir," he said, "from an Italian poem—"

"Yes, by Calitri."

"Yes, sir. The ship was named the *H.M.S. Amaranthine* when she was first built. Then she was captured by the Dons and given the name *Esperanza*; and then, when she was retaken, she was given the name of *Promise* by Admiral Oakes— I am not sure why, sir."

"Fascinating." West felt it a good sign. Oakes had given him a ship to which he had a personal connection of some kind. It bode well for the granting of his request. Of course, he already had faith in his old friend, or he would not now be standing on the deck of a Navy frigate. But West had learned that faith and certainty were not the same as the absence of doubt.

Kenmare then offered some comment about the honour of serving under West, the man who had saved England from a Spanish invasion. "I had a fine crew behind me, and that was what mattered," West answered. "I trust I will again." He had made no speech upon assuming command, as some captains did, but he knew that those words would end up being passed along to everyone on board. "Have you served on the *Promise* long, Mr. Kenmare?"

"Ever since she was given her new name, sir. I did not know her in the *Amaranthine* days, but I have been her first lieutenant as long as she has been the *Promise*. Mr. Teal served here three years as midshipman. Mr. Rede and Mr. Lang are new to the ship."

"Well then, I trust we shall have ample opportunity to come to know each other, and the *Promise*. How goes the provisioning?"

At this, Kenmare and West launched into a lengthy discussion regarding the technicalities, and difficulties, of provisioning a ship for what was presumably a long voyage. West knew that the process would occupy most of their attention for the coming days; but he also took the time to invite the officers to supper in his cabin. Acceptance was, of course, immediate.

"Would you like to see your cabin, sir?" asked Kenmare.

"Yes, thank you."

The other lieutenants returned to their work, while Kenmare led West below to the cabin. The captain's cabin on the *Promise* was small but cheerful. It was painted a creamy yellow with soft blue trim, colours that West liked immediately; and that was important to him, as he was a man deeply aware of colour. It was furnished only with a cot, the previous captain having taken the rest of the furnishings with him upon his

CHRIS FASOLINO

retirement, but that did not matter. "My things will be arriving by boat from my inn," West said. "See that someone brings them down here."

"Aye, sir."

"And ask the steward to bring me a cup of coffee."

"Aye, sir."

"And Mr. Kenmare— I look forward to serving with you."

"And I with you, sir." Kenmare smiled warmly and left.

West stood alone in his cabin and looked out the window. He tried not to consider how he felt at being back on a Royal Navy ship; the emotions were too contradictory to make self-analysis either useful or pleasant But then the steward arrived with his coffee, and West was able to focus his attention on a his new visitor.

To his surprise, and fascination, the steward was Chinese. "Pilgrim Chang, sir," he introduced himself. "Captain's steward." He wore slacks and a shirt that buttoned up to the neck; both were made of black silk with a faint inlaid pattern, and they gave an impression simultaneously sober and exotic. The man's face was unlined but not young, and his black hair was tied back in a queue. He gave his unusual name without self-consciousness, but as he handed West the coffee and exchanged pleasantries he spoke the kind of broken English called pidgin. Regretting this impediment to conversation, West found himself staring out the window again; and as he did so, he noticed the reflection of Chang's movement as he picked up a book that had been laying on the cot. It was a somewhat surreptitious motion, not meant to be seen; but the reflection and West's keen eyes had spotted it.

"Is that book yours, Mr. Chang?"

"Aye, sir. Left it early. Sorry, sir."

West smiled. "You have no need to apologize, Mr. Chang, but I trust you will permit me the assumption that your English is as fluent as mine."

"Beg pardon, sir?"

"I took note of the book when I came in. Boethius' treatise on music theory, in the original Latin. A fine choice; his observations on music as an expression of the harmony that is possible between humanity and the rest of the Universe are undeniably profound. But I find it hard to believe that your Latin is better than your English."

West saw surprise and indecision in Chang's face, and he realized the man was wondering whether to speak the truth or make some excuse for the book. West added: "I do find it easy to believe that pidgin has its advantages, and you have my word that I will not reveal this matter. But permit me my scepticism."

At last, Chang smiled. "I accept your word, sir, and thank you. You are a perceptive man; Captain Mayhew never made that discovery. I trust you are not offended, sir."

"Not at all; I am sure there will be times I shall envy you. I am also sure that so learned a man will make an exceptional steward."

"The two do not necessarily follow, but if I may dispense with false modesty, then yes, sir, I am a fine steward."

West sipped his coffee. "Your coffee certainly speaks on your behalf. I trust that, when we are alone, you will do me the complement of speaking freely. I look forward to discussing Boethius with you; and I would very much like to hear about your homeland."

"Yes, sir. And thank you, sir." Chang smiled again, bowed formally, and left. West smiled, too, as he drank his coffee. He was delighted with his steward and looked forward to his further acquaintance. He was also admittedly pleased at having discovered the ruse. Most officers would have assumed the Latin book to have been left by the previous captain. But West had a great respect for the learning of the Chinese civilization; and he had keen eyes, and, by chance, a window.

As usual, West's sense of self-gratification was quickly replaced by another reaction: amusement with himself for having such a flight of vanity. Fortunately, both feelings were pleasant, and by the time he had finished his coffee and gone back on deck, his deeper and more conflicting emotions were forgotten in the pleasure of the moment.

The scene on the deck of the *Promise* added to that effect, for it was a scene of such busy order that West felt himself simply happy to be back on a ship. Casks of rum were being loaded on board and carried down below. They were needed. A sailor's rum ration was the best part of his day, and not without reason. Navy rum was a fine drink. West knew fine wines and port as well as any officer, but his favourite drink at sea remained the simple rum of the lower deck; although, with the privilege of command, he dispensed with the addition of water.

West spent a few minutes in conversation with Kenmare about the provisioning. His thoughts of rum had reminded him to order that an ample supply of lemons and limes be taken aboard. West was familiar

CHRIS FASOLINO

with the new medical theory that the juice of citrus fruit served to prevent scurvy, and he put some faith in it. Scurvy had often plagued the ships of explorers on long voyages, and he was eager to avoid that peril if he could. The citrus juice could be added to the men's rum rations, giving a fine flavour and keeping them healthy as well. "Aye, I've drunk rum with lime juice in the West Indies many a time," said Kenmare, as West explained the idea. "Never knew I was keeping myself in good condition that way." West smiled.

Then, Teal approached with the news that captain's belongings had arrived and were being taken to his cabin. West returned to the cabin to make sure everything was laid out properly. There was an eastern carpet to be put upon the floor, rich in its hues of turquoise and red. There was a desk and chair carved of rich, dark wood. There was a bookcase with books in several languages. There were private stores of food, spices, and liquor which were delivered to Chang. And, strangest of all to the eyes of the men, there was a bird in a cage.

It was not the presence of a bird that was strange, but rather, its dull appearance. Captains who kept pet birds chose parrots or similarly bright, colourful creatures. This bird was admittedly exotic, but it was neither bright nor colourful. Its plumage was white and brown and taupe, and its head was mostly white. It sat on a perch in its wire cage, looking out with intelligent yellow eyes at the sailors who carried it in and placed it, at West's instructions, on the desk.

"May I ask what kind of bird it is, sir?" asked Acting-Lieutenant Teal curiously.

"You may," said West. "It is a southern thrush, a species native to the New Hebrides, and his name is Autolycus."

"Yes, sir," said Teal, looking unenlightened. West fancied that Rede— or Chang— would be more likely to understand the Shakespearean reference in the name.

The rest of the day was uneventfully busy. Kenmare had arranged the provisioning of the ship with all the efficiency and professionalism that the gleaming white decks suggested, and he apparently had no difficulty in adding citrus fruit to the provisions. West believed they would soon be ready to sail; the process had, after all, been going on for some days before his arrival. Of course, the question of where they were to sail to remained unanswered, for both captain and crew.

Supper with the officers was pleasant, and it gave West further opportunity to study their personalities and peculiarities. Chang prepared an excellent meal of lamb with apple-and-herb butter and roasted potatoes; he handled English cooking as well as any innkeeper in Britain, and far better than some. A bottle of West's claret was opened, and finished, with the meal; afterwards, port was served, accompanied by good Stilton cheese. West found his own appetite to be excellent; and among his men, Kenmare, in particular, seemed to have an unreserved enjoyment for good food and wine.

Of all his officers, Kenmare was the man whom West was most quickly coming to like. The youthful eyes in the aged face had an almost poetic quality. He spoke of Captain Forrest Mayhew, whom West was replacing, with great respect, tinged with pity. Although Kenmare did not say so openly, West gathered that Mayhew had been declining; he was an old man and left the *Promise* to retire in Sussex. Kenmare's sensitivity to the plight of a good captain in such a decline was endearing—especially as it seemed unmarked by any self-consciousness regarding his own age. West had no idea how old Kenmare was, and he was not sure that Kenmare had any idea, either.

Rede fulfilled West's expectations as to his literary bent. When the topic of the pet bird came up, and West mentioned its name, Rede immediately smiled and said: "Though I am not naturally honest, I am sometimes so by chance."

"It sounds as if we will have keep an eye on our second lieutenant," laughed Kenmare.

"Merely quoting a previous Autolycus, sir," said Rede.

"That he is," West confirmed. "I named my bird after a clever thief from Shakespeare."

"If I may ask, sir," said Kenmare, "why do you keep that sort of bird? I know them to be hard to come by, but they are none so fair as others— if you'll forgive me, sir."

"Of course— you're quite right," said West. "But there is one thing about a southern thrush that is truly colourful, that is, if one could hear a colour. The bird's laughter."

"Laughter?"

"Yes. The sound a southern thrush makes is loud and trilling, and it sounds like laughter. There's even a fine old story attached to it."

"I don't suppose you would care to tell us the story, sir," said Rede hopefully.

"I would indeed care to." West smiled. Earlier that evening, he had brushed aside Rede's questions about his last battle with the Spanish. He knew his reticence had been taken for modesty when it was nothing of the kind; but he wanted to show that, while there were some things he would not speak about, neither was he going to be a silent, dour commanding officer. He knew himself to be a good storyteller, like many a Scotsman. And as he launched into the story of the southern thrush, he could see in the faces of his listeners that this was one talent he still had.

"The natives of the New Hebrides tell this story of the beginning of the world. They say that there was a time when all was dark. There were men, and there were animals, but there was no light. It was like a long night without end. And nothing seems quite right on a long night. So the fish could not swim, the men shivered in the cold, and the black sky was closed even to birds.

"But upon the horizon dwelt an old man who was the keeper of a great tree. And one day that tree bore a glistening golden blossom, and the old man knew that it was a flower that could light the world. So he asked the King of the Sky to raise up the flower so that the shadows would be dispelled. The King of the Sky gave his assent; but he said that first, he wanted everyone to know about it, and so he sent the old man away from the horizon and into the earth, to spread the word.

"But everything was still dark. The poor old man was stumbling around, trying to tell everyone about the light, but in the midst of that, it was still dark. And then, all of a sudden, he heard a wonderful sound. In a small tree near at hand, there was a southern thrush, laughing and laughing.

"And then it happened. A great golden light in the sky, streaming out from the horizon. The shadows fled away and the earth and the seas rose up to embrace what they saw. Because the flower from the great tree had been set on a path through the sky, and it was the sun, rising for the first time. The fish could swim, the men felt warmth, and the blue sky was open to the birds.

"And so they say that the day the southern thrush cries— the day it weeps instead of laughing— that's the day you give up hope. But not before. Never before!" West looked about him with a twinkle of lightning in his eyes. The officers smiled. West reached for the port.

II.
Sealed Orders

*I*t was two days before word arrived from Oakes. During those days, West felt an underlying anxiety that could not be entirely relieved by discussing provisioning with Kenmare or music philosophy with Chang. In the end, he resorted to his tin whistle. The officers and crew of the *Promise* saw for the first time what would become a familiar sight during their voyage: the Captain standing upon his quarterdeck playing the tin whistle. Among some, the sight caused private smiles and hidden laughter; among others, raised eyebrows. But there were times when the music was so plaintive that nearly everyone was moved by it. Forgetting that it was the Captain's tin whistle, they listened as they would to a musician in a tavern, absorbed in the music purely as music. The tin whistle looked like a child's plaything, and it was strange to see it played by the master and commander in his gold epaulettes. But there were moments when none of that mattered.

The arrival, at last, of the Admiral's letter was preceded by such a moment. West was playing an old Irish folk song, one that was both wistful and well-known. The sound of the whistle was sweet and sad, and most of the men on the ship had the words of the song echoing in their mind:

> *I wish I was in Carrighfergus*
> *Only for nights in Ballygrant*
> *I would swim over*
> *The deepest ocean*
> *Only for nights in Ballygrant.*
> *But the sea is wide . . .*

And here the music of the flute rose to a higher pitch, and, more importantly, a peak of yearning.

But the sea is wide
And I cannot swim over
Neither have I
The wings for to fly.

And then the music ceased. Teal was waiting near the edge of the quarterdeck, attempting to catch West's eye. Absorbed though West was, it chanced that he saw the young lieutenant. He lowered the tin whistle, hoping this was the news he had been awaiting.

"There's a packet of sealed orders for you from the Admiralty, sir," said Teal. "And a man from the East India Company, along with his secretary. He says they are to come aboard, sir."

West raised his eyebrows. The second sentence was a surprise. He put the tin whistle in his belt, and followed Teal.

There were two men who had climbed from the ferryboat to the deck of the *Promise*, all while West had been in his music. One of them, the secretary, handed West a sealed package with all the conventional words of honour. West took it and held it in his hand.

The other man stepped forward and said, "I am Francis Gilbraith, and I represent the East India Trading Company." He appeared to be in his early thirties, with light brown hair and a wisp of a moustache. He wore a black suit, a white shirt, and black cravat, all of excellent quality. He carried himself with a pompous air of self-distinction, and West immediately decided that he was just the sort of man who would irritate sailors. Nonetheless, West shook his hand and introduced himself. Something surprised him then, and he cast his eyes downward to try to get a closer look at Gilbraith's hands. However, the man immediately clasped them behind his back. West wondered if that was merely an affectation. The man's handshake had revealed something that did not fit. Someone like Gilbraith should have soft hands; but instead, they were mildly calloused. Unable to examine the hands further, West looked into the eyes of the East India Company representative, searching for any uncertainty that might suggest deception. But there was no uncertainty there— only the same supercilious quality that his bearing had suggested.

"This is my secretary and personal servant," Gilbraith went on, gesturing to the man next to him. "We will be traveling with you on your voyage to assess the trading possibilities of the islands you seek to find. It is all explained, so I understand, in your orders." He nodded to indicate the packet West held.

"Seek to find . . . well, I am looking forward to a long voyage and so I can hardly complain of repetition. Does your secretary and personal servant have a name?"

Gilbraith gave West a puzzled look; he was obviously surprised by the captain's air of courteous irony, and seemed to be trying to decide whether or not he should be insulted. Then he pressed on, apparently without having reached a conclusion. "His name is Nile Carrin," he said. Carrin was a much older man, probably in his early sixties. He had grey hair and light eyes, and his manner was subdued, almost studiously discrete. When West reached out to shake his hand, he seemed surprised, and then offered his hand with a nervous air. The fingers were slightly calloused, but the hands were not, all of which fit with his role as a secretary.

"Welcome aboard the *Promise*, gentlemen. I will now withdraw to my cabin to read these orders. Mr. Teal, please make Mr. Gilbraith and Mr. Carrin comfortable while they wait. Have my steward bring them some coffee, if they wish."

"Aye, sir. Where shall I put them, sir?"

"I am sure they will be content to wait here on deck." West was really not at all sure of that, but he did not wait for any response from Gilbraith.

Having retired to his cabin, West eagerly broke the seal and opened the package. There was a formal letter from Admiral Oakes, which he quickly scanned. It gave him orders for a voyage to the Blue Isles in the South China Sea, much as he had wished. There was, however, the addition of a representative from the East India Company, Francis Gilbraith, who would be accompanied by a secretary and who would help to evaluate the commercial possibilities of the venture, and of possible subsequent voyages to the archipelago. West was not pleased by this; he had hoped to have a free hand. While Gilbraith could in no way supersede West's authority, his report might have considerable repercussions on their return to England; the power of the East India Company could not be ignored. But it was still too early to make any assumptions. He did not even know what they would discover in the Blue Isles. Oakes had given him most of what he asked for; problems with Gilbraith could be dealt with as they arose.

There was a second document within the packet. This one was, not a formal set of orders, but rather a private note from Oakes to West, written quite informally. West read it eagerly.

My dear friend West,

As you can see, your Voyage to the Blue Isles is beginning. But even an Admiral has limitations. My colleagues were surprised by your decision to turn down a promotion to Commodore. I need not tell you that they look upon such lack of ambition as rather suspect. In any event, I did obtain for you the assignment to sail the Promise to the Blue Isles on a mission of Exploration. However, the addition of this fellow Gilbraith was insisted upon. It was put forth that, since the benefits of your mission would be largely in the way of trade, a representative of the East India Company would be necessary. However, I believe there may be more to the matter than that. I recommend, privately, that you keep an eye on Mr. Gilbraith, as I am not certain either of his motives in this or of the motives of those who recommended him for the mission.

I also wish to warn you that your Voyage of Exploration is not entirely open-ended. I myself told you that I feared the days of Exploration past; many of my colleagues on the Admiralty Board hold that view even more strongly. It is, of course, my hope that this voyage will prove restorative to you, and that upon your return, you will reconsider the offer of appointment to Commodore. However, if you are truly set upon being an Explorer, then as your Friend I must tell you that the Royal Navy may no longer be the place for you. It was for that reason that I gave you the Promise, of all ships. It is an aging ship— though a fine one— and I believe I could allow a private individual to buy it if he wished. Say, perhaps, a distinguished Captain who has earned prize money, and who may yet earn even greater riches exploring the South China Sea. I could then grant such a man a letter of marque as a Privateer, with the Freedoms that such a commission offers.

I am, of course, going against the good of the service in suggesting all this; but Friendship and Loyalty compel it of me. I am entering the Winter of my own life, and near to hauling down my flag; and I well know that there is more even than Duty that a man must think of. And if the truth be told, a certain resemblance in your character to that of another valiant friend— one who was lost in battle long ago— may give me added motive to look to your Health and

Happiness. Whatever you decide and wherever you sail, best wishes and God-speed.

Gervaise Oakes

West read and re-read the note. A privateer: that opened up new possibilities. Privateers did have great freedom; many were little more than pirates, but why not a privateer who served as an explorer, charting a course of his choosing to the edges of the map? He smiled, and fingered his tin whistle.

In time, he returned to the deck to find Gilbraith and Carrin waiting impatiently, which did not trouble him. "It seems you will be sailing with us," he said. "Mr. Teal will find quarters for you. I trust you have luggage coming over?"

"I am going to send Mr. Carrin back for it. Perhaps you can send some of your sailors to assist him."

"I will do so. I trust you have considered the fact that space is limited on a frigate; but if necessary, you can deal with that matter when your luggage has arrived. Mr. Teal, please see to Mr. Carrin's departure, and then find a cabin for Mr. Gilbraith."

"Aye, sir."

"And tell Mr. Kenmare I wish to see him in my cabin."

"Aye, sir."

It seemed only a moment before Kenmare was there. "Have you met our guests, Mr. Kenmare?" West asked.

"Aye, sir," said Kenmare with a look of distaste.

"I have Teal attending to their needs, but I am going to ask you to keep those needs in line. The secretary, Carrin, is returning with their luggage. Do not go out of your way to insult these people, but discard whatever you feel is unnecessary. Also, Gilbraith is going to complain about his quarters." West was certain that was inevitable, regardless whether the man was genuine or not. If he was genuine, he would not be satisfied with any quarters that could be provided aboard a frigate; if not, he would know that such dissatisfaction was an essential part of the role he was playing. "Assure him that they are the best we can offer. If he persists, or if he is unreasonable in any other way, remain firm and direct him to my authority if necessary. I will, of course, support you."

⚓ CHRIS FASOLINO

Kenmare smiled. "I am sure that is kind of you, sir, but I can handle Mr. Gilbraith."

West smiled back. "Well, now, on to more exciting matters. We have a long voyage ahead of us, Mr. Kenmare. As a matter of fact, we are going to go where few of our countrymen have gone before. The *Promise* is now a ship of exploration." As he spoke, he thought of Oakes' words about privateering. And he hoped they would find treasures enough on the voyage to let him purchase that freedom.

West went on to describe the mission to Kenmare, who seemed as excited by it as his captain was. "Inform the other lieutenants, as you have the opportunity," said West. "I will address the crew once we are at sea."

"Aye, sir."

"When can we be ready to sail?"

"Within a few hours, sir. And the wind is fair for the Atlantic."

"Then let me know as soon as all is ready; and we shall make good use of the fair wind." He paused. "And send my steward to me, when you have a moment."

"Aye, sir."

When Pilgrim Chang arrived, West was pouring over a map on his desk. The map was an old one, and the parchment was browning; but it showed the South China Sea in a joyful splash of turquoise, and the Blue Isles marked in deep cobalt. It was unusual to see land marked in blue, but West supposed it fit with their name.

Of course, in studying a chart of the South China Sea, West was looking far ahead; but there would be time enough to chart his course south through the Atlantic, around the Cape of Good Hope, and through the Indian Ocean. Now, his eyes were on the prize.

"Thank you for coming, Mr. Chang."

"Aye, sir."

"Keep this to yourself for now, but we are sailing to the Blue Isles, in the South China Sea, on a voyage of exploration. I was wondering if you knew anything about them?"

"The Blue Isles? I do not know the name."

"Well, that is what the English call them. Take a look at the map."

Chang did so, and recognition immediately dawned in his eyes. "Ah yes." He proceeded to give the name of the isles in Mandarin, which

West found lyrical in quality but difficult to pronounce. "I have never been there, and indeed few Chinese of the modern age have. These islands are said to be nearly surrounded by perilous reefs."

"That is what has kept English ships away, too. Our task will be to find a way through." West was smiling faintly, eager for the challenge. "I hope to use the skills of local boatmen— fishermen and the like— once we approach the area. I think you may prove an unexpected help, Mr. Chang. Do you know the languages of the area?"

"Some of them, sir. It is also quite likely that some people there will speak Mandarin, which is of course my native tongue."

"Excellent. How about the Isles themselves? Do you know anything else about them?"

Chang smiled. "They are said to be rich in pearls and jade." West nodded. "They are also said to resemble an earthly paradise."

West raised his eyebrows. "A paradise?"

"Yes. It is a matter of legend, of course; but I have heard the story told, that any man courageous enough to sail to the Blue Isles will be rewarded by those who dwell there."

"Rewarded, how?"

"I do not know. But the Isles are said to be a place of pristine beauty, and the people peaceful and wise. It sounds to me like a myth— or, more aptly, a retelling of the most ancient human wishes. My people also have the story of the Peach Blossom Stream, which is really much the same."

"Yes, I believe I understand, though you must tell me sometime about this Peach Blossom Stream. Nonetheless, it is our mission to try to sail to the Blue Isles; so perhaps we shall be rewarded."

"We can hope so, sir."

"Thank you, Mr. Chang. I will be going up on deck now. The winds are favourable, and Mr. Kenmare assures me that we will soon be ready to sail." At that moment, the southern thrush laughed— and in a kind of response, so did West. He did not seriously believe it to be a good omen for the voyage. He could not help but think it a blessing, though; and the laughter was still ringing through his thoughts as he stepped onto the deck in the sunlight, and gave orders for the *Promise* make sail.

III.
Captain and Crew

*T*he first few weeks of the voyage, as the *Promise* made its way south-west into the Atlantic, were blessed with fair winds and fair weather. For West, there was an idyllic quality to this early stage. There was a freedom in being at sea again, and a kind of wonder as well. West could stand upon the deck and look up to see the white sails billowing above him, brushing the face of the clear blue sky. He could look down at the water and see the white foam leaping joyfully in response to the frigate's passage. And he could contemplate the adventure before him, knowing that he was sailing to the edge of the map, in search of things new and noble.

His comrades proved to be a blessing as well. West was honest enough with himself to know that this was largely because of the luxuries that his rank granted him; he could maintain a degree of reserve and privacy and still be thought of as warmly approachable by the standards of commanding officers. Certainly, his interaction with the crew was limited. Early on, he had the men assembled on deck, and he gave them a brief speech from his quarterdeck, describing the mission to the Blue Isles. West used glowing but simple terms, applying his skill as a storyteller, and the speech was received with cheers. It was followed by the distribution of the day's rum ration, which West knew to be a far more exciting event for many of the sailors.

West's contact with the lieutenants was considerably more extensive. He soon found himself re-examining his early concern about Teal, for the lad abandoned his ingratiating air as soon as he saw that it failed to ingratiate him. The defining moment, perhaps, came after West's speech to the crew. Teal took the opportunity to inform his captain that the speech was "stirring to both the men and the officers" and had been met with a withering look. From then on, he maintained an air of simple professionalism with the captain, which West greatly preferred. West still wondered whether the early attempts spoke ill of Teal's character and therefore retained some questions about him; he neither liked nor trusted sycophants. But at least Teal ceased to be an irritation.

The third lieutenant, Wade Lang, had been quiet during the first dinner West had had with his officers; but after a few more such occasions had been shared, he began to open up. West learned the Lang had, indeed, begun on the lower deck. He had been promoted to midshipman after diving into a raging sea to save his former first lieutenant, who had been swept off the deck by a rogue wave. (When Lang told the story, Kenmare said: "Feel free to do that again if it be needed.")

The promotion, of course, had opened up a new set of challenges for Lang. He found himself a midshipman in his forties; and while he was literate, he was quite uneducated by the standards of officers. Still, he had benefited from thirty years of experience at sea; and West deduced that he had a good memory despite his lack of formal learning. As a midshipman, he had applied himself to the books in order to supplement his practical experience; and he therefore came to take the examination for lieutenant. "It was seamanship as got me through, sir," he said of that experience. "If it had been all on mathematics of navigation, I'd have stood a thrush's chance in a gale." West had never heard the figure of speech before, though it was certainly vivid enough; it sounded as if it had been invented by some colourful novelist. All in all, West found Lang to be a man who inspired confidence, as well as a man of bluff good humour.

He could tell that his second lieutenant, Rede, was not quite of the same mind, however. Rede's polished, upper-class demeanour made him a sharp contrast with Lang; and it was the sort of contrast that could cause friction. The second lieutenant seemed to typify the increasing trend to the idea that formal education and personal gentility were desirable or even required traits for Naval officers. West disagreed with this trend, despite the fact that he himself could be said to have both the desired traits; he was willing to accept an officer like Wade Lang or an officer like Cato Rede. However, he could tell that Rede was somewhat uncomfortable with the third lieutenant. It was not that there was any open hostility between them; Rede was always relentlessly polite. But West could perceive an air of discomfort about him when Lang told a tale or a joke. He might laugh if it was appropriate to do so, but he would laugh a trifle too readily to be natural. On the other hand, when his sense of humour was genuinely affected— say, perhaps, by a dry quip or a literary reference from the captain— he would merely smile with a moment's twinkle in his eyes. At least he was not trying to ingratiate himself, West noted; but he hoped that Rede would come to judge Lang justly, and not allow himself to be trapped by superficial distinctions.

Aside from this, West liked his second lieutenant; and oddly, he felt sorry for him. There was always a certain tension about Rede, and while it doubtlessly added to his issues with Lang, it was considerably broader in nature. There were times when West could see him unbend. After a meal, with a glass of port in his hand, Rede could appear to become less guarded. But West was certain that the effect was only comparative. The truth was, West was a man who recognized scars when he saw them; and he saw them in Rede, though he was not sure from whence they had come.

Of all his officers, the one who West came to like the most was Kenmare. The first lieutenant was, quite simply, an easy man to like. He was a fine storyteller with a wealth of experience to draw on. He could speak lyrically of his home on the Irish coast— which, from the way he described it, reminded West of his own home on the coast of Scotland; and he could speak just as freely of the coasts of Africa, the cities and the exotic marketplaces of India, and the taverns of the West Indies. He had never yet been to the South China Sea, and he shared West's enthusiasm for their current adventure. He also shared West's enjoyment of Navy rum; and it become common for West and his first lieutenant to while away evenings in the captain's cabin, each with a tumbler of rum in his hand, sharing stories old and new. (Old, when Kenmare would repeat himself— the only sign of age, beyond white hair and wrinkles, that West had yet seen about the man).

West also liked the fact that Kenmare had been virtually born and brought up at sea. Even during his earliest boyhood, he had spent considerable time on a fishing vessel that his father had owned, sailing the Irish coast. He seemed to carry the memories of those days clear and bright in his mind; and he had gone so far as to fit out the *Promise* with a fishing net. "If we ever find ourselves running low on provisions, it's a fine thing to have, sir," he explained. West agreed, and wondered why more ships were not similarly equipped. Even if the captain and the lieutenants were ignorant of such matters, there would always be men on the lower decks who could work a fishing net. Kenmare's idea showed practical wisdom.

The possible mote in the eye of shipboard life was Gilbraith. West had rather dreaded the prospect of having to include him on such occasions as the dinners with the officers; he was, however, consistently saved by Gilbraith's seasickness. The East India Company representative had proven to be quite susceptible, and his secretary, who seemed to be a painfully nervous and withdrawn personality, was loathe to do anything without him. West was pleased by the situation, but he wondered about it nonetheless, and devised a number of possible explanations in his mind.

One explanation, of course, was to take it all at face value: seasickness was hardly an uncommon complaint. But it also occurred to West that Gilbraith might be as reluctant to mix with the ship's officers as they were reluctant to have him do so; in that case, seasickness would be a readily accepted excuse. And then there was the matter of their quarters.

West's suspicions about Gilbraith had led him, quite early in the voyage, to consider having his quarters searched. This would have to be done surreptitiously, of course; but he felt certain he could trust Chang with the task. He would be highly perceptive, and as steward, he could easily plead an excuse even if he was caught. But the fact that Gilbraith spent so much time in his quarters limited the options in that regard. West did not give up the idea; it was to be a long voyage and the opportunity would surely present itself. But because Gilbraith's actions served to at least delay West's plan, West could not help but wonder if Gilbraith had somehow anticipated it and acted accordingly. He knew the thought was somewhat irrational, but he also knew that he did not trust Francis Gilbraith.

Chang was, indeed, the other principle figure— from West's point of view— aboard the ship. West enjoyed his discussions with Chang, which began with Boethius and music philosophy but soon moved to the culture of China. Culture was the operative word, for West's attempts to probe Chang's own history were futile; Chang had the strong sense of privacy that might be expected from someone who had been reluctant to admit that he spoke English, and whenever West's line of conversation became too personal, he would guide it, with gentle courtesy, back to the realms of the intellectual and aesthetic.

CHRIS FASOLINO

Nevertheless, West learned much about China that was of great interest. He was especially pleased when Chang brought out a book of Mandarin poetry and attempted to translate the complex characters for West's benefit. The captain found himself quite drawn to the lyrics of Li Po, whom Chang described as a brilliant and eccentric figure who his countrymen had called, with a touch of humour, "the banished immortal." His work seemed to combine the wistfulness of the Scotch-Irish folk music West knew so well with flights of fanciful imagination beautiful to contemplate.

All in all, then, the beginning of the voyage of the *Promise* was fair sailing in every way. It only changed when Rede began practice with the guns.

The practice was of course necessary; although West hoped that they would never have to use the cannons in battle, the men and officers had to be ready to defend the ship if some unexpected danger arose. At Rede's request, therefore, West gave permission one morning for the exercises. The guns would be run out, fired, and run back in; the whole maneuver would be timed and then repeated until it could be performed smoothly and quickly. West had seen the maneuvers a thousand times before; but he was quite unprepared for how it would now affect him.

As the guns were run out, he stood on his quarterdeck, watching and listening, perfectly content. Kenmare stood next to him, his blue eyes darting between the men, the cannons, and the watch that he held in his hand. No sooner had the guns started to fire, than West felt a wave of fear come over him. The ship around him seemed distant and hazy, as if his vision was clouding; even Kenmare, who was standing next to him, seemed far away. He heard the roar of the guns, and he felt that they were not the guns of the *Promise*; they were the guns of his old ship, no, the guns of the Spanish ships, as they met in battle on the coast of Andalusia— West's last battle, the one that had nearly cost him his life.

West managed to keep his face expressionless, though it was so pale that Kenmare asked, "Are you all right, sir? You look a mite ill."

"Quite all right, Mr. Kenmare. The maneuvers seem to be off to a fine beginning, so I will leave them under your supervision. I will be in my cabin if you need me." West's voice sounded hollow and distant in his own ears.

"Aye, sir."

West returned to his cabin and shut the door. His hand was shaking; a reaction he had struggled to keep in check during the walk from the quarterdeck. It was good, at least, to be alone; if he was to be unmanned by fear in this way he did not want his officers nor his men to know it. But what did it mean? What was this reaction that had come over him? His wound, serious though it had been, had long since healed. Furthermore, when the real battle had taken place, West had felt very little fear; his whole being had been absorbed in action and in doing his duty. Yet now, long afterwards, in the safety of his cabin, he was close to panic.

It was impossible to reason out, since he could not think clearly. He looked at the bottle of rum on the desk but rejected it; West was no Puritan but he had no intention of using alcohol as a crutch. He picked up an old volume from the bookshelf and began to thumb through it quickly, looking for something to distract himself; but the pages might as well have been blank, and he threw it on the desk in frustration, nearly upsetting Autolycus' cage. At last, he lay down upon his cot and, to his own astonishment, began to sob, silently but bitterly.

He lay there for some half an hour after the maneuvers with the guns had ceased, thankful for the silence but still weak and shaken. Then a knock came at the door; a most unwelcome thing. "Who is there?"

"Chang, sir."

West sat up on the cot, pleased; he was keeping Chang's secret, so Chang could certainly keep his. "You may enter."

"Door locked, sir," said Chang in pidgin.

Of course; West had locked it when he had returned to his cabin. He got up and opened it. Chang entered, bearing a mug and a carafe and closing the door behind him. "I brought you some chocolate, sir," he said. "I thought you might need it. It is quite harmless, but it does have some restorative properties, you know."

West looked at him quizzically as he laid his burdens upon the desk. "How do you know? And what do you know?"

"I saw you grow quite pale, sir, when the guns began firing. Do not be concerned; none of your officers would have known what was happening. But I have read of this thing. I know, of course, that you were wounded in battle. Such a reaction is not unusual."

Impressed by the man's perception, West sat down and accepted the mug of chocolate; it was rich and warming. Chang continued, "It is in the *Odyssey*, as you know, sir."

"It is?" West said.

"The banquet where the minstrel sings of the Trojan War."

"Of course— Odysseus puts his cloak over his head and . . . weeps."

"Yes, sir. Odysseus was a strong man, and like you, he was from a warrior culture. But he was briefly overcome when his mind went back to things he had experienced."

West smiled faintly. "A warrior culture, eh? You mean the British or the Scottish?"

"I would think both, sir. Am I mistaken?"

"Well, all cultures may be warrior cultures, and barbarian cultures too, compared to the Chinese."

"I do not believe the latter, sir. But it is true that we have always drawn a distinction between the arts of war and the arts of peace; and we have, for the most part, accorded the latter greater honour."

West sipped at the chocolate again. "What do you suggest I do?"

"I have no suggestions, sir. But I would propose that you should neither feel ashamed nor surprised."

"Very well." He was silent awhile. "I knew an Admiral once who had served in the East Indies. He said that when he had first arrived there, he had found the heat quite oppressive. But when he came back to England, he liked to sit by a roaring fire, even in the summer."

"Then you think—"

"I must be able to think clearly if there is a crisis, so as to defend my ship. Tomorrow, there will have to be another practice at the guns."

There was another practice the day after that as well, and the day after that. At first, Rede was pleased; but eventually, he was surprised, as the crew's efficiency with the guns was already becoming exemplary, and this was in theory a peaceful mission. Nonetheless, West continued to order further practice. At first, he would remain in his cabin during the maneuvers. Then, he started to come out and observe them silently from his quarterdeck. Finally, after about two weeks of daily practice, he called a halt and told Rede to return to the usual schedule for such matters.

Only Chang knew the reason for it all; everyone else on the ship began to think that the captain suspected there would be more danger on this voyage than seemed apparent. As for West, after he told Rede to belay daily practice with the guns, he strode to the side of the ship and looked out over the waters.

The past two weeks had left him exhausted, but they had been successful. He was grateful for Chang's support during the time. Now, on this last morning, he had been able to stand on the quarterdeck, listen to the guns, and solve tactical problems in his head. The fear was under control. And the relief he felt now, looking out to sea, was overwhelming.

He had found himself remembering his last battle over and over again during the past two weeks, and feeling far more frightened than he had at the time, when his life actually was in danger. Now, though, he could look out to the grey sea and know that, although his scars were still there, their pain would not overwhelm him.

Yet there was one more step that Chang suggested, when they were alone in West's cabin that afternoon. "I am the only man aboard who does not know the story of your battle," Chang said. "Perhaps it would do you good to tell it now."

"And I thought you were the only man aboard who did know my story," said West with a smile. "Nonetheless, you may be right. I think that I can now tell the story, briefly at least, and put that part of my life somewhat farther behind me.

"I was, at the time, the Captain of a frigate called the *Sea Unicorn*. I was patrolling the western Mediterranean and the Atlantic coasts beyond, when word reached me of a secretive shipbuilding project on the Spanish coast. The word came, actually, from fishermen. Spain and England were not officially at war at the time, and I always tried to maintain good relations with the Spanish fishing vessels I met, buying part of their catch from them and using them as a source of information. The fishermen did not know what the project was; they only spoke of the large shipments of timber that had been sent. Their words were innocent and ill-guarded, and as it happened, saved many lives in the end, Spanish as well as British.

"I sailed to the coast of Andalusia to investigate, and there found a deserted harbour with two Spanish frigates at anchor. It was clear to me that there was some secret there; so, rather against the protests of my First Lieutenant, I went ashore myself to investigate."

"Yourself, sir?"

"A mission of espionage, if you like. I am fluent in Spanish, and like any good storyteller, I have some improvisational ability. The *Sea Unicorn* dropped me farther along the coast with civilian clothing and a purse full of gold; I obtained the right kind of clothing, and hired the necessary servants, carriage, and so on, in a small village. I thus became Don Esteban Zapata y Quijana, a Spanish nobleman who had taken up commerce after falling upon hard times. The elaborate nature of the story helped ensure that I would be believed; no one would expect a British officer to go to such great lengths in the way of creative detail. Fortunately, they do not know the Scots very well.

"It was also fortunate that Don Esteban Zapata y Quijana had business interests in the timber and resin industries so essential to shipbuilding. This opened the way for him to acquire a great deal of information during his sojourn on the Spanish coast. I learned that the Spanish were secretly building an invasion fleet on the shores of that harbour."

"They were going to attempt an invasion of England?" Chang asked. "A new Spanish Armada?"

"That was what the British press later took to calling it. In fact, the three frigates were to guard a number of transport ships for troops. It was the transport ships that were being built. The plan then was to sail around the western shore of Ireland and then go north to land somewhere on the Scottish coast. This would allow them to bypass the might of the British Navy and instead fight what would be primarily a land war.

"It was a bold scheme, but a reckless one. Even assuming that they landed successfully, they underestimated the kind of opposition they would face. They hoped for Jacobite support from Scotland, but my people would have been divided in their response. Some would have joined the Spanish, and some would have defended the English. And if the invaders managed to march south into England itself, they would have been quite overwhelmed by military and popular opposition. I discovered that the entire plan had originated with a man named Count Vega, an aristocrat capable of great brilliance but plagued by a fatal grandiosity. In any event, I was convinced that the plan to invade England would ultimately fail.

"However, I also knew that the attempt would have disastrous results. There would be great loss of life on both sides; and much of the damage might be wrought upon my own homelands on the Scottish coast. I was therefore determined to do all that I honourably could to stop the attempt before it began, laying down my life if necessary.

"I therefore returned to the *Sea Unicorn* and dispatched a cutter to carry the news to another Navy ship, and thence to Whitehall. However, I could not wait for reinforcements; if the transport ships were finished and the fleet began to sail, even the Royal Navy might not be able to catch them; their sweep around Ireland was potentially so wide, and their destination on the Scottish coast so vague, that no certain blockade would be possible. I decided to take the *Sea Unicorn* into battle, to defeat the two frigates in the harbour and then send a force of Marines ashore to burn the fleet that was under construction.

"Of course, the odds were two to one; but then a great storm arose, and that gave me an idea. We anchored and waited out the storm, hidden farther along the coast, and my ship endured it well. When it was over, though, I had the sails and the rigging deliberately frayed, so that it would appear that we had been badly battered. Then, we limped into the harbour as if merely seeking a place of refuge to repair after the storm."

"Did that not give you a disadvantage in the battle, sir?"

"Not really, because the battle had to be joined at such close quarters. It was three ships in a harbour; the speed of maneuver would not be nearly so important as on the open sea. The element of surprise was far more useful. And I knew that my ruse was in full accord with the rules of war and with a gentleman's honour."

"So you met in battle, and you succeeded despite the odds."

"Yes." Here West's eyes grew far away. "My idea to surprise the enemy worked well, and of course, British gunners are more efficient than Spanish gunners, or French ones for that matter; it is because we spend so much time out at sea, you know. When it comes down to broadsides— as this battle quickly did— we always have the edge. The close quarters of the harbour helped us in that respect, too.

"There was a boarding party, though, toward the end. As their own ships were battered, a group of Spaniards launched themselves onto the deck of the *Sea Unicorn*, with pistols and swords in their hands. I saw

CHRIS FASOLINO

one of them aim his pistol at me; I saw a puff of smoke; and then I felt a kind of thudding pain in my side. Everything seemed to go cloudy after that; the last thing I can remember is the fire, the tawny fires from shore as the landing party from the *Sea Unicorn* burned the invasion ships. That meant we had been successful; and I was pleased to think that I had known that, before I was about to die.

"But then, of course, I did not die. I was borne back to England, wounded— a wounded hero, as they said— and honoured and all, and then I went back to my home to recover." West smiled now, a smile tinged by pain but not defined by it. "That was the real reward— my home is a place of great beauty. For a long time, I never thought I would leave it.

"And yet, here I am, at sea again."

"An explorer, now, though, sir," said Chang.

"Yes," said West. "An explorer."

The days that followed, up until the encounter with the pirates, found West relieved of some of his mental and emotional burdens, and once again pleased to be at sea. Kenmare drilled the crew with the sails and the rigging, and West found this pleasant to watch. The wind and weather continued favourable, and this caused odd grumblings among many of the men, and even their officers. Their concern was voiced by Lang: "As like as not we will pay for all this later." Sailors were often superstitious, but West merely smiled at their concerns.

There were, in the meantime, some further developments with Gilbraith and his secretary. It began with Gilbraith apparently experiencing a respite from his seasickness; he walked about on deck, apologized to West for his indisposition, and invited himself to dinner. "My officers have duties that will prevent them from attending," West answered, not wanting to burden them with Gilbraith's company. "However, you are welcome to join me for dinner in my cabin. I trust your secretary will accompany you?" Gilbraith answered in the affirmative, and when the two of them arrived that evening, they found Teal acting as steward. Chang had other duties.

Teal seemed nervous as he brought in the meal Chang had earlier prepared— a beef stew with potatoes and carrots— and then opened a bottle of claret. West attributed it to simple concern over the potential embarrassment of dropping something, and he was surprised when, as soon as Teal had left, Carrin said: "I believe I know that lad."

West and Gilbraith both looked at Carrin; the aged secretary was normally so quiet. "Well, not him really, but his family," Carrin clarified. "His name is Teal, you said?"

"Yes, Alexander Teal."

"I knew an Alexander Teal in London. He was an elderly man— the lad's grandfather, perhaps. There is some family resemblance about the nose." Teal's hook nose was his most striking feature. "Indeed, the Mr. Teal I knew was the guardian of his grandchildren, so your young officer was probably quite affected by the events."

"Mr. Teal has not spoken much of his family."

"I do not blame him. His grandfather was a wealthy merchant who ended by having to declare bankruptcy. He had become involved in the latest tulip craze in Holland; invested all his savings into trying to acquire rare bulbs. I do not think it was just a matter of financial gamble either; from what I saw, the man was as obsessive about tulips as any Hollander."

"Really?" said West. He was intrigued, and he was beginning to feel that he had his first insight into his youngest lieutenant's character, provided Carrin's words were true. "How did you meet him?"

"I was a court clerk for a time, before I took service with the East India Company. I remember the man giving testimony in the bankruptcy hearing. This was perhaps a dozen years ago."

"You must have a fine memory, then."

"Mr. Carrin has an infallible memory," said Gilbraith. "It is one of the reasons he is so excellent a secretary."

"I imagine the trait would be useful," said West with a smile, taking a sip of his claret. He found conversation rather easy during the meal; he simply maintained an air of polite geniality while remembering the purpose of the occasion. Carrin said little else during the evening, but Gilbraith enjoyed talking about himself, and West allowed him to do so. He heard something of Gilbraith's accomplishments in the East India Company and the noble connections of his forebears. West tried to note all that was said, but suspended belief. Even if Gilbraith was genuine, he was clearly exaggerating out of vanity.

As Teal came back and forth to perform his duties as steward, no one said anything to him regarding Carrin's remarks. But West wondered if there was any chance that Teal, too, remembered Carrin. It seemed unlikely; yet, if as a child he had been in the courtroom when his grandfather was deposed, perhaps every detail would be etched in his memory. Perhaps even the face of the court clerk. It would account for his nervousness. But then again, there was no need to account for his nervousness. And there was no need for his suspicions of Gilbraith to affect his view of the acting-lieutenant. Teal's actions could likely be taken at face value, even if Gilbraith's could not.

What about Carrin? Was there some reason for him to make up the story? There, West's suspicions of Gilbraith were relevant; if one suspects the master, one might suspect the servant as well. But he could not think of any reason why a story about the Teal family finances might benefit either Gilbraith or Carrin.

As Gilbraith continued to ramble on, West's thoughts wandered off to the tulipomania that had apparently cost the Teal family so much. It was a phenomenon that had combined elements of a classic financial bubble with a genuine aesthetic enthusiasm. Love of the exotic had played a role, too, and West certainly understood that. Tulips had come to Holland from Turkey, where the bulbous, brightly-coloured flowers had been called *dulbend*— turbans. It came to be believed that Turkish sultans considered them the world's greatest treasures. Soon, tulip bulbs became a source of great wealth for anyone who could obtain them; West had read that three tulip bulbs could buy a fine home on the canals of Amsterdam. At least, they could until the tulip market crashed. The most dramatic cycle had come over a century ago; but more recently, there had been a similar outbreak of the craze that had led to the same result. It must have been then that the Teal family fortune was lost.

Gilbraith and Carrin took their leave after the cheese and port. West had Teal put a cork in the unfinished bottle of claret and clear the dishes; then he, too, left. West poured himself a tumbler of rum and sat back to await Chang's report.

But before Chang arrived, Teal came back with a message from Kenmare. "Mr. Kenmare's compliments, sir, and there's a storm on the horizon. He has shortened sail in the hopes that we do not run into it, sir."

"Thank you, Mr. Teal. You may give my compliments to Mr. Kenmare when you return. But I would like to ask you something first. I do not mean to pry, but Mr. Carrin told me that he knew of your family; he spoke of your grandfather's misfortune in the tulip markets."

"Aye, sir." Teal seemed mildly surprised, and then his face suggested he was lost in the past. "That's why I came to sea, sir— after I was a bit older, that is. I needed to make my own way, sir."

"I understand. You started under Captain Mayhew, on this ship?"

"Aye, sir."

"And in time, he made you Acting-Lieutenant. I imagine you were frightened when you first came to sea, under those circumstances; then you grew comfortable under Mayhew's command. Is that not so?"

"I suppose so, sir."

Teal looked uncomfortable as soon as he had said it, and West added: "Believe me, there's no shame in admitting fear." Then he nearly smiled at the irony, since he had been so careful to hide his own fears from his officers and crew. "In any case, my purpose in talking about this is to reassure you. I imagine that the change in command on this ship— the first change in command that you have known— renewed your anxieties. You need not answer; it would be a natural reaction. I know you have already noticed that I do not care for having people try to impress me. But that is all right, because you do not have to. Do your duty, and it is then my duty to see that life on my ship gives you no cause for fear."

Teal stared at him, his eyes glittering. "Aye, sir. Thank you, sir."

West was beginning to feel he had gotten through to Teal. He added: "I think I understand your grandfather, by the way. I once heard of a Dutch book called *The Tulips of the East for the Enjoyment of the Noble-Minded*. They were not just valuable. They are beautiful and exotic. Any explorer would understand."

"Aye, sir." Teal paused. "Perhaps it is fitting I am here, then, sir."

"Perhaps it is. My compliments to Mr. Kenmare, as I said."

"Aye, sir."

Chang arrived not long after Teal left. He closed the door behind him, and immediately asked, with real concern, how the meal had been; Chang took great pride in his duties as captain's steward.

"Your beef stew was excellent," said West with a grin. "But you must make me a Chinese dish sometime."

"I do not really have the necessary spices aboard ship, sir. Perhaps when we arrive at the Blue Isles."

"Yes. Now— about your mission."

"It was fortunate that one of the keys you gave me fit the lock of Mr. Gilbraith's sea-chest."

"I expected it would." When Kenmare had condensed Gilbraith's luggage before the voyage began, he had issued the East India Company representative a ship's sea-chest in place of the enormous trunks he had brought with him.

"It was in the sea-chest that I found the only item of interest. There, in amongst his fine clothing, was a book— *Voyages in the South China Sea*, I believe is the title; it was written by an Italian explorer named Nazzareno Primo. The book is in Italian; because it is so like Latin, I had some understanding of it, but I do not really know Italian and that did limit how much I was able to read in the time I had."

"Of course. I do know Italian, and I will have to try and think of a way to obtain the book from Gilbraith. I presume it had some material on the Blue Isles?"

"Yes, sir. Primo claimed to know something of the history of the islands. He says that there is an aboriginal tribe there along with, I was curious to see, a Chinese element. It was not clear to me whether they are separate or whether they have intermarried. The Chinese are said to have arrived during a great age of exploration for their people; I presume the reference is to the treasure fleets of the Ming dynasty."

"Yes, well, we shall have to talk about these treasure fleets— they sound fascinating," said West, his eyes bright. "But I do not understand why Gilbraith should keep this book hidden. Did you find anything in it that the East India Company might not wish a ship's captain and company to know of?"

"Yes," said Chang. "I saw a sketch that seemed significant, and I copied out the passage below it to show you. Here it is." He handed West a sheet of paper, and the captain read aloud, translating from the Italian (which Primo himself wrote in a rather idiosyncratic manner):

Isolated though the Blue Isles are, they are home to what must be considered one of the great treasures of the high seas. It is an heirloom of their royal family. It is called the Pearl of the Long Ages. This pearl is not only of great size but of most extraordinary colour: peacock-green, with hues of glistening gold as well. I really cannot describe its beauty. The way the two colours merge together, shifting and changing in different lights. In the sunlight they are blinding in their vibrancy; the moonlight, like rich tropical seas; the firelight a warm glow and the starlight softly caressing. Of all the wonders I have seen in my travels it is perhaps the grandest.

"The sketch above was of the pearl, and shows it is of great size," Chang said. "Though from that description, the size seems of secondary value compared with its colours."

"Yes," said West. "Well, now we know what the East India Company's interest in all this is. This is not simply a voyage of exploration, at least not to them. To them, it is a treasure hunt."

IV.
The Fortress

The island of St. Helena was ringed with steep cliffs where seabirds soared. At a break in the cliffs was a harbour, and there stood a fortress, with a small town behind it. Atop the fortress flew the British flag. At anchor in the harbour were two small Navy cutters and a merchantman. Approaching them, and coming in from the sea, was the *Promise*.

The arrival of the *Promise* at St. Helena meant that the ship had already travelled a substantial distance: from England to the South Atlantic. It also meant that provisions were needed. St. Helena was a small and sparsely populated island, and its only importance was as a place where ships on long voyages could take on food and fresh water.

West stood on the quarterdeck as the *Promise* anchored. He noted the two cutters in the harbour, both small vessels with their names were written in letters of gold upon their hulls: the *H.M.S. Snowdonia*, which West recognized as being named after a mountain in Wales, and the *H.M.S. Albatross*. One of them was probably the ship that had transported the garrison of the fort and might bear them away when they were relieved. The other was presumably making a stop for provisions, as the *Promise* was. That would be true of the merchantman as well. Each of the ships had a handful of men at watch on their decks, but they seemed quiet; doubtless most of the men were ashore.

West ordered the signal midshipman to inform the fort of their intentions. In response, the fort raised several signal flags of their own, acknowledging them and inviting a landing party ashore. West had been a signal midshipman himself once, and he could remember and interpret most of the combinations of flags; nonetheless, the midshipman read them aloud to Kenmare, who relayed them to West.

"Thank you, Mr. Kenmare. Prepare the landing party, if you please."

At that, Gilbraith entered the conversation. He had been standing on deck along with the officers as St. Helena came into sight; and now, he asked, "Do you wish me to join the landing party, Captain West?"

West looked at him. "Is there any particular reason I should, Mr. Gilbraith?"

"I am a merchant, sir. You may wish my assistance in the provisioning of the ship."

Kenmare stifled a guffaw. "I think we can manage all right, thank you kindly, sir."

"Yes, Mr. Gilbraith, whatever your experience in commerce, my officers are far more experienced in the ways of the sea. They certainly do not need your assistance with the provisioning." He paused and allowed Gilbraith a moment to attempt to conceal his injured pride. "However, you have my permission, and indeed my encouragement, to accompany them to the fort so as to bring the greetings of the East India Company to the commander of this distant garrison. Think of it as something of a social occasion. Mr. Kenmare, I will ask you to prepare and command the landing party."

Gilbraith looked a trifle confused, but nodded. "Very well, sir. I will bring my secretary with me, if you please."

"As you wish."

West noted Kenmare's disappointment at having Gilbraith included in the landing party, and as soon as the East India Company man's back was turned, West winked at his first lieutenant, as if to say, "trust me." He would explain everything to Kenmare later. For the moment, he added: "Give my compliments to the commander of the fort; you may tell him that I will come ashore later to greet him." West had been prepared to lead the landing party himself; it was only Gilbraith's desire to go ashore that had made him assign the task to Kenmare instead.

The rest of the preparations were taken care of by Kenmare, who selected Wade Lang and several sailors to accompany him. They set off in the jolly boat, with the sailors rowing toward shore. "Mr. Rede, I will be in my cabin. Please contact me if there are any developments from the landing party that I should know of."

"Aye, sir." Rede seemed faintly surprised that West would not remain on deck to supervise events more closely, but West, of course, had his reasons. He returned to his cabin, at first, only for a moment, to obtain the spare key. This was followed by a rapid trip to Gilbraith's cabin, followed by a return trip with a book in his hand.

Once he was in his own cabin again, West stood at his desk— he was too excited to sit down— and began a hasty examination of the book about the South China Sea. The passage on the Blue Isles was relatively brief, so he was able to absorb it quickly. The existence of the Pearl of Long Ages was doubtlessly the reason the East India Company representative wished to keep the book secret; the rest of the material dealt with history, culture, and landscape. The Italian captain confirmed Chang's description of the Blue Isles as paradisiacal in their beauty. West smiled, more and more pleased that Admiral Oakes had sent them on this particular mission of exploration. The book described the treacherous coral reefs surrounding the islands, but Primo was irritatingly silent on the question of how he had found his way through. West would have to solve that problem himself.

The book referred to the Chinese element upon the Isles as stemming from the time of "that nation's great armada of exploration." That must have been the treasure fleet Chang spoke of; West would have to ask him for more information about it. According to Primo, a captain of this fleet had sailed away from China after the fleet was disbanded. (Disbanded was the word used, but it seemed strange to West— why would a great fleet be *disbanded?*) The Chinese captain, who apparently became an outlaw by doing so, had found a place of sanctuary on the Blue Isles. He married the daughter of the local ruler, and from their offspring came the current royal family of the Blue Isles. This same captain was said to have discovered the Pearl of Long Ages, apparently presenting it to the ruler in order to win his daughter's hand in marriage. The captain's name was given as Alishan, and he was clearly a folk hero to the people of the Blue Isles. West thought he sounded like an interesting character.

The people were described most favourably, as being gracious and gentle. They had a knowledge of Chinese culture and language that they had acquired through Alishan and his men. More importantly to Primo, they also had a strong sense of hospitality. While the Pearl of Long Ages was their great treasure, their islands were also said to be rich in "lesser pearls" (any other pearl would be lesser) as well as "an abundance of jade and spices."

Lastly, and perhaps most intriguingly, Primo said: "This is a place to make music about." West thought about that and smiled.

Suddenly, an urgent knocking came at the door. "Come in," West said.

It was Teal. "You are needed on deck, sir. The landing party is in danger."

West left the book on his desk and quickly followed Teal, wondering what kind of danger they had found on the isolated island of St. Helena. When he arrived, he saw a man with a speaking trumpet standing on the parapet of the fort. The man was dressed in tattered white slacks and an even more tattered white shirt, topped with a fine vest of claret velvet. A cutlass and a pistol were at his side. Several other men were crouched behind the parapets, readying the three massive guns with which the fortress was equipped.

"He says that he is in command of the fort, and our landing party has been taken prisoner," said Rede, his voice even but his eyes troubled.

"He is a pirate, I assume?"

"Aye, sir. He wants to know what we will trade for our men."

"Does he now? Mr. Teal, fetch me a speaking trumpet." West's air of confidence came primarily from confusion. He had been called so quickly from a contemplation of the Blue Isles in the distance to an immediate, and unexpected, confrontation, that he could not yet feel any emotion. He would simply take the obvious course and hope that an idea came to him.

The speaking trumpet arrived, and West strode to the bow of his ship, calling: "Who are you, and what do you mean by threatening men of the Royal Navy?"

"My mates call me Crimson, because of the colour I wear. And what I want is what I can get." The man's voice was English.

"Then your mates are colour-blind," said West, "for there's more than a trace of burgundy in that vest. As for what you can get— release my men at once, and perhaps you may not hang."

"That will not be good enough, Captain. I am in command of this fort now. Your men are my prisoners, along with those who are left from the garrison and the crew of the *Albatross*. You will also have noticed these small popguns beside me." He gestured ironically at the fortress's cannons. "I think myself strong enough to demand more than the lack of a noose."

"How could you have captured the fort? I see no signs of battle."

"Because I captured the fort with guile. My men and I took the sloop *Albatross* at sea and sailed it into the harbour here, dressed as British officers. We were welcomed into the fort with all due respect."

"If that story is true, you must have another ship. Where is it?"

"Lost in the battle with the *Albatross*. There was a spark near the powder kegs— our own ship exploded. But most of us had already boarded the sloop, so the *Albatross* is our ship now."

"Very well." West suspected that there was, in fact, a pirate ship lurking somewhere nearby— not in the harbour, obviously, but along the cliffs of the island. If it were close enough, it might attempt to block the *Promise* in the harbour, and West would then face an attack from two sides.

"So, what I want are ship's stores, guns, your rum of course— whatever ye have."

"Our ship's stores are nearly empty; that is why we are here." West looked at the fort with its guns. It was essential that it be neutralized, and quickly. But how? And how could they attack the fort without endangering Kenmare and their men— as well as the other prisoners?

"I admit I would rather have seen another merchantman. But you must have something of value."

"You captured the merchantman here, then?"

"They fell into the same trap you have."

"And the men posted on the decks are actually yours. Clever, Crimson. You seem to have done things quite thoroughly." It was then that the idea came to him. West lowered his voice and added: "But I must—" Then he dropped the speaking trumpet. It clattered to the deck. He leaned over and picked it up. Then he stood up and faced Crimson again. "I ask for parley. I will come to the fort to speak with you. Provided that you give your word I shall not be taken prisoner."

Rede stared at his captain, and there was a moment's silence from Crimson, as if the pirate could not believe his opponent's incredible stupidity. Then Crimson answered: "You have my word."

"Very well." West's voice was suddenly weak. Even with the speaking trumpet, it was not clear whether it had carried. He repeated the phrase, louder, and then dropped the speaking trumpet on the deck again, this time with an attitude of carelessness. "Mr. Rede, have a longboat prepared for me. Send one of the men to row; that will be all."

"Captain, I must protest. You cannot believe—"

"I assure you, Mr. Rede, Crimson and his men will not lay a hand on me. Carry out my orders."

"Aye, sir. May I at least clear the ship for action, sir?"

"Absolutely not. In fact, tell the men on deck to look as slovenly as possible."

"Slovenly?"

"Yes. Go against your grain and make things look unprofessional here. Mr. Teal, tell the ship's surgeon that I want to see him immediately."

"The ship's surgeon, sir?"

"You heard me."

When West arrived on the shore and stepped out of the longboat, he looked very frail. There was pallor in his face, his eyes were glazed, and he seemed disoriented. His naturally thin build and narrow features added to the impression. With the sailor walking silently at his side, he entered the fortress, led by two of Crimson's men carrying pistols and cutlasses.

The pirates led him through the antechamber and around a corner to the stairwell. Then they went up a flight of stone stairs, until they emerged on the parapets, where Crimson was standing by the cannons. "Welcome, Captain West," he said. "Another hostage is always useful. Now tell me what your ship has to offer."

"Hostage? You said I would not be taken prisoner."

"And you believed me. Now, can I profit by your ship, or should I just open fire?"

West looked increasingly confused. "You do not understand. What did my men tell you about the condition of my ship?"

"They said they had come ashore for provisions. What are you talking about, Captain?"

"We should not have come ashore at all, I know. That is, we should not have come into the harbour."

"So you have discovered."

"I do not mean because of you. But it is a terrible thing to die of thirst when you are already dying anyway. We needed provisions desperately. Although I suppose even that would not have mattered."

"Dying anyway? What do you mean?" Suspicion— and alarm— were beginning to dawn in Crimson's eyes.

West stared up into the sky. "It is so warm here." He started to take off his uniform coat. Then he looked straight into the pirate's eyes. "Water," he said. "Just give me water."

"Why? Are your provisions as low as that?"

"It has been a long time since we made port. We should not have come here . . . Should have stayed out at sea . . . But this place is so isolated I thought it might be all right. And my crew was suffering so. Water, I said!"

"Captain, what is wrong with you?"

"Oh, I am just dying of thirst." West began to laugh hysterically. Then, as Crimson stared at him, he collapsed. The uniform coat fell away, and the boils on West's neck could be seen. Crimson cried out and drew back, his own face pallid.

"The scoundrel has come into port with the plague!" he said. "Gather the men, quickly. We must flee this place!" Within moments, West and the sailor were alone on the parapet.

West opened his eyes and handed the sailor his telescope. "Monitor their escape. I think I had best continue to lie in a faint; it would not do to have someone look back towards us and see me up and about."

"Aye, sir."

"The *Promise* would have them covered if they tried to reach the sloops, so I imagine they will head inland and try to find their other ship. Let me know when the exodus seems complete."

"Aye, sir. And very nicely done, if I may say so, sir."

"You may. We will show anyone who tries to take our rum, eh?"

The sailor, a good-natured fellow named Senecal, grinned broadly. West smiled and lay back down.

The pirates retreated quickly. Seamen of all sorts feared the plague, which could sweep through a ship— or a fortress— bringing swift devastation. The pirates fled overland, through the village and into the mountainous countryside. Returning to the sloops must have seemed too risky, since the *Promise* had them covered. As it was, they were apparently making their way overland to rejoin the pirate ship whose existence West had deduced. Once the sailor told him the retreat had been made, West climbed up the fort's topmost tower and took out his telescope. He could see it from there. It was in a small inlet, close to the main harbour but shielded by the cliffs that ringed the shores of the island. The ship was a great Spanish galleon, old and huge. It had three decks and probably nigh on a hundred guns. That meant that it carried between three and four times more cannons than West's frigate did. A single, sustained broadside from the galleon could sink the *Promise*. However, the galleon would be far less manoeuvrable than the frigate, and West hoped that if it came to a fight, that he could use his advantage of speed to even the odds.

Crimson and the pirates who had fled the fort were climbing over the cliffs, beginning to make for the galleon. It would be a steep climb down, but they would be able to make it; West could see through the telescope a place where the mountains levelled out somewhat, and he was certain the pirates would find it. Whether they would be welcomed back aboard was another matter. They would have to explain their retreat, and unless the pirates on the ship saw through the ruse, Crimson and his companions would surely be left marooned on the shore.

West shut the telescope and climbed down from the tower. "Well, let us see about releasing the prisoners," he said, and the sailor followed him down into the fort.

It was easy enough to find the jail cells; they just kept going down. Hewn out of the stone below the fort was an underground prison. There, in cavernous spaces of dank grey rock, locked behind iron bars, were a number of faces both new and familiar. West took a set of huge black iron keys off a great hook and began unlocking the cells. There were Kenmare, Lang, and the sailors from the *Promise*. The two lieutenants greeted West with amazement. "How did you manage this, sir?" Kenmare asked. "And so quickly as well? But— I must say, sir, you look fair to drop."

West grinned. "Yes, that all goes together. I will explain when I can. Help me release the other prisoners." The survivors from the garrison of the fort, the two sloops, and the merchantman were released as well, all offering expressions of gratitude that West pushed aside in the urgency of the moment.

"Who was in command here? Who can tell me what happened?"

A Navy lieutenant stepped forward. "Lieutenant Brian Baird, sir. Our captains are still prisoners of the pirates, sir."

"Where are they?"

"They were taken to the pirate ship— do you know about the galleon, sir?"

"I saw it from the tower."

"Yes, sir. The pirates sailed in on the sloop *Albatross* and gained entry as Navy men. Took us by surprise, they did. The merchantman, *Miller of the Dee*, was caught in the same trap that they would have tried on you."

"Yes, I had gathered all that. So, when they captured the fort, they moved your captain to the galleon?"

"Yes, sir. They moved their prisoners from the *Albatross* to the cells here, save for their commanding officer. And they brought the merchantman captain there, too. They figured if something went wrong at the fort, they would still have the commanding officers as hostages."

A young midshipman, apparently from the *Albatross*, piped up: "Please sir, my captain was wounded when the pirates attacked us. He might be in bad shape, sir."

"You should also know, sir, that the pirate captain is a very different sort from that fellow Crimson who was left in charge here," continued Baird. "It was the captain who talked their way into the fort; we thought he sounded upper-class even for a Royal Navy captain, sir. Aristocratic, really. But I am sure he can be quite ruthless, sir."

West nodded, but he could not help taking note of the fact that the prisoners had been spared and apparently not mistreated; perhaps this aristocratic pirate captain was to be a civilized opponent.

West said aloud: "Clearly, we must mount an attack on the galleon. Lieutenant Baird, gather all the men who are in fit condition and man the two cutters. Leave enough men behind to guard the fort, though— the pirates may try to retake the place by a land assault once they realize that they had been tricked. Oh, there will be a few pirates parading around on the decks of the sloops and the merchantman; you will have to take them into custody. Then, make them ready to sail— and to fight. The galleon is of formidable size; my frigate will be grateful for your assistance."

"Aye, sir," said Baird, and moved into action.

West looked around him and then took Kenmare off to the side. "Where are Gilbraith and Carrin?" he asked.

Kenmare's usual genial face showed contempt. "Gilbraith panicked as soon as our landing party was taken captive, sir. Told the pirates he had information for them that he would trade for his life. What it could be I cannot think, sir; perhaps something about his own Company's trading routes, or perhaps some bluff. Anyway, that quiet secretary of his gave him a look that would freeze a man's blood. Said if Gilbraith were wise he would dare not speak. So the pirates took them both off to question them. I do not know to where, sir."

"Baird!" West called. "Are there any smaller cells here— for just one or two prisoners?"

"Aye, there's one such cell over there, past the guard station, sir."

West hurried in that direction and found a wooden door that he had strode past on his way to the main cells. He tried the keys until one fit. The door opened. It was dark inside. West grabbed a lantern from the corridor and held it so that its ruddy glow was cast into the cell.

There, Nile Carrin stood blinking in the light. And Francis Gilbraith lay on the floor, dead.

"What happened here?" West stepped forward. There seemed to be no sign of violence upon Gilbraith; then he noticed a tear in his sleeve and a cut on the arm below. On the ground next to him lay a dagger.

"It must have been poisoned, sir," said Carrin quietly. "One of the pirates stabbed him with it, and he fell down."

"Why did they do it?"

"He said he had information for them, sir. I told him not to tell them anything, but then the pirates brought us in here. Mr. Gilbraith said he would give them information on the shipping routes of the East India Company in exchange for his life and his freedom. They were listening. But then Mr. Gilbraith saw that one of them had that dagger on his belt. I saw him looking at it. I do not know if he felt remorse at betraying the Company, or if he just acted on impulse. He was very panicky when were taken captive, sir. But for whatever reason, he tried to grab the dagger; they struggled over it, and it ended with the pirate cutting him there."

"And then he simply collapsed."

"Yes, sir. Poison, sir, as I said."

West knelt down to look at the wound. Yes, there was no doubt that Gilbraith was dead from poison; there was no other mark on the body, and the wound itself was nothing of any consequence. West considered picking up the dagger, but he realized he was not entirely sure what to do with it. He decided he would simply lock the door behind him and tell Baird to dispose of it carefully. Now, there were other matters to attend to. That meant that Gilbraith's body would have to be left here for the moment as well. But there was no help for it.

West paused a moment, though, wondering about Carrin's words. Was that really all Gilbraith had said to the pirates? West knew that he had had information that might be more valuable even than shipping routes. Perhaps he was simply holding it in reserve. And what of Carrin? He had tried to stop Gilbraith from talking. Was it simply loyalty to the East India Company? Did Carrin know about the Pearl of Long Ages? For that matter, was Carrin somehow involved in Gilbraith's death? There were no other witnesses, save for the fleeing pirates. Perhaps Carrin's entire account was untrustworthy.

Finally, West shrugged off all the questions, at least for the time being. There was a pirate galleon not far away, where honest seamen were being held hostage. That was his next task. Carrin walked out of the cell, and West followed, closing the door behind him.

But as West was being rowed back to the *Promise* with his companions, he looked around him and thought about Gilbraith. As much as he had disliked the man, he felt a moment's melancholy; St. Helena must be an unexpected place for anyone to die.

V.
The Clouded Leopard

*A*s the *Promise*, the *Albatross*, and the *Snowdonia* left the harbour, they turned east, and it was not long before the pirate galleon was visible, sailing south. The wind had veered southward and was freshening; the galleon was seeking to make the most of these favourable conditions. West ordered the royals and top-gallants of the *Promise* unfurled, and the sloops followed suit. Once this had been done, speed was on the side of the Navy vessels.

West stood on deck, looking at the galleon through his telescope. The impression of size that it gave was enhanced by the great forecastle built high above the main deck. The design was quite archaic, and the ship itself was probably very old; galleons like this were built during the Age of Exploration. More modern vessels, like the *Promise*, were far more manoeuvrable. Nonetheless, the size and firepower of the galleon would make it formidable in battle.

West's only hope, if it came to battle, was to remain at the outer edge of cannon range and manoeuvre the *Promise* so that a broadside could be fired at the galleon's stern. There were several cannons mounted there that would return fire, but the frigate would avoid the devastating effects of a broadside. Of course, the pirate captain would attempt to counter this by tacking and changing position. But the *Promise* would be able to tack far more quickly; hopefully, she could remain in line with the galleon's stern.

West had ordered the sloops along in the hopes that he could use them to provide some tactical advantage, but he had now discounted that idea. In the face of the galleon's numerous heavy cannons, the sloops would not stand a chance of avoiding destruction. West had already had the signals sent up ordering them to remain out of range. They would serve instead by swooping in and picking up survivors if the worst case scenario took place and the *Promise* was sunk.

For that was a real possibility if battle was joined. Even the bow cannons of the galleon were heavy enough to do real damage. The size and weight of the galleon, which made it slow, also made it strong. At the long range at which West wanted to operate, it would take more than one broadside to the bow to do sufficient damage. In the meantime, the *Promise* might be sufficiently raked as to reduce her speed of tacking; a skilful shot from one of the bow cannons could easily knock down a mast, for example. That would, immediately, be the end of the battle. The galleon would then swing around and deliver a broadside that would cripple or sink the frigate.

There were also the lives of the hostages to consider. The men who they were trying to rescue would have little chance of surviving such a battle. If the pirates did not kill them, the guns of the *Promise* might.

All this, however, was assuming that battle was the outcome of this chase. That was not necessarily so. If the pirate captain wished battle, he could turn about at any time and engage the *Promise*; he had not done so. And despite the odds in his favour, there was good reason for him to want to avoid an engagement. If he were a clever man, as he seemed to be, he would surely anticipate West's strategy: it was by far the best way for a single frigate to attempt to engage a galleon. He would know that there was at least a chance of it being successful, and a probability that some damage would be done. Most importantly of all, there was virtually nothing for the pirates to gain. The *Promise* was no merchantman; she had no cargo to plunder; she was even low on provisions, which was what had necessitated the stop at St. Helena in the first place. A shrewd pirate captain would barter with the hostages in order to avoid battle; and a shrewd frigate captain would listen.

West continued to look at the galleon. Its hull had no paint, and was made of dark wood, old but strong. There were windows in the forecastle. Looking at them through his telescope, West could catch a glimpse of a furnished, probably well-appointed interior. No doubt this was the cabin of the captain whom Baird had described as aristocratic. The rudder was quite large, another archaic feature; and atop the forecastle was a beautiful copper wheel. The flag from the mainmast was not the skull-and-crossbones that one associated with pirates, but rather a flag that West had never seen before. It looked as if it was based on a family coat of arms. It showed, against a claret field, an argent sword and a golden flower.

"She's a rare sight," said Kenmare, suddenly standing at West's side, and referring to the galleon. "Like something out of another age."

"Like something out of the Age of Exploration," said West with a smile.

"May I ask what your plans are, sir?" With some captains, that would have been an unwise question; but Kenmare knew West well enough now to be confident that he was on safe ground. West answered by quickly detailing both his battle strategy and his willingness to negotiate.

"Sounds wise, sir. And if I may say so, the way that you handled the situation at the fort was quite something. I imagine men will be speaking of that for a long time to come."

"Ah. Well, it seemed the thing to do."

"How did you manage to look so ill, sir?"

"Belladonna in the eyes, a trace of powder on the face, courtesy of our ship's surgeon; he also had something he rubbed on my neck to make it look red and blotchy. Truth to tell, it still itches. But at least it fooled Crimson."

"Aye, that it did." Kenmare chuckled. At that moment, the pirate ship began to swing about. West thought that they were about to go into battle after all; he was pleased that the practice with the guns had done their work. He felt a healthy fear of death or mutilation, but not the unreasoning fear that he been stricken with before; at least not in any way that he could not control. As for his ship, she was already cleared for action. And when he looked to the sides, he saw the sloops obeying his orders and falling back.

But then he saw the figure of Crimson standing on the forecastle deck with a speaking trumpet at his lips. "My captain requests parley!"

Apparently, the captain had seen through West's ruse of carrying the plague; Crimson and his comrades had been allowed back on board. More important, though, was the matter of parley. West handed Kenmare his telescope and picked up his speaking trumpet. "The request for parley is accepted, and your captain is welcome to come aboard."

"Do we have your word that he and his party will not be harmed or taken prisoner?"

"Unlike some of us, Crimson, I know what parley means."

A few minutes later, a longboat left the galleon and rowed toward the *Promise*. The galleon, meanwhile, had continued to turn about, stopping when her stern faced that of the *Promise*. West could see a name painted on the stern hull in silver letters: the *Clouded Leopard*. A curious name. West believed it to be a real creature, a kind of leopard; but the word "clouded" also suggested something mysterious, or, at sea, perhaps threatening. Meanwhile, the longboat reached the side of the *Promise* and the captain came aboard, accompanied by two lackeys who were dressed much as Crimson had been, but without the fine vest. The captain, though, was indeed a different sort of figure.

"I am Captain James Clarion, of the *Clouded Leopard*," he said with grave courtesy. He spoke the King's English and did so like a nobleman.

"Captain Sir Bowman West, of the *Promise*."

Clarion's manner of dress was almost as old-fashioned as his ship. He wore a long coat of burgundy velvet, very rich in both material and colour. Below it were black trousers, and upon the pirate captain's head was a great black velvet hat with a plume of white feathers. The man's features were also striking. The face was drawn and craggy, with a sharp nose and heavy black eyebrows. The skin was deeply tanned, but the eyes were a clear pale blue with a trace of violet. West found those eyes arresting; there was an undeniable melancholy in them.

"Captain West, it is a pleasure to meet you. May I congratulate you upon your successful ruse. While Mr. Crimson is not a difficult man to fool, your ingenuity is all that I would have expected from a man of your reputation."

West smiled at the pirate's manner and decided to respond in kind.

"I thank you, Captain Clarion, and I must also compliment your abilities, as shown in your capture of the fort. The game, however, is now up. I must request and require that you release your hostages and surrender yourself and your crew for the judgment of the crown."

"A well-spoken request that you know well I shall not consent to. But perhaps we might discuss these matters in more comfort in your cabin."

"Of course, Captain. Please follow me; I will have my steward bring us some port. Mr. Kenmare, please make these gentlemen comfortable." West gestured at the ill-dressed, scowling pirates who stood upon the deck.

"Of course, sir," said Kenmare, grinning broadly at the whole scene.

In the cabin, Chang poured glasses of tawny port and then departed. Clarion sipped at his glass appreciatively. "A fine vintage," he said. "Though I confess I have always favoured white port, myself."

"And I favour Navy rum," said West. "But now, to the matter at hand."

"Yes," said Clarion. "To speak honestly, Captain West, I have something that you want, and that you cannot get by battle: the lives of the hostages. Captain Fieldstone, the commander of the fort; Lieutenant Downs, the commander of the *Albatross*, who unfortunately sustained injury to his right arm when we boarded his vessel; and the captain of the merchantman, a rather nervous fellow whose name I do not recall. Should you attempt to attack my ship, I would not be surprised if these men proved to be among the first casualties of battle. However, I think we may be able to reach an accommodation."

"Well, that might be possible; provided of course that the hostages are released and the stolen stores returned."

"I have no great desire to carry Messers Fieldstone and Downs, and the said merchant captain, across the seas with me. The stores might be another matter. In any case, Captain, any negotiation which is followed by a battle is little more than a waste of time. If we are going to fight— a conflict in which I rather have the advantage— then for my purposes, we may as well do so now."

"If you are looking to avoid battle, then, what do you propose? You have attacked a Navy vessel and fort, kidnapped Navy officers and British citizens, and you are not willing to surrender yourself for arrest."

"All true. However, as I said, I would have the upper hand in any battle between us. If you attempt to capture my ship and take my men and I into custody, to await an appointment at Execution Dock no doubt, the affair is likely to end with your own fine ship rotting at the bottom of the South Atlantic. That would be unfortunate. I am sure you do not wish to undergo that sea change and have your bones made of corals, rich and strange though it all might be."

"It is refreshing to meet a pirate who uses Shakespearean references in his threats. Let me respond with this verse: *A great while ago the world began, with heigh-ho, the wind and the rain.* You forget, Captain Clarion, the inexorable hand of time that touches us all— even ships. The *Clouded Leopard* is a vessel that any historian would be fascinated by. In

✴ CHRIS FASOLINO

battle, however, it would be as easy to outmanoeuvre as— alas! I lack a simile. But you seem an intelligent enough man to understand the tactical situation, even without literary device."

"If you seek a simile, I will give you one: your ship would be a falcon fighting an elephant. I grant that the frigate is swifter and more manoeuvrable. That does not mean it will be able to make an impact. On the other hand, should I be fortunate enough to aim a broadside, then the falcon will be trampled by the elephant.

"Captain West, I will tell you my proposal. In exchange for the hostages, you will give my ship a four day head start before attempting any pursuit— should you wish to offer pursuit, that is."

"Such a start would make pursuit impossible, even as slow as the *Clouded Leopard* is; unless, of course, you see fit to confide your destination. However, I do not think such an agreement could be acceptable to me. The stolen stores would have to be part of the exchange, as well."

"Ah, but what sort of pirate would give up what he has stolen?"

"The sort of pirate who knows that I am perfectly capable of damaging his ship even if I lose the battle. You must understand, Captain Clarion, that my ship is low on provisions. We came to St. Helena to re-stock. If this is not possible, we will be in sore straits. Therefore, if you are unwilling to return the stores you have stolen from the fort, I really have no choice but to enter into battle. You said you were aware of my reputation. Do you really think your *Clouded Leopard* is going to escape damage? Is it your plan to send me to the bottom of the ocean while you are left stranded in these isolated waters? Or will you listen to reason?"

Clarion sipped his port. "You are a fine orator, Captain West. Let me make you this offer: the hostages, along with the stores from the fort. The cargo of the merchantman I will retain."

West pretended to consider that, though it was precisely what he had expected. He sipped his own port. "You know, this really is a fine vintage. As to your offer, Captain Clarion, I believe that it would be acceptable." He stood up, and Clarion did likewise. They shook hands. "A four day head start, provided the conditions are met. You have my word."

"Then I will send the hostages over in a longboat. The transfer of the stores will take rather more time; naturally, our truce will continue during that time."

"Naturally."

"Then I may tell that it has been a pleasure to speak with you, Captain West." Clarion smiled mysteriously. "Perhaps we will meet again someday. Stranger things have happened upon the seas."

"Perhaps so." West eyed him keenly, and thought he saw a trace of irony in the pirate captain's melancholy blue-lavender eyes. But what that meant he could not tell.

VI.
Stories and Rum

West did not see Clarion again during the time that the prisoners and stores were being returned. When the transfer was complete, the *Clouded Leopard* sailed off on a southerly course, and the *Promise* returned to St. Helena.

The ship's surgeon of the *Promise* treated Lieutenant Downs and was pleased to report that the injuries to his arm, which had been caused by a pirate's cutlass, would heal. Both Downs and Fieldstone, as well as Atkins, the merchant captain, offered their compliments and gratitude to West. In addition, Fieldstone expressed agreement with West's judgment not to enter into battle with the *Clouded Leopard*. "I may be biased because it was my neck in the noose," he said, "but I think you did the right thing, Captain West. It would have been most unwise to set your frigate against that galleon. Most unwise."

The officers were returned to St. Helena, where the *Promise* divided the rescued stores with the fort and the other ships. The matter of fresh water was also attended to, and fresh vegetables and meat were obtained. The interior of St. Helena was lush and fertile, despite the forbidding nature of its coastline. There were farmsteads that offered produce and a clear stream that ran down to the sea. During the next few days, the *Promise* was well-provisioned.

West remained in the harbour for a full four days, in order to avoid even accidentally breaking his word to Clarion. Then, the journey continued, with morale at a high point. Not only was there a greater variety of food to be enjoyed, but there was also the marvellous story of West's single-handed recapture of the fort. The captain's ingenuity and daring were praised among the officers and in the lower decks. West was aware of this and somewhat amused by it; but he could not help but be pleased with the confidence and loyalty it engendered.

Chang's morale was at something of a high as well. After having been reduced to serving out simple rations, he was now able to cook again. He also had the opportunity to study, along with West, the book about the South China Sea that had been appropriated from Gilbraith's sea chest. Gilbraith had been buried ashore and would never reclaim his book.

This is not to say, however, that the *Promise* was now free of all things East India Company. Carrin remained aboard. In fact, he informed West that he would now act in Gilbraith's stead as representative of the Company, stating that there were likely instructions to this effect in West's official written orders. West had checked the orders again and found that this was indeed the case. He found it noteworthy both that Carrin was so insistent and that he knew what the orders said. The act of subservience— West was more and more convinced that it was an act, just as he was convinced that Gilbraith, in some way, had been acting— was slipping away from Nile Carrin. Nonetheless, Carrin kept to himself as the voyage continued. He did not ask for Gilbraith's book; probably they were at a stalemate there, for if he confronted West about the book's disappearance, he would have to explain its secrecy. And he did not offer any particular reason for his solitude. The others aboard the ship could only guess as to whether it was indisposition, as had supposedly been the case with Gilbraith, or some natural diffidence. More importantly, West still had his questions about Gilbraith's death; but it seemed that no answers were forthcoming.

After they rounded the Cape of Good Hope and turned north into the Indian Ocean, the weather began to change. The favourable conditions that had prevailed for much of the trip— aside from the occasional brush with the edges of an Atlantic storm— gave way to grey skies and foul winds. For weeks, the *Promise* had to beat about the coast, making little or no progress. All the while the sea and sky were grey. West would have taken to port if he could; but South Africa was under the control of the Dutch East India Company, and given the elements of trade and treasure in his mission, he had no intention of making landfall there.

In time, the wind died away. Then, finally, it was replaced by a faint northward zephyr. The *Promise* was able to resume her course, slowly now, but with perceptible movement in the right direction. It was then that Chang to came to West with his idea.

CHRIS FASOLINO

West was on deck at the time. He was staring through his telescope at the distant coastline on the port side of the ship. It was a fair enough morning; the clouds, at least, were scattered. The *Promise* was moving north under all sail at some three knots. "I wish that breeze would pick up, sir," said Kenmare.

"Yes," West agreed.

Chang approached with coffee for the captain. "Mebbe Captain wants coffee in his cabin, yes, sir?" he asked. West knew this to mean that Chang had something to discuss with him. He nodded and followed his steward back to his cabin. As soon as he shut the door, Chang said, "I have been considering the material in Gilbraith's book, and I have a somewhat imaginative suggestion to make." He handed West the cup of coffee almost absently, too absorbed in his idea for the usual courtesies, a phenomenon that West well understood.

"What is it?"

"I have the impression that the Chinese influence is significant in the Blue Isles. The people there clearly view this Alishan as a hero. In particular, I might say that the influence of the Chinese treasure fleet has therefore been significant."

"Yes, I agree with that impression. As a matter of fact, Mr. Chang, I have been wanting to ask you to tell me more about this treasure fleet."

"Yes, sir. My suggestion rather concerns the treasure fleet. I understand you are planning to make landfall along the East African coast at some point?"

"Yes. Since we have been delayed by the winds and the weather, I want to re-provision before we cross the Indian Ocean. There is a place called Port Tawny that is something of a haven for British ships."

"Port Tawny?" asked Chang with a raised eyebrow.

"The name was something of a jest." West smiled. "It was coined by an eccentric and possibly inebriated English adventurer, Sir Frank Crisp, who explored the region while hunting big game."

"Ah, the inscrutable English sense of humour, with its attachment to puns. Even the great Shakespeare was plagued by it."

"So he was," West laughed.

"In any case," Chang continued, "since we are visiting East Africa, I have an idea that I wish to share with you."

"What is it?"

"There is a kind of animal that is highly valued by the Chinese. The treasure fleet brought one home to the Emperor. This creature is considered to be one of the 'celestial animals'— rare, special, and auspicious. If you were able to capture one and bring it as a gift to the Blue Isles, I think you would ensure that your diplomatic mission would be well-received."

"A fascinating suggestion, Mr. Chang. And what is this animal?"

"We call it the *quilin*. It is said to resemble a deer in the form of its body yet have a tail like an ox. Its neck is like a pine tree. It has hooves like a horse and a horn like a unicorn, save that there are two horns, soft as velvet. It is said in poetry to have "luminous spots like a red cloud or a purple mist" and to observe a celestial harmony in its every motion. Its tongue is a deep and regal purple, and its voice is like the sound of a bell. I am sure that this description is sufficiently distinctive, sir."

West raised an eyebrow. "It sounds like a creature from a fairy tale. How am I to find this wondrous beast?"

"Europeans call it the giraffe," Chang answered with the trace of a smile.

"Now that sounds more achievable. You said that this animal was brought back as a gift for the Emperor?"

"Yes, sir. The *quilin* is believed to appear only in times of great peace and prosperity. The Emperor Zhu Di took advantage of its appearance to name Beijing as the new capital. I am sure that the arrival of a *quilin* in the Blue Isles would cause its bearer to be viewed with great favour."

"And why is the giraffe considered so valuable?"

"It is believed to be the gentlest of creatures, treading so carefully that it does not even trample down the grass. It therefore expresses the benevolence of heaven— that is the part about observing celestial harmony with its every motion. The creature is, of course, very exotic to the Chinese. The treasure fleet sailed as far as Africa to bring back rare animals, along with other treasures. Since our own ship is also travelling to Africa, the possibility of a *quilin* came to me."

"But would we be able to keep it alive all the way to the Blue Isles?"

"We would certainly have to lay in a supply of its food, sir, but the journey by ship to China was at least as far, and yet the creature did survive to be welcomed by the Imperial court."

"Fascinating. I love the idea, Mr. Chang, and I thank you for it. I will assuredly take some time at Port Tawny to look for a giraffe— or, rather, a *quilin*."

"Yes, sir. Thank you, sir."

On the way to Port Tawny, there were two events that would later stand out in West's mind. The first was an evening of entertainment for the crew. Sailors with musical talents were called upon to put them to use, with the crowd usually joining in, so that singing seemed to echo from the deck up to the sky. "The Jug of Punch" provided a fast-paced, rousing conclusion.

It was very early in the month of June—
As I was sitting in my room—
I heard a thrush— in an ivy bush—
And the song he sang— was the Jug of Punch!

To West, the song was like a set of Chinese boxes. The thrush was singing the Jug of Punch, and that was the name of the song. So the thrush was singing about himself singing the Jug of Punch, and so on and so on. Not that the sailors were thinking of that; they simply enjoyed the music and good cheer, and that was as it should be.

The second event was a supper with the officers in the captain's cabin. The meal was finished with Stilton cheese, along with port for Rede and Teal and Navy rum for West, Kenmare, and Lang. At that point, West reminded his lieutenants that, on the first such occasion they had shared, he had told the story of the southern thrush; and as if on cue, Autolycus had turned to peep out at them from his cage. Then West said: "I think it is your turn this evening. Or at least, we can share the privilege."

"What do you have in mind, sir?" asked Kenmare.

"I think we should each tell a story tonight. We are sailors, after all— so we all have stories to tell." West took a sip of rum.

"A fine idea, sir," said Kenmare. "I don't believe I have ever told you all about the time I visited Marrakesh, and I think that is as good a tale for tonight as any." Without a trace of effort, he launched into his story; and West could see the other lieutenants trying to listen and think at the same time.

"Many years ago, I was third lieutenant in a ship called the *Regulus*, in the Mediterranean. The time came that we docked in Gibraltar, and I spent that evening ashore with some of my mates. I came back aboard rather late, and, if I recall, singing. Well, my mates got me back to my cabin, and I slept like a felled oak. The next morning, a midshipman woke me up and told me the captain wanted to see me.

"As you can imagine, I was none too pleased with the timing. My head was throbbing and my limbs were weak. Nonetheless, I did what I could to make myself presentable— a quick shave and a change of uniform— and I went to my captain's cabin. I knew I was not the most spruce young officer in the fleet, not that morning, anyways; but my captain was a kind man, and though I felt a bit sheepish, I was not afraid."

West happened to glance at Rede's face at that moment, and saw there was a far-off look in his eyes. He noted it.

"Well, when I got to my captain's cabin, I was in for quite a surprise. And I did indeed wish that I could have done a better job of making myself presentable. For there was another captain with him, and there was a young woman— and not just any young woman at that.

"She was dressed in a flowing robe of green and gold silk, with a kind of silk shawl about her head. She was tall and stately, her skin was dusky, and her eyes were black. She was an Arab maiden, and my captain introduced her as the Princess Morgiana of the Sultanate of Morocco.

"Well, I was so taken aback I couldn't do much more than nod and say 'yes, sir' and try not to stare. Turned out that the other captain, his name was Burton, he commanded a frigate that had just fought a ship full of Barbary pirates. The pirates had sailed out from a patch of fog and attacked, but they ended up taking the worse part of the bargain for all that. Captain Burton had a well-trained crew; they cleared for action in just about no time at all, turned about, and started firing broadsides at the pirate vessel. Before long the mainmast was down and the sails were in tatters. That threw them into confusion, of course; and the Navy men took that time to come alongside and board her.

"Before long, the Barbary ship was captured. Captain Burton sailed her back to Gibraltar as a prize. There was all manner of rich cargo aboard; silks, spices, even some gold. But richest of all was a captive the pirates had taken from their own people- the Princess Morgiana. They hadn't laid a hand on her, pirates though they were; they were holding her safe return for ransom, for her family was rich and noble. Once the

British rescued her, Captain Burton gave her the hospitality of his own ship and saw to it she was treated with every courtesy.

"All that was amazing enough; but when my captain told me my task, I could hardly believe my young ears. I was to take the Princess Morgiana back to Morocco to reunite her with her family. We were to sail to Casablanca, just across the straits and then southwest down the coast; so I was to be given a small brig, the *Starfish*, to carry out the mission.

"I will not forget what my captain said to me then. 'I've chosen you for your discipline, Mr. Kenmare,' he said, and he eyed me up and down with a twinkle of amusement in his eye. 'The quality may not be apparent at the moment, but I know I can trust you to bring the Princess safely home.'

"Well, I gave him my word that I would, and I picked out a small crew who I knew would be just as respectful. We outfitted the *Starfish*, and both my own captain and Captain Burton sent a supply of luxuries along, for the comfort of the princess, they said.

"Finally we were ready, and the princess herself came aboard. I'd love to tell you that she looked around and complimented me on a trim little ship. But she did nothing of the kind. Just swept across the decks as lordly as you please. Went to her own quarters and stayed there while we sailed away from Gibraltar.

"I thought she would probably stay there for the whole trip. For awhile she did; I would bring her meals into her, with all the little comforts that the captains had furnished, and never a word would she speak. But when we came nigh on Casablanca, she was out on deck, looking at the shores of her homeland. But she was not wearing that silk robe anymore. Or if she was, it was underneath the veil. For she was veiled now— a great heavy black garment, so that she did not look like a woman at all, but just a shapeless form. 'I suppose you'll be happy to be home,' I said to her.

"Well, she just said, 'yes.' Just the one word, in English, with a fair musical voice; but no more. She just kept looking at the land that got closer and closer— or I guessed that she was, for I could not see her eyes.

"We landed in Casablanca, and disembarked amid the fair city with all its white houses up against the blue Mediterranean. I left a couple of men to guard the *Starfish*, and then I had to arrange transport the rest of the way to Marrakesh. Before long, myself, my men, and the princess were riding south on camelback. I hired a guide who showed us how to ride the beasts; but nasty ill-tempered creatures they were."

"I have heard they are prone to spit," said Rede with an expression of some distaste.

"Aye, that they are; you do not want to come in spitting distance of a camel, and their spitting distance is a lot farther than ours. But we made do. I will never forget the way the princess looked upon hers. She rode that lanky, yellow creature as gracefully as if it was a fine horse. And when I ventured to tell her so, she spoke to me for just the second time. 'The camel,' she said, 'is our ship. The ship of the desert.' I thought about that for a long time afterward. And I always thought, I am happy to be an Irishman. For I would rather sail a ship through the blue waters than ride a camel through the dun sands any time.

"There was something wondrous about that journey. We went down a desert road, and on the one hand was a vast stretch of flat sand, very bright and hot with the sun beating upon it. On the other side of us, the sand kind of rose up, and it turned into great mountainous dunes. Sometimes the wind would come and whip sand into our eyes and blow at the princess's veil without ever uncovering her face. I had heard that there were great whirlwinds that prowled the desert, and that the sand would be blown upon travellers and they would be lost forever. But we made a safe enough journey and faced no such dangers as that.

"And so we came to Marrakesh. A very different city it was from Casablanca, to be sure. Casablanca is all white, and open to the sea. Marrakesh is surrounded by a great stone wall, and it is all red. The red city, they call it— for the stone that they used has a ruddy colour. A beautiful place it is. I remember seeing a snake charmer at one street corner, with a cobra coming out of the pot next to him. We passed by a marketplace, too. It was a great open-air market, with glistening wares of bronze and gold. And there was a rack of spices there, spices that were every colour you could imagine, orange and red and green and even deep blue and bright pink.

"Then we came to the palace of Morgiana's family. Her father came out to greet her; a great chieftain, dressed in fine robes and a turban. I presented to him the greetings and respects of the captains, and he thanked me, and bid me thank them. His English was a bit halting, but

CHRIS FASOLINO

he said, 'You have brought my daughter home. Come now and feast with us.'

"And so my men and I had the chance to attend a Moroccan banquet. Quite an affair it was, I can tell you truly. We ate in a beautiful courtyard that seemed to be in the centre of the palace. The whole floor was tiled with marble, and the walls round about had tile mosaics that must have taken someone forever to make. There were trees here and there in the courtyard, and one of them bore scarlet flowers. There was a fountain, too, with a blue tile basin, and the water just bubbled down in amongst the mosaics with a sweet noise.

"And the food! There was no drink, I am afraid, save tea; but do you know, the food actually made up for that. There was a great roast lamb with savoury spices; there was chicken cooked in a kind of clay pot, with lemon and green olives; there was something like a Cornish pastie, only with sugar and cinnamon, as if they could not decide if it was to be for a meal or a sweet; and there was a kind of grain that they called *couscous*, that they served many different ways. There was a child who walked about while we ate— a girl so young that she did not wear the veil— and she bore a kind of lantern with her that gave off a light mist. The mist carried the smell of oranges, and she kept dousing that upon us; apparently that's what they do for honoured guests. I did not much care for it while we ate, really. There were already so many good smells from the food. But when the meal was done, and she came around once more, I started to get the idea. The smell of oranges was sweet in the hot North African night, with the stars beginning to come out above us in the dusky blue sky.

"And that is really the end of my story. We were given hospitality for the night, and the next day, we started back for Casablanca and the *Starfish*, and then for our own ship. And as for the Princess Morgiana, from the time I handed her back to her family, I never saw her again, if you could say I saw her at all while she was under the veil. In all the time I knew her, I had only heard her speak twice. But we took her safely back to her home, and it was an adventure I will not forget."

Kenmare fell silent, and the others looked at him. "I think Mr. Kenmare is a hard act to follow," said West.

"Aye, that he is," said Lang. "But I have one for you, sir, if you'll pardon me." He was looking now at Kenmare. "Do you know why God made whiskey?"

"And why was that, Mr. Lang?"

"To keep the Irish from conquering the world!"

Kenmare's laughter was as loud as anyone's in the moment that followed. "Well said, Mr. Lang. But since you're so quick to speak, perhaps you would like to tell the next story?" Lang nodded unabashedly in answer to his First Lieutenant's question, and West saw Rede look slightly relieved.

Lang began: "Well, this is none so fine a tale as Mr. Kenmare's, but perhaps it will make you smile. I was on a cutter once, the *King Alfred*, being commanded by a Lieutenant Ford. Well, we took a gentleman from the diplomatic service aboard once. We were starting from London and we were supposed to ferry him to Amsterdam.

"The gentleman's name was Mr. Coachman, and he was what you might call a bit of a stiff. He was a bit— as I said, a bit of a stiff." Lang hesitated and then ploughed on. He had clearly altered what he was going to say. West was fairly sure that Lang had unthinkingly been about to reference Gilbraith, only to remember that the man had met an untimely end and it would not do to speak ill of him. Rede, however, stiffened; stiffened being the operative term. He was apparently taking Lang's hesitation as an insult to himself— as if the Third Lieutenant had been about to make a jibe at him. West was sure that was not the case, but thought idly that there might have been some truth in it; Rede was obviously a touchy man. And there was that tension Rede had with Lang, that West had noticed before. It clearly had not changed.

Lang continued: "At first, he didn't make too much trouble. But as soon as we had sailed down the Thames and made it out to sea, the man went into a kind of panic. He was a young man and he had never been to sea before, it turned out. And he was just madly frightened that we would run into a storm, or an enemy ship, and somehow sink. He was seasick, too, of course, and I'm sure that made it all worse. Anyway, he was storming about on deck something fierce, and nobody was quite sure how to calm him down.

"Well, Lieutenant Ford figured out a way. He saw Mr. Coachman near the rail, ranting on about something and waving his arms about; and he came over to him. Mr. Coachman turned to look at the lieutenant, and he said something to him, I don't rightly recall what. But the

lieutenant didn't say nothing back. He just walked over to Mr. Coachman and pushed him over the side.

"Well, we all just stared at him. The lieutenant hadn't changed his
expression at all, neither when he pushed him in or afterwards. He just
stared at the diplomat who was flailing away down in the water. Then, just
before the cutter passed him by, he said to me: 'All right, Lang, fish him out.'

"So I did, and Mr. Coachman thanked me and went back to his cabin
to dry off. Later on he came back out, stood on deck, and looked around
a bit, as calm as you please. So I says to Lieutenant Ford, 'Lieutenant, sir,
what's come over that fellow? Ever since you pushed him in the water he
seems much happier.'

"And the Lieutenant, he says to me: 'I think Mr. Coachman figured
out the ship isn't so bad!'"

Everyone laughed, and Lang looked pleased. In fact, he decided to
press on with another story.

"You might like this one, too— I have to throw in another since mine
was none so fancy as Mr. Kenmare's. I was in a tavern once in Naples,
along with a few of my mates, when three sailors from a French ship
walk in. They looked like they had already visited a few other taverns
and wanted to start trouble. So one of them walks over to me and says,
'The King of England's a poltroon.'

"Well, I didn't say nothing, just kept on drinking. My mates did the
same.

"The next one comes over and says, 'The King of England's a scally-
wag.' I still didn't say nothing, just kept on drinking.

"Finally the last one comes over with a big silly grin on his face, as if
to say, 'this'll get you.' And he says: 'The King of England is French.'

"Well, now I just couldn't help myself. I looked up at him and said:
'That's what your two friends have been trying to tell me!'"

Lang was rewarded with further laughter. "There was a bit of brawl
after that, but we did all right," he concluded. West, who was beginning
to think it time to press on, nodded to Rede.

"Well, gentleman, I do not have the gift of the gab like Mr. Kenmare,
nor the gift of humour like Mr. Lang," began Rede apologetically. "However, since it is my turn, I suppose I can tell you something about why I
came to sea. That may not sound like an interesting story, but it has a
most interesting character: Admiral Hawke."

"You were inspired by Admiral Hawke?" said Kenmare politely, as if trying to conceal a conviction that this was going to be a dull story.

"Not only that, sir; I met him." At that, everyone's attention became much more focused.

"My parents own an inn and pub in Bristol called The Old Stand," said Rede. "When I was growing up, I always wanted to go to sea, because of all the sailors who would come through the pub. I would fetch them food and drink and listen to their stories, and it always seemed such a grand adventuresome life. Then, too, I was the second son, and the innkeeper's life was marked for my elder brother. So I had to make my own way somehow, and the sea was the way I chose.

"Well, one day, a very well-dressed man came into the pub and said to my father: 'Admiral Hawke is outside and wishes to know if you can accommodate his party. There will be a dozen men.' My father did not believe him until he glanced out through the window and saw a fine coach on the street.

"Then he said, 'This is just a humble place, sir. We have good ale and plain food and little else.' My father would not speak disparagingly of his ale, no matter what the circumstance." Rede smiled slightly; he was becoming wrapped up in his own memory and forgetting his audience, and his tale was all the better for it.

"The man said: 'That is all the Admiral wants.'

"So my father said: 'Then it would be an honour.' The man left and he came back in with party of officers. In amongst them was the Admiral himself. I was standing at the bar, and I just stared at him. He carried himself with a fine air; as dignified as anyone, yet somehow right at home in the Old Stand.

"Well, I brought them their ale and their food. I remember Admiral Hawke drank porter. And when they got up to leave, and he gave me a coin and his thanks, I had to tell him: 'Sir, I hope to be a Navy man someday. I hope to go to sea.'

"He looked at me and smiled. Then he reached down into his pocket again. He took out another coin and tossed it to me. 'If you want to go to sea, you should have that coin, lad. I picked it up on a voyage long ago.' I looked down at it and saw to my astonishment that it was a gold doubloon. I stared up and murmured my thanks, and the Admiral smiled again, and strode out of the pub.

"Needless to say, I never spent the coin. I still carry it about with me— right here." He reached down into his pocket, took out the gold doubloon, and passed it around for everyone's admiration. Lang handed it back to Rede, and Rede put it back in his pocket.

At that point, Teal began to look nervous. Kenmare smiled at him encouragingly. "Now then, lad, why not tell us how Captain Mayhew came to name you Acting-Lieutenant? That would be a fine tale."

But Teal only flushed. "I do not think I could, sir." He paused. "But if you like, I will tell you about a man I met once who made a kind of impression on me. He was a famous man, too, though none so famous as Admiral Hawke; and he was someone who surprised me.

"His name was Captain Burroughs." Everyone nodded; Burroughs had been famous enough. Kenmare's eyes were far away. West realized that Kenmare knew the story. Teal's brief time in the service had been spent entirely on the *Promise*, and Kenmare would surely know most of his stories.

"Captain Gideon Burroughs came aboard the *Promise* to take passage from Gibraltar back to England, because he was retiring. He had been commanding a ship of the line, and he had of course had a long career, and was a really renowned man. Of course. So when he came on board, I was looking forward to seeing him and seeing what he was like.

"He looked like a distinguished older gentleman. He had a fine speaking voice and seemed to always be very courteous to everyone. But after supper one evening, he and Captain Mayhew decided to play a game of chess. They had been talking about it during the meal. Apparently Captain Burroughs was a great chess player. Anyway, they got started here as the rest of us officers were leaving— this was after I had been made Acting-Lieutenant, you see.

"The next morning, Captain Mayhew asked me to bring Captain Burroughs his breakfast. And when I did, I saw the strangest thing. Captain Burroughs was crouching over his cot, and on the cot was the chessboard. I saw him move the black castle a few squares forward. Then he moved the white knight. He was playing chess with himself!

"I left him his breakfast, and he thanked me, but didn't seem to pay much attention. He went back to his game. Later on, I asked Captain Mayhew who had won the game last night. He said that Captain Burroughs had, naturally. Captain Burroughs was a famous chess player.

"That night, Captain Burroughs refused to come to supper in Captain Mayhew's quarters. He had me bring his food into him. And when I did, he was still at the chessboard. It was set up all differently; it was a different game. But he was still playing chess with himself.

"I told Captain Mayhew about it, and the next day, he asked if Captain Burroughs would play another game with him. But Captain Burroughs refused and would not come out of his cabin. He just kept playing chess with himself.

"As the voyage went on, it got even worse. I would bring him his meals and take them away again, and he hadn't even touched them. He was not eating. His eyes were red, his face was drawn, and his bed untouched. He was not sleeping. All he was doing, day and night, was playing chess with himself.

"It was Mr. Kenmare who finally stopped him, with Captain Mayhew's permission. Mr. Kenmare walked into Captain Burroughs's cabin, picked up the chessboard and the pieces, and put them in a big canvas bag. Captain Burroughs grabbed at them and tried to protest, but Mr. Kenmare just said he was acting under Captain Mayhew's orders. Then Mr. Kenmare walked out on deck and threw the bag into the sea.

"Captain Burroughs had followed him on deck, and when the bag went into the water, he just stared. Then he went back to his cabin and shut the door. And it was so strange, but it seemed we could hear the sound of sobbing. Then, at last, Captain Burroughs slept. And when he got up, he would eat again. He even took his meals with Captain Mayhew and the officers, quietly, but he was there. Of course, no one ever brought up chess again.

"In time, we brought him back to England. But when he left the *Promise*, that was the last I saw or heard of him."

"Fascinating," said West.

Teal nodded gravely. "Yes, sir."

"Throwing the chess set overboard was my idea, I'm afraid," said Kenmare. "Perhaps it was a bit harsh, but I could not think of any other way to break through to him. And I was afraid he would die slumped over that chessboard."

"I wonder what happened to him," said West. "I had heard that Burroughs retired, but I have heard nothing about him since."

"Nor I," said Kenmare. "Of course, none of this was all that long ago. Captain Mayhew retired himself not long after that— in a rather better state of mind, happily— and then you came aboard, sir."

"And then we set sail for the Blue Isles."

"Aye, sir, and then we set sail for the Blue Isles."

West smiled. "Well, gentleman, I thank you all for your fine stories."

"What about you, sir?" asked Kenmare.

"Me? The one about the southern thrush doesn't count?"

"Well, that was some time ago now," said Kenmare.

"Very well," said West. He took a sip of rum. "Here's a story for you all, then. Of course, as much as I enjoyed all your stories, I never said they had to be true. So I think I will tell you a fairy tale, the kind that my parents told me when I was growing up." That was true; West's parents had told him fairy tales. But he did not see fit to tell his officers that he had written this particular fairy tale the week before. "This is called 'A Summer's Tale.'"

In the old days, when people still listened to the sound of the waves on the shores and knew what they meant, there was a kingdom known as Greensward. And Greensward was a fair land, with meadows the colour of emeralds and stony cliffs at the edge of the sea. There were trees in that land from which golden flowers blossomed; and there were running rivers that sang like birds. There were warm, sunlit days and cool, starlit evenings. Thus it was that the people of Greensward rejoiced, and they made music that became renowned throughout the earth.

But then it came to pass that a plague fell upon the land, a plague that men called the Grey Death. Those upon whom the plague came knew that their end was nigh, for the plague was feared in all places, and its sign was manifest. First, the man lost his ability to see in colour; and therefore was the Grey Death so named. Some few days after this, he would slip into a deep sleep from which he could not be awakened. And the end of his life would soon follow.

But there was a nobleman in Greensward who was in truth a bold man. He was called North because of the place where he dwelt. And though fear of the plague, for his people's sake and his own sake, ran deep in his own heart, yet he determined to fight against it. So he called the wisest men of the land to his side, in the Eld Castle which is by the sea. And unto them he said: 'O you sages of the land, how may this Grey Death be halted? For truly it is spoken that for every plague that ails the sons of men, some countermeasure does exist, even though it be far away or undiscovered.'

And the wise men responded: 'You speak truth. For even the dreaded Grey Death, a cure exists. But whether it can be attained is another matter. For the healing, the only healing, is from the brightening Flowers of Colour in the Rainbow Isles. Those Isles lie in the midst of the western sea; but no chart tells where, for it is long years since any of the sons of Greensward have journeyed to their distant shores.'

At that North said, 'Nonetheless, journey there I shall.'

And then the oldest of these old men spoke, in a voice so thin and frail that it could barely be heard. 'Should you make the voyage,' he said, 'there is one ship that you must take. An old ship, one that some men may not even think seaworthy. But it is the one to choose, and I will show it to you.'

North then clasped the old man's hand in friendship and honour, and bade him do so.

He led North to the silver strand where Greensward tumbled into the ocean. And there, perched upon the shore, was the ship. It was indeed an aged ship, but through the wood was long weather-beaten, it was still unwarped. North climbed aboard and walked across the deck. 'She will be strong enough for the voyage,' he said.

Then he looked up at the sails, and saw that they were tattered and worn. And he would have given orders for new sails to be fitted, but the old man stayed him from his course. 'Mend the sails, but do not replace them,' he commanded, 'for the ship must be kept intact, lest its memories fade.' So North ordered that the sails be mended straightaway. And when the work was done, they were unfurled upon the mast, and lo! The ship shone in the sunlight, and all who looked upon her knew that she was ready for to sail.

Then the old man gave to North these parting words:

'There is good reason for my counsel, that you should choose this ship, and her even as she was. The ship itself knows the way to the Rainbow Isles. She has travelled there before, and though men may forget a path through waters, a ship does not. Take her out to sea under full sail, and she will bring you to your destination. And for the sake of all Greensward, I wish you fair winds and following seas!'

Then North began his voyage. And sure enough, when he found himself in the open sea, the ship seemed to choose its own course. And when he stood upon the deck and looked out at the horizon, he felt hope, like sunlight on his shoulder; and he believed that soon, the Rainbow Isles would appear.

Lo! A great storm, that turned the sky black and rent it in two. And great bolts of lightning flashed from the darkness, and the wind blew with the breath *of ice. All around North's ship, the sea was in turmoil. Great waves rose and fell, and the ship was tossed about. North stood on the deck, staring straight ahead and seeing nothing, so impenetrable were the shadows.*

And then the wind grew fiercer still, and its fury was terrible. North had taken in his sails and was grateful for it; yet he feared now for his own person, and he had to struggle to keep his footing, such was the force of the gale. His fears soon proved to be well-founded. A wave of exceptional mightiness arose beneath the ship, and it seemed to leap upward. Amidst the sudden motion and the keening of the wind, North felt himself falling. He pitched into the sea and felt himself immersed in freezing waters pitiless. He rose, gasping for air, and struggled to reach his ship, even as it was borne away from him by the tempest. And then his mind's eye closed and he knew no more.

When he awoke, the storm had passed. There was no sign of the ship, yet the sea all around him was tranquil and blue, as indeed was the whole sky above. His hands were touching something that was not water, something that felt sleek and strange; and as he looked at what he touched, he felt great surprise. For he was being borne along by two silver dolphins.

One of the dolphins swam ahead, and turned, and looked at him. It seemed to be laughing. There was a purple seashell in its mouth. It came toward North and pressed the seashell against his face. North did not know what it was doing, but he could not help laughing. Then, the dolphin placed the shell in his open mouth. To North's astonishment, the shell dissolved on his tongue and tasted like honey, and he swallowed it.

The dolphins then began to utter clicks and whistles; and to North's even greater astonishment, he found that he understood them, as if it was a language in which he was fluent. 'I am Quicksilver,' said the dolphin who had given him the shell. 'This is my mate, Songbreeze. We have delivered you from the storm.'

'Then you have my great thanks,' said North. 'But how is it that I can understand you?'

'The seashell we have given you bears the gift of knowing our language.'

'And you can understand me?'

'The languages of men are not very difficult, though they are often inadequate in expressions of beauty. But tell me, whither do you journey?'

'To the Rainbow Isles. I must find the Flowers of Colour, to save my people from a deadly plague.'

'Ah, we have visited the Rainbow Isles many times. We can bear you there."

'Then I thank you again, as indeed would all the people of Greensward.'

'We must warn you, though,' said Songbreeze, 'the journey may be perilous for you. For we must pass through the White Mist.'

'Ah, yes,' said Quicksilver. 'For us, it is harmless, as dolphins are immune to its effects. But for humans, it is quite deadly. We will have to make as much of the journey underwater as possible. I hope you can hold your breath.'

'It seems I have no choice but to try,' said North.

'Then let us go.' The dolphins bore him forward through the waters, until they came to a place where the waters themselves could not be seen. There was a cloud of white mist before them, obscuring both sea and sky.

'Do not be afraid as we go through,' said Quicksilver. 'Like the Grey Death, the White Mist can be healed by the flowers of colour. We will remain underwater as much as possible. Your danger will thus be limited, although so will your air. But we will surface as we must so that you may breathe. Now, cling to us tightly.' Quicksilver and Songbreeze dove under the water, with North holding fast. He kept his eyes opened and marvelled at the blue world through which they travelled. But then, the need for air began to choke at him, and he feared that he would perish beneath the water. Finally, at what seemed to be the last possible moment, the dolphins came to the surface.

North gasped at the air, and breathed in and out; but it was cold and bitter. He could see nothing save white, and the mist felt cold and clammy on his skin. When he looked at his hands, though, he felt the gravest fear; for they were as white as leprosy. In another moment, they dove beneath the waters again. And as North looked at the blue around him, he remembered that the dolphins had told him not to be afraid.

So the journey went; moments of gasping at the clammy air, followed by passages through the water when he could not breath at all. But then, at last, they came up out of the sea, and the air was no longer cold. They were at the shores of an island. Yet, no sooner had he satisfied his longing for air, then North felt fear clutch at his heart.

'Have we passed through the White Mist?' he said.

'We have, and your courage has been rewarded,' said Quicksilver. 'We have fulfilled your quest, and the Rainbow Isles are before us.'

'All that I see is grey and black and white,' said North. And then he realized that he himself had carried the plague with him. 'I am near death,' he murmured.

'Yet nearer still the cure.' The dolphins swam forward and placed him upon the strand. There was a grey field before him, with grey flowers.

'I greet you, wayfarer,' said a soft voice beside him. He turned, and saw a pale maiden standing nearby. She looked at him for a moment, and then turned to the dolphins. 'I greet you, Quicksilver and Songbreeze,' she said.

'And we greet you, Daughter of the Sun.'

'You need not fear for your wayfarer. I will care for him.'

'We know you will. Farewell then, to you, Daughter of the Sun, and to you, North.'

'May the seas before you be the purest of blues,' said the maiden. The dolphins leapt above the sea in a tribute to joy, laughing as they did. Then they swam away.

North turned to the maiden, and saw that she had plucked one of the grey flowers, and she was holding it out to him. He took it.

'Breathe in its scent,' she said.

He did, and felt for a moment as if he were inside a flower. Then, he saw that the flower in his hand was no longer grey; it shone like a flame. But everything else was still grey.

'Again,' said the maiden.

He breathed in again and look about him, and the ocean was a vibrant blue, and the sands were warm and golden. The rest of the island was a green field, glowing with flowers of every hue imaginable, many of them of the same fiery appearance as the blossom in his hand.

'Again.'

North breathed the flower again, and he felt warm, and his skin lost its pale hue and returned to the colour of life.

'Again.'

And then colour flooded into North's memory, and he saw the dolphins making their great leap, and they were glistening silver, and the water sparkled blue and green and turquoise.

The maiden before him was beautiful. Her hair was burnished gold, and gold were her eyes, and her skin had a warm, rich hue. Her robe was as yellow as the sunlight, and she wore an azure cloak about her shoulders.

'Who are you?' he stammered.

'I am the Daughter of the Sun,' she said. Even her voice was golden, the rich gold of a cello's music.

'Do you rule this fair island?'

At that she laughed, and the sky rang with the sound. 'No one rules here, save the Creator of all,' she answered. 'Yet I come here often, when I tread the earth. I am the Daughter of the Sun, and I ride the sunlight wheresoever I will.'

North thought upon that, and then he saw a sight on the shore that he had not yet taken notice of. 'My ship!' he cried. For there it was, nestled upon the sands with sails unfurled.

'Yes. It found its way here.'

'Then I will be able to journey home.'

'I do not think it wishes to leave. Yet fear not, mortal! I myself will bear you home, under my wings and upon the light of the sun.'

Then North knew that Greensward would be safe, and the Grey Death would be defeated utterly. With a joyous heart he bent to gather the Flowers of Colour. And he gave thanks to the laughter of the dolphins and the warmth of the sunlight— the blue and the gold— and the love from which they sprang.

Bowman Balfour West reached the end of his story.

It was not the kind of story anyone would expect the captain to tell; or then, again, perhaps it was. In any event, West was a good storyteller. He could see it in the eyes of his officers. They were not wondering why he had told the tale, as they perhaps were when he had begun; they were wondering upon the tale itself. The face of Alexander Teal was strangely wistful. Wade Lang looked content, like a man lost in a happy memory of childhood. Cato Rede bore a furrowed brow, as if he was trying to solve a puzzle; but there was a faint smile about his lips, as if he appreciated the beauty of the puzzle even while he did so. And the eyes of Jonathon Kenmare were glistening.

"That was a Summer's Tale, gentleman," said the captain of the *Promise.*

VII.
The Safari

*P*ort Tawny was an enclave of land on the coast of East Africa, ideally situated for catching the trade winds to India. It was considered British by virtue of a treaty with the sultan who held sway over much of the coast. The port included a cove where ships could dock, warehouses from which they could be re-supplied, and lodge where their officers were customarily provided hospitality.

Sir Frank Crisp, the adventurer who had founded the enclave, sometimes claimed to have named it after a pride of lions he had seen in the area, since a lion has a tawny mane. On other occasions, he claimed that the long grasses of the savannah, with their occasionally tawny colour, had been the inspiration. But as West had indicated to his ship's steward, it was in fact quite obvious that the name was a pun regarding Sir Frank's favourite beverage.

As the *Promise* sailed along the coast, West enjoyed watching the shoreline from his quarterdeck, telescope in hand. The grey waters that prevailed farther south had been changed to aquamarine. The coast was sandy and sometimes lined with palm trees. At times, small boats could be seen fishing near the shore. They were small and flat, almost like rafts. Each had two masts that met at their tip, forming a triangle, and supporting an irregularly shaped white sail. Each such craft would carry three or four African villagers, who would be casting their nets into the sea.

When the *Promise* turned into the cove of Port Tawny, West was able to look at the lodge that Crisp had constructed. Near it were the warehouses, square white buildings made from blocks of crushed coral. The lodge was made of dark wood, with a great colonnaded veranda and an arched roof. West knew that officers would sometimes go big-game hunting during their stopovers, and the building looked like it fit that purpose. He himself planned on hunting of a different sort. He was going to try to capture a living, healthy *quilin*.

There was a sloop at anchor in the cove; its name was the *Androcles*. There were no other ships in sight. "Have you been here before, sir?" asked Kenmare, approaching the quarterdeck.

"I have not, Mr. Kenmare. I wager that you have, though."

"Aye, sir. I wonder if Captain Pimlico is still in command here. He was always noted for his hospitality."

"Then we can hope that he is. I imagine we will be invited to dinner in the lodge."

"That would be usual, sir."

"I would like you to come with me. You can leave Mr. Rede or Mr. Lang in charge of re-provisioning, I expect."

"Aye, sir. That would work out fine."

"Good. I have a rather unusual idea that I want to share with the commander here, and as you know him, it may be well to have you along. In a manner of speaking, I want to go hunting."

"Oh, there would be nothing unusual in that, sir. Many of the officers go hunting while they are here."

"The game, in this case, is going to be somewhat different. I want to catch a live giraffe and bring it on board with us." West smiled at Kenmare's surprise. He had made the statement without any explanation purely for the pleasure of seeing his First Lieutenant's reaction. Then, of course, he expanded, describing what he knew of the Blue Isles, the Chinese influence, and the likely effect of a giraffe.

"Fascinating notion, sir," said Kenmare with approval. "It's a bit like your trick with the plague."

"I don't know that I follow you, Mr. Kenmare."

"Well, neither is the sort of thing that just anyone would think of. And the first one succeeded quite well. This one might give us an advantage, too, if we can pull it off."

"Thank you."

"The problem I see, sir, is getting the giraffe all the way to the Blue Isles. Keeping it alive, I mean."

"Yes, we will have to find out what sort of thing they like to eat and make sure we pick plenty of that up, here, as well. The matter of water worries me, as giraffes must drink a great deal. But I have been studying the charts— there is a chain of islands in the middle of the Indian Ocean where we can add in a stop. That should get us to India, and from there on, we will be travelling mainly along the coasts, anyway."

"Yes, sir. That sounds as if it could work." He grinned. "You might just be turning the *Promise* into an Ark, though!"

"Yes," said West, returning the grin. "Very well, then." By now, the *Promise* was well into the cove. "Prepare to drop anchor, Mr. Kenmare."

"Aye, sir."

When West and Kenmare were rowed out to the lodge for dinner that evening, the sun was beginning to dip toward the horizon. Its golden light was scattered upon the waters. The air was still hot, as might be expected this close to the equator. West, who rather enjoyed a tropical climate, did not mind. And Kenmare did not seem to notice; he was too busy talking about the upcoming meal to give heed to the temperature.

They landed at the small quay and walked up the path to the lodge. A tall, black-haired man, holding a gold-tipped wooden cane, greeted them on the veranda. "Welcome to Port Tawny," he said.

"It is good to see you again, Captain Pimlico," said Kenmare. "I was wondering if you would still be here."

"Aye, my leg hasn't been the same since it was wounded in battle off Madagascar. This has become something of a permanent posting for me. I can't say I mind, though. Lieutenant Kenmare, isn't it?"

"That's right, sir. This is my commanding officer, Captain Sir Bowman West, of the *Promise*."

"Captain West, your reputation precedes you. It is an honour to have you here. I am Captain Patrick Pimlico."

"A pleasure to meet you, Captain Pimlico. You seem to have a beautiful place here." He looked at the countryside around him. Savannah, dotted with trees, seemed to stretch out as far as the eye could see. Beyond the warehouses was a small stream that rolled down to the sea.

"Yes, the place does have its appeal. And Mr. Kenmare may have told you that we pride ourselves on keeping a fine table for British travellers."

"Yes, Mr. Kenmare did mention that." West looked at his First Lieutenant mischievously. "And he mentioned it. And he mentioned it." Kenmare grinned.

"Well, we will do our best not to disappoint him. This way, please."

Pimlico led them in through a pair of large wooden doors and a stone-flagged hall. They came to a large dining room with a floor of polished wood and a great wooden table. There was a great stone fireplace as well, but in view of the heat, it was not in use. The walls looked like the same sort of dark wood used on the outside of the lodge. They were adorned— inevitably, West thought— with hunting trophies. The head of a male wildebeest stared down from one wall. Several huge elephant tusks were also mounted. West had rather mixed feelings about that sort of thing. He had never seen an elephant in the flesh, and he would have much preferred to see the tusks in their natural setting. But there was no time to think about that, for Pimlico was introducing him to his other officers. There was one lieutenant and a Colonel of the Marines, along with their men. It was a small group here at Port Tawny, and seemed quite informal, as one might expect. Pimlico had obviously served here for years; perhaps some of these men had as well.

Pimlico also introduced them to a civilian, and West's interest was piqued by the name: Sir Galen Attenfield. This man was a renowned natural historian. West studied him, thinking that he was just the man to help them with their mission.

Attenfield wore the kind of khaki garb associated with safaris. He had greying hair, a wiry build, and a speaking voice that immediately sounded distinguished. "I have heard of your work," West told him. "You have travelled to some amazing places."

"I am pleased to say that my life has never been dull. For the past few months, I have been here at Port Tawny, studying the creatures of the savannah. It has been an enjoyable experience, and Captain Pimlico's hospitality has, of course, been excellent," Attenfield said.

"Why, thank you, Sir Galen. It has been a pleasure to have you here," Pimlico answered. Addressing West, he said: "I have accompanied Sir Galen on some of his expeditions, as my leg permits. It is quite fascinating to see him at work in the wild. Though I am not sure I would have the patience for some of his research."

"Patience is rather a requirement of my field, but it does have its rewards. I have spent a great deal of time on this trip observing a creature called the hammercop, or lightning bird. It is hardly the most attractive of Africa's animals, but its behaviour is rather unusual."

"The lightning bird? It sounds as if it would be a most flamboyant creature."

"You would think so, would you not? Its appearance is actually rather dull. It is the behaviour that is flamboyant. I became interested in studying it as a result of hearing what the natives said about it. Africans believe it to be the king of all birds."

"And why is that?"

"Because it builds such an enormous nest. For the size of the bird, the nest is huge. It takes a long time for it to be built, and it is very wide and very thick. There is, so far as I have been able to determine, very little reason for it. The nest is obviously very stable, but there are many birds of a similar size that rear their young successfully in far smaller structures. It is as if the lightning bird feels that it needs a palace."

"Hence, its role as king," said West.

"Precisely. Also, the nest is so huge that other birds sometimes come to investigate it. They will even steal some of the building materials while the lightning birds are off gathering more. That, at least, is what I have observed. If you watched what was going on only a little less carefully, you might think that the other birds were bringing building materials in as opposed to taking them. And that, too, is part of the story; that the lightning bird is king because all the other birds help it to build its palace. There is an element of truth in it." Attenfield smiled. "But I am afraid I tend to ramble when I discuss my work."

"On the contrary, your work is most fascinating to me." At that moment, Pimlico's butler announced that dinner was served. They sat down, but West contrived to remain near Attenfield so that he would have opportunity during the meal to discuss giraffes.

For the moment, West turned his attention to the food and drink, which seemed to be all that Kenmare had described. "I try to bring some local fruits and spices into the cooking here at the lodge," Pimlico said. "And because we are on the trade route to India, we benefit from a supply of Indian spices as well." There was a savoury stew that combined beef and lamb, seasoned with curry leaves and turmeric and topped with mango chutney. There was roast chicken that had been delicately spiced with cinnamon, nutmeg, black pepper, and lemon juice. There were loaves of bread as well as grilled flatbread. There was a great dish of rice seasoned with a highly spiced curry sauce. There was rich brown ale from newly opened casks, and a local drink distilled from coconut milk. Pimlico explained that the hot climate made storage of wine virtually impossible. Kenmare enjoyed the ale, however, and West tried the coconut liquor, which proved to be unexpectedly fiery. They both sampled all the dishes and did justice to the spread.

"So where are you bound for, Captain West?" asked Pimlico.

"The South China Sea," said West. "The Blue Isles."

"That's unexplored territory."

"The very reason we're going," said Kenmare.

"You are an explorer, then, Captain West?" asked Attenfield.

"Such is my ambition."

"An ambition that I understand well. If your life had taken a different turn, perhaps you would have been a natural historian."

"I believe it is possible," said West honestly. "Indeed, I will be taking up your profession, at least briefly, during my stay here. It is a matter in which I would appreciate your help."

Pimlico said, "Captain, if your interest is in hunting, I have a man who can guide you."

"Please, Captain Pimlico, I would hardly ask Britain's greatest natural historian to be a mere safari guide. My interest is not in hunting. Actually, what I am talking about is part of my mission."

"How so?" asked Attenfield. Pimlico looked curious, as well.

"My destination is the Blue Isles, and my mission is one of trade and diplomacy. I have learned that there is a great deal of Chinese influence in the society of the Blue Isles. This dates back to the fifteenth century, when China had ships of exploration sailing the seas." Although Chang had spoken of the size of the treasure fleet, West moderated the information, lest his audience disbelieve him. "During that time, one of the treasures that this fleet brought back to the Emperor of China was a giraffe. Apparently, the Chinese believe it to be a most special animal— a sign of peace and prosperity. I believe that if I were to bring a giraffe to the Blue Isles as a gift for the archipelago's rulers, my mission would be received far more favourably."

"A gesture of goodwill," said Attenfield. "That is a noble idea, Captain."

"I have heard that the Blue Isles are rich in jewels," said Pimlico. "Trade might well be profitable there, and such a gift could open the way.

There may be something to your thinking, Captain." He smiled. "Still, it is a first. Transporting a giraffe on a Royal Navy ship! I don't think there is anything in the Articles of War about that."

West joined the laughter. "Probably not. What do you think, Sir Galen? Is it possible?"

Attenfield looked thoughtful. "It might be. Capturing it certainly would be. The question is the sea voyage. Yet, you say that a giraffe was brought back to China in the fifteenth century?"

"Yes."

"How did you find that out?" asked Pimlico.

That put West in a bind. He could not very well cite his Chinese steward who pretended not to speak English. "It was recorded in Chinese histories," he said, assuming that was how Chang knew.

"Well, I would certainly be inclined to trust that," said Attenfield. "I have always thought that westerners who think Europe the centre of all learning would do well to take a look at the Chinese." West nodded. "So, the voyage to China would have been somewhat farther. I believe you have a frigate, Captain?"

"Yes."

"Then it would also have been much longer. I would not think that there was any ship on the seas in the fifteenth century— even one built by the Chinese— that could match a modern frigate for speed. Apparently, then, it is possible.

"Giraffes generally eat acacia and combretum leaves in the wild, but those kept in captivity have successfully been fed alfalfa hay. Would you be able to provide that sort of thing, Captain Pimlico?"

"Certainly. Many ships carry livestock, and we have the necessary supplies."

"That sounds encouraging," said West.

"Water may be the issue, though," continued Attenfield. "I have travelled on enough ships to know that fresh water is always a problem, and a giraffe would need a great deal of it."

"I have given that some thought, Sir Galen." He described the plans that he had told Kenmare about.

Attenfield nodded. "There is, of course, no way to know for sure. As Captain Pimlico said, this does not come up very often. However, I think it is plausible."

"Then would you be willing to help me capture one?"

"Yes, Captain, I believe I would."

West smiled. "Thank you, Sir Galen."

"This should prove a memorable trip, Captain West," said Pimlico. "But now we must give our attention to dessert. Besides the cheese and the port, there is local fruit, as well as a kind of trifle that my chef makes with mangoes instead of berries. Captain West, would you care to try some?"

"Certainly, Captain Pimlico."

"As for Lieutenant Kenmare, I already know what his answer is likely to be."

Kenmare looked down at his empty plate. "Well, I didn't like mine at all," he said wryly. "But I will give the trifle a go, Captain, if you pass some this way."

The next morning, after coffee on the veranda, five men rode out on safari: West, Attenfield, Pimlico, Rede, and Lang. The second and third lieutenant had been chosen to assist in getting the giraffe back to the ship because they both knew how to ride. Rede had learned as a boy, when he had to bring supplies back to his parents' inn; Lang had simply tried it once while on shore leave and found he took to it immediately. The ability to ride a horse was, of course, far from universal among sailors. West himself was a skilled rider, and mounted the chestnut stallion Pimlico gave him with ease and confidence. It was with regret that he had parted from his own horse, Rocinante, when he left his home in Scotland.

At his belt, West carried his telescope and a pistol, though he hoped he would not have to use the latter. Lang carried a several sections of one-inch line brought from the *Promise*. Pimlico had brought a cleverly contrived cane of light wood that folded up so he could carry it at his belt. He rode with ease, the ability apparently unaffected by his injury.

They left in the grey hour before dawn. The air was warm but not yet hot. They rode out into the savannah, where the long grasses were broken only by the occasional tree. West found the baobab trees, with their bulbous, intertwined trunks, to be fascinating. As they continued riding, with Attenfield setting the course, dawn began to break. West was treated then to a wondrous display, both in sight and in sound. The golden light of the sun turned the grasses of the savannah green and yellow. The still air came alive with the call of birds and the chatter of monkeys. They mounted a rise and saw below them a herd of zebra grazing, and West marvelled at the creatures with their patterns of black and white. There were small gazelles to be seen, as well; graceful and elegant creatures with fawn-coloured coats. In a tree nearby, a group of monkeys seemed to be playing, jumping in the branches. West looked at one through his telescope and was almost startled to see the creature looking straight back at him.

"If we go around the herd of zebra and then turn to the south, we will come to a watering hole," said Attenfield. "That will be a good place to look for giraffes, especially as there is a stand of acacia trees nearby."

West nodded, and the party spurred their horses forward. They made a wide circle around the zebras, which were grazing peacefully. Several of them looked up at the humans, but beyond that, they paid them little heed. "Is it true that they are impossible to tame?" West asked.

"Yes," said Attenfield. "No man has ever ridden a zebra."

West looked back at the herd, his eyes dangerously bright, before deciding that he should probably stay focused on looking for a giraffe.

They continued riding through the long grass. The sun was climbing higher now, and it was beginning to grow hot. "What's that over to starboard, sir?" asked Lang.

They turned and saw a cluster of grey shapes in the distance. "A herd of elephants," said Attenfield. West eagerly took out his telescope and trained it on the animals. They were impressive creatures. Among them he noticed a calf, and one of the adults— presumably the mother— was stroking it with her trunk.

"They seem to be affectionate with each other," West said.

"They are. Elephants are very sociable creatures— the females, that is," Attenfield said. "They will actively help each other at times. I once saw a calf trapped in the mud near a watering hole. Not only did its mother try to help it, but several other adult females joined her. Eventually, they were able to raise it out of the mud with their trunks."

"Wonderful." West was delighted with the image. "They live in groups, then?"

"The females and the juvenile males do. There is always a matriarch. Their memories are, of course, proverbial. Therefore, experience is useful to them; the matriarch knows where to go for food, water, and minerals."

"Minerals?"

"They will sometimes consume dust from mineral deposits. Apparently, it provides some sort of supplement to their diet of vegetation."

They rode on, and in time, they saw the watering hole in the distance. "As we get closer, we will have to approach carefully," said Attenfield. "A watering hole is a place where all animals must go. The result can sometimes be volatile— lions and zebras do not drink together in peace."

"So it's a bit like a tavern in a neutral port, eh?" said Lang with a laugh.

The watering hole was open to the savannah on two sides; the other two sides were more wooded. As they rode closer, West trained his telescope on the trees. Birds with brightly coloured plumage were perched there. He did not see any great nests, though; apparently this was not the domain of the lightning bird.

Suddenly, there came a great roaring sound from within the trees. The birds immediately took to flight and scattered into the air. Attenfield pulled back on his reigns and drew his horse to a stop, and the other men followed his example. The roaring sound was repeated.

"Lion?" asked West.

"Rather worse, I'm afraid," said Attenfield. From his demeanour, the word 'afraid' did not seem accurate. He spoke with a dry, stiff-upper-lip manner that would have done credit to any captain in the Royal Navy.

A moment later, a great bull elephant came crashing out through the trees. The smaller trees were shattered like matchsticks. The elephant continued his charge unabated, out onto the grasslands. Then it seemed to stop and look around.

"Turn about," said Attenfield. "It's in musth. I will explain the details later, if I have the opportunity. For now, let it suffice that it is a dangerous creature." They wheeled their horses about and turned to beat a retreat, but the elephant saw them and came charging straight at them. The horses raced forward through the grassland, with the great bull elephant running behind, his pounding footsteps seeming to shake the earth.

"I thought you said they ate vegetation!" Lang called out as they rode.

"It is not trying to eat us," said Attenfield. "But a bull in musth will attack anything. They are most unpredictable."

"Should we try our guns?" shouted Pimlico.

West was looking forward, urging his horse on; but at that moment, he heard a sound from behind him. He turned to see that Lang's horse had stumbled. Horse and man were both on the ground. A moment later, the horse stood up. Lang stood up more slowly, apparently injured in his leg; and by the time he reached out to grab at the reigns, his horse had bolted across the savannah. West wheeled his own horse around, as did his other companions. Wade Lang was standing in the path of a charging bull elephant.

As the creature came closer and closer, its full enormity was apparent. The very sound of its strides was like thunder. Its great ears flapped at its side as it ran. Its white tusks seemed outstretched, as if it was going to run Lang through; but in fact they were far above his head. His real danger was in being trampled by the grey monster, like a rowboat in the path of a ship of the line.

West knew that his pistol would do no good against the creature. Pimlico, who was used to the dangers of the savannah, carried a rifle. He took aim, but before he could fire, Rede guided his horse right into the path of the elephant. The others had all been farther ahead, their horses having continued to run for a moment after Lang's had stumbled. Rede was the closest to his injured shipmate, and he acted without hesitation.

The horse's eyes showed that it was frightened, but Rede held it tightly on course. He swung into the elephant's path and over to Lang; Lang leaped up, his expression one of pain as a result of the injury that he was ignoring. As soon as Lang was sitting behind him, Rede relaxed his hold on the reigns, and the horse immediately darted forward, out of the path of the elephant. The creature pounded onwards, trampling over the place where Lang had stood a moment before.

Pimlico readied his gun, but Attenfield held him back. The elephant was not turning to pursue Rede and Lang; nor was it turning toward the other three men. Instead, it continued charging forward, almost blindly. Finally, it stopped at a baobab tree which it ferociously attacked with its tusks. West stared in astonishment as the elephant grappled with the tree as if determined to pull it up by the roots.

"They are quite unpredictable in this state," said Attenfield. "Now, while it is distracted, would be a good time to leave."

"I couldn't agree more," said West. They joined Rede and Lang, and together, the five men rode back toward the lodge. "We must get Mr. Lang another horse, in any case."

"And after that, we can make a try to the north," said Attenfield. "There is another watering hole in that direction. It is a bit farther off, but it is also a likely place to find a giraffe. And hopefully there will be no elephants in musth in that direction."

"Hopefully not," agreed West. "Fine work, Lieutenant Rede. You are a brave man."

"And I owe you my life, sir," said Lang to Rede. Lang seemed rather shaken by the experience, understandably, and genuinely grateful.

"Merely doing my duty," said Rede, but he looked pleased.

The area to the north of the lodge revealed a different aspect of the savannah. The grass became shorter and sparser as they travelled, giving way to large patches of red dust. "The elephants that come up this way end up being reddish in colour," Attenfield remarked, "as a result of rolling in the dust."

They passed a rocky hill where a cheetah looked out at them. The yellow, spotted animal had been taking its ease, it seemed, but it shifted to a crouch at the approach of the riders. "Surely it's not going to attack us?" Rede asked.

"Not at all," said Attenfield. "It is simply readying itself for flight, if it should be necessary." Sure enough, as the humans passed by, the cheetah remained alert but motionless.

As they continued on, they noticed huge mounds of red earth with vaguely pyramidal shapes. "Termite mounds," said Attenfield. The land grew more and more dusty, and then the process began to reverse itself. Patches of green sprang up amid the red. The grass became taller and more lush. Finally, they approached the watering hole. It was smaller than the one to the south, and it was set against a stony cliff. As they approached it, Attenfield extended his arm, the hand pointing to the edge of the cliff. Around its far side, a giraffe was approaching, coming toward the water. "Our timing seems ideal," he said.

As West began to consider his next move, he noticed several other creatures drinking from the water. Their heads and upper bodies closely resembled the zebra they had seen, with black and white stripes; but their hindquarters were brown, making them look like horses. West was reminded of the kind of composite animals that often appeared in mythology. "What are those?" he asked.

"Quagga," said Attenfield. "You do not often see them this far north. In the south, there are vast herds of them— though hunting is beginning to take a toll."

"Strange name," said Rede.

"They make a kind of coughing sound that some of the African tribes found rather amusing. They named them for that— quagga quagga."

West nodded and turned his attention to the giraffe. "Mr. Lang, knot the rope into a noose and then pass it to me."

"Aye, sir." Lang ably complied.

"I am going to take my stand near the cliffs. If I can, I will capture the giraffe while it is drinking. If not, I shall have to try to climb the rocks in order to do so. Sir Galen, would you be so kind as to ride with me?"

"Of course, Captain West."

"I would ask the rest of you to please follow but remain at something of a distance." The words 'ask' and 'please' was for the benefit of Pimlico, who was West's equal in rank. Technically, in fact, Pimlico had seniority, as he had held his rank longer. West knew already that Pimlico was an officer of rather informal nature who was not about to throw his weight around. Nonetheless, it would have been bad form for West to address him the same way he would address Rede or Lang.

They rode together to the cliffs, coming around behind them and approaching the giraffe. West stared up at the creature. Intellectually, he had known the height of giraffes; but now that he saw one for the first time, he was beginning to question the idea of actually transporting one by ship. Aboard a frigate, space was limited even for humans. How could this unbelievable creature, with its neck like a tree, possibly be brought from Africa to the South China Sea aboard a frigate? Regardless of what the Chinese admiral had accomplished, it seemed impossible.

He looked with regret at the beautiful creature, with its spots like purple mist and its gentle eyes. He could understand why the Chinese viewed it as a celestial animal. But he could not imagine it aboard the *Promise*.

The giraffe spread its forelegs apart, its hooves upon the sand near the water, and bent its front knees. In this awkward posture, it lowered its enormous neck and drank from the watering hole, spreading its lips apart and revealing a purple tongue. West watched with both astonishment and regret.

"Sir Galen," West said at last, "I do not think this can work." He explained his doubts, and the natural historian nodded thoughtfully.

"There is another option," he said. Attenfield spoke slowly and seemed to be moved by some strong emotion. It was the first time West had seen him show emotion, and he wondered what prompted it. "I was somewhat reluctant to mention it, however, I believe it is worthwhile. In establishing contact with less developed societies, we English have, all too often, been lacking in the good form that characterizes our relationships with each other and with our fellow Europeans. As a man of science, I want to see more explorers like you, Captain West— men who will come bearing true gifts that matter to the people they encounter, and not Grecian gifts that serve as a trap in the end. Showing such honour to the people of distant lands will truly open up the frontiers of science, so that an English natural historian may be welcomed in any land to which his curiosity takes him."

"I fully agree with you, Sir Galen. But your words are mysterious as well as wise. What is the other option? And how do our feelings about good form relate to it?"

"They relate, Captain West, because I believe you are worthy of the gift I am going to give you; or, rather, the gift that we are both going to give to the people of the Blue Isles. Come. Let us return to the lodge."

When they had done so, Attenfield silently led West past the warehouses, to the area where the stream ran through the savannah. The banks of the stream were dotted with trees and overgrown with brush. There, near the water's edge, was a wooden fence.

Still silent, Attenfield opened the door to the enclosure and gestured for West to follow him. Inside was a pair of animals that West had never before seen. At first glance, they seemed like a mirror image of the quagga. They had black and white striped hindquarters and legs, and their body and head were a luminous brown; though the face was lighter in places, almost grey. The rich and varied hues of the coat reminded West of storm clouds he had seen in the tropics.

As he looked more closely at the heads of the creatures, it also became apparent that they bore a striking resemblance to the giraffes. They had narrow faces, large ears, and gentle eyes. The male had a pair of soft horns. As they moved quietly through the enclosure, heedless of the presence of the men, the gracefulness of their movements was clear. As the female nibbled delicately on some of the shrubbery, a long, dark-coloured tongue was visible. However, unlike the giraffes, they were no taller than the men.

"What are these creatures?" breathed West.

"They are a species previously unknown to Europeans, which I discovered on an expedition which took me to the south and into the interior. The pygmies who hunt them for food call them *okapi*." Attenfield rubbed his chin. "I was not willing to bring them north and subject them to the English climate; nor could I find it in myself to shoot such gentle creatures, even as specimens. I therefore decided to keep them here for the remainder of their natural lives. Then, I planned to preserve the bodies, make the voyage home, and present them to my comrades at the Royal Society. It would undoubtedly have been considered one of the great discoveries of my career. I believe that these animals are very rare, and it may be generations before a European looks upon them again. However, my laurels are already more than I desire; I pursue natural history for its own sake. And I believe that your mission would be a nobler purpose for the creatures." Attenfield gave a wan smile. "That is, if you think they could pass for *quilin*."

"I am certain that they could, Sir Galen; and they are indeed celestial animals. I thank you, sir." West reached out and shook the hand of the great natural historian. "It will be an honour to bring this gift to the Blue Isles."

VIII.
The Consulate

*T*he voyage across the Indian Ocean was novel only because of the okapis on deck, but that was novelty enough. When they had returned to the *Promise* with the animals, Kenmare had said: "Why, two of them! I'm happy the Chinese do not like elephants."

To which Lang replied wryly, "I agree, sir. I agree."

The two okapis were rowed out on the largest boat the *Promise* had. Once the boat was alongside the frigate, cords of thick rope were tied about each okapi, under the belly; and they were then hoisted onto the deck in much the same manner as cattle. The animals seemed remarkably calm, and once they were on deck, they looked about them with curiosity and seemed content. West saw to it that they were immediately fed and watered, and that no doubt helped, as well.

The okapis were a source of great wonder for the *Promise*'s crew. They gathered around to stare at them, both as they were being raised to the deck and once they were safely tethered there. Some of the sailors gazed in astonishment; others spoke excitedly to their fellows, wondering what it all meant. Kenmare allowed them a few minutes, looking on with tolerant amusement; but eventually his patience ran out, and he ordered them back to their work. There was still much to be done when it came to re-provisioning.

The okapis seemed content during the voyage, as well. They were well-fed and well-watered; the latter was thanks in part to an uneventful stop at a group of small islands near the centre of the Indian Ocean. The islands were uninhabited and fairly barren, but one of them held a stream of fresh water. West often watched as the okapis were fed and watered; he was astonished by their long, dark tongues, which seemed the finishing touch to a colourful and exotic animal. In addition to their hay, they enjoyed apples and carrots, much as horses would, and it was a pleasure to West and Kenmare, as well as to a number of the sailors, to give them such treats. As for their environment, they seemed quite happy to be on deck. That meant that sailors had to be assigned to keep the area clean, of course, and Kenmare was quite particular about that.

The weather was fair. Indeed, West spent a great deal of time on deck himself, watching the placid animals or looking out at the blue-green waters of the Indian Ocean. His once-pale features were soon deeply tanned from the warm sun. And the trade winds blew them onwards to the coast of India.

Soon enough, that coast came into view, and the *Promise* made her way around the southern tip of the subcontinent and through the Gulf of Mannar. On the starboard side was the island of Ceylon, famous for its rubies. West was excited by the prospect of visiting India. He had been there only once before, as a young lieutenant. It seemed very long ago. Furthermore, he had been much farther north then, in Calcutta. Now, they would be visiting the famous Coromandel Coast, a fabled land of spices.

The coasts that West studied through his telescope seemed green and lush, and the water was a rich blue. As they approached the city of Madras— or Fort St. George, as the East India Company called it— and entered its harbour, there were all manner of vessels to study. Small local fishing boats; British merchantmen in plenty; and some Navy vessels as well. The *Promise* itself made a great showing as she sailed in and dropped anchor. Everywhere, on the decks of other vessels and on the quays, people seemed to be pointing and staring in astonishment at the strange creatures on her deck.

Kenmare immediately met with the port authorities and began making the arrangements for re-supplying the *Promise*. As this was to be their last major stop prior to the South China Sea, they had to prepare for the future. West hoped that after they left Madras, they would need to stop along the coasts of southeast Asia only for fresh water.

Kenmare reported that the authorities were as cooperative as he could ask, but apparently, they quickly spread the word of the *Promise's* arrival— and the arrival of her captain. An hour or so after Kenmare had returned, a small boat rowed out to the *Promise* bearing a message for West: he was being invited to dinner at the Admiralty House. West sighed at that and would have liked to refuse. He had been looking forward to seeing the marketplaces of the city. He remembered, however, a resolution he had come to regarding Alexander Teal, and therefore gave his acceptance. He then informed Kenmare of his plans, adding, "Do you think you can leave Mr. Rede in oversight here? I am beginning to feel we make a good pair for these sorts of events."

"Why, yes, sir. Thank you. Mr. Rede is a capable man, and from what they told me, most of what we need will be loaded on board tomorrow, anyway."

West considered bringing Teal with him as well, but decided that the lad's actual presence would not be necessary. So when the time came, it was he and Kenmare who set off to the Admiralty House.

A carriage had been sent for them, and during the ride, West stared out the window, trying to see whatever he could of the city. It turned out not to be much, since their destination was not far from the harbour. West glimpsed the large brick warehouses near the shore, and, as the carriage progressed up the narrow streets, sections of smaller brick and timber residences, some of them inns and some of them private homes for well-to-do foreigners. This was clearly not the native section of Madras; West would have to find that on the morrow, when he returned to his plans of exploring the marketplaces. The carriage soon stopped at the iron gates of the Admiralty House; the gates were opened, and they proceeded up a drive paved with white stone. When they stopped and got out, West looked up at the house, a red brick building fronted with a line of tall palm trees. There were large windows flung open but curtained within to keep out insects. There was a garden that began in front of the palm trees and stretched around the side of the house, presumably continuing in back. It was planted with tropical flowers that bore great blossoms; their soft petals were red and yellow and royal purple. As he walked toward the white doors, West could not help but stop to look at a bird with brightly coloured plumage perching upon one of the blossoms. He did not know what kind it was, but it was a vivid green like the tail of a peacock, and the flower upon which it stood was scarlet. He breathed in the scent of the flowers. The air was heavy and damp and hot. He noticed that Kenmare was at the door, looking back at him with an amused expression. West joined him, and they went into the house.

An Indian servant took their hats; they were happy to hand them over. As much as West was enjoying these hot climates, the captain's hat could be a nuisance, and it would be a fine thing if uniforms were not made of wool. He suddenly realized that when he became a privateer, he would have to dispense with the uniforms anyway. Another benefit. He pictured himself standing on his quarterdeck, telescope in hand, but dressed in slacks and a shirt of light cotton, perhaps in some lighter shade of blue.

The servant led them to a large reception room, and he was jolted out of his reverie by the sounds of the chatter and laughter of the guests. Kenmare immediately saw a face he recognized, and looked pleased. "It's Captain Belmont, sir of the *Pegasus*. I have not seen him in years." West nodded, and Kenmare went over to his old friend, his face beaming.

There were several dozen people there; some of the men were in uniforms and others in civilian clothing, while the women wore gowns in many colours. None of those colours, however, compared to the colours of the flowers outside. On the other hand, it was pleasant to see women again after so long a time at sea. West would need to take care that he did not become too distracted, as many sailors, captains included, were wont to do while ashore.

The room was paved with marble tiles that were creamy rather than white, creating a warm appearance. The walls were paneled in dark wood and adorned with paintings. One of them was a Canaletto and presented an incongruous image of Venice's Grand Canal. Another, which drew West's interest more strongly at the moment, was by some unknown artist, but it portrayed India's Taj Mahal. The painting was in the western manner and clearly was the work of some European traveler. It portrayed the eastern masterpiece lovingly, the great white dome surrounded by the delicate minarets, all fronted by a reflecting pool. Looking at it made West wish he was spending more time on the Subcontinent.

"Greetings— Captain Sir Bowman West, is it not?"

West turned to see a figure in an Admiral's uniform, with a broad, whiskered face and a wide smile. "Yes, sir," he answered.

"I am Admiral Taylor. It is a pleasure to meet you."

"Likewise, and may I thank you for your hospitality." They shook hands. "You have a beautiful home here."

"Thank you. What brings you to Madras, Captain?"

"I am on my way to the Blue Isles, on a mission of trade and exploration."

"The Blue Isles? That's the South China Sea, isn't it?"

"That's right."

"And they told me you are in command of a frigate."

"Yes, sir. The *Promise*."

"Whatever for?"

West was not sure what to make of the question. "I was on leave for some time after the battle in Spain, recovering from my wounds. During that time, my former First Lieutenant was promoted to Captain of my old frigate, the *Sea Unicorn*, as per my request."

"No, no," said Taylor. "I don't mean, why are you not in your old ship? I mean, why have you not been promoted? You are the man who stopped the new Spanish Armada. They should have made you a Commodore, and yet they did not even give you a ship of the line! It's absurd!"

Taylor spoke with some feeling. Now that West understood him, he was not sure whether to be amused or embarrassed. He decided to answer as simply as he could. "I am happy to have this assignment, sir."

"Well, your modesty does you credit, West," Taylor said. His predictable misinterpretation made any explanation on West's part quite unnecessary. He did, though, add some words of encouragement. "Your time will come soon enough, I am sure. You will be hoisting your own flag as Admiral someday."

"Thank you, sir, but I rather doubt it."

"Of course you will, of course you will." Again, Taylor mistook his words as evidence of modesty. West was definitely starting to feel amused now.

"There is one thing I would like to ask you, sir," he said. "I have an Acting-Lieutenant on my ship; he was promoted from midshipman but has not yet been able to take the lieutenant's examination. Given the number of naval officers here in Madras, I was wondering if that could be arranged. Who knows how long it will be before we return to England? Yet, with captains here to ask the questions, and an Admiral to approve the promotion, why could he not take the examination here?"

"A fine thought, West. Why make the lad wait, eh?"

"Precisely, sir."

"Well, I think we can arrange that. I will speak to some of the captains here tonight. It's an interesting idea you have. When I was a boy, my captain made me Acting-Lieutenant after a successful cutting-out expedition; but I had to sail halfway across the world before we had returned to England and I could take the examination. This notion of giving the examination wherever there are enough captains available might be of some value to the service."

"I thought perhaps it might. Thank you, sir."

"No need to thank me. The idea speaks well of you. Now, make yourself at home, West."

"Yes, sir." West happened to notice one of the other guests, a tall man with a white suit, a white shirt, and a burgundy cravat. "Who is that, may I ask, sir?" He gestured discretely toward the man. Taylor made a rueful face.

"The Spanish ambassador to the British Raj. Now that we are at peace with the Dons, I can hardly avoid having him at some of these events. Needless to say, we're careful about what we discuss around him. His name is Velazquez— Domingo Velazquez y Torres."

"I thought he looked familiar." The man had been an aide-de-camp to West's old enemy, Count Vega. Once, well before the battle against Vega's armada, West had met the Count at a diplomatic event. This man Velazquez had been with him then. His presence here was probably meaningless, but it brought back memories. He tried to focus on the memories of the diplomatic meeting, which had been mostly harmless, and not those of the later battle.

Meanwhile, the noise and the bustle continued. Taylor had moved off to speak to someone else, and West realized, idly, that his own work was now done. He had come here to see that Teal could take his examination, and that had now been set in motion. He made his way toward the other end of the room, where double doors opened to the back of the garden. The opening was curtained with white linen, but glimpses of the garden could be seen, West walked toward it.

His walk was interrupted by one of his fellow officers. He was young, probably in his early thirties; he was holding a glass of whiskey, and his tongue seemed already loosened with drink. He introduced himself as Cosgrove, commander of the sloop *Ice Bear*. It had apparently been named for the great white bears of the north, but the name sounded out of place on the coasts of India. "This is my first command, Captain West," Cosgrove said after West had introduced himself, speaking in a confidential whisper that was heard by half the room.

"Best wishes, then," said West.

Cosgrove drew another man into the conversation, with the careless gregariousness produced by alcohol, introducing him as Captain Shreve. Shreve was standing by the wall with a glass of claret in his hand, looking uncomfortable. But he shook West's hand and murmured pleasantries. He was clearly sober, at least, and appeared to be in his middle forties. "Heard all about your battle with the Dons," he said. "Good show."

"Thank you, Captain Shreve," said West.

"Yes, Captain West here was quite the hero," said Cosgrove. "What brings you to Madras, West?" West briefly explained his mission. Then Cosgrove asked about West's ship. "I am commanding a sloop, myself— the *Ice Bear*," he repeated.

"The *Promise*."

At that, Shreve looked surprised. "One of my officers was being transferred to the *Promise*, before I left England. A man named Cato Rede."

"He is my Second Lieutenant," said West with a smile. "A fine man."

"I am pleased you find him so." Shreve's voice and expression was dour. "I was about to offer my condolences."

West raised an eyebrow. "Why?"

"I found Mr. Rede to be somewhat lacking. His manner bordered on the insubordinate."

"I find that hard to believe."

"Well, perhaps I cured him of it."

"Can you give me an example of this . . . insubordination?"

"I once ordered a particular course to be set along the coast of France; Rede came to me afterwards, in private, and told me that he'd studied the charts and feared my course would take us into shoal water."

"And?"

"And what? He was questioning my orders. Sure enough, we came near shoal water, but we made our way out all right. It was none of his business, anyway— he was the gunnery officer."

"Ah, so you're that kind," said West. Shreve looked puzzled, and West did not explain. "Well, I have found Mr. Rede to be an exemplary officer— one of the best I have ever served with."

"Well, I always maintained discipline in the *Dauntless*. Rede may have picked up something after awhile. If he is a fine officer, you have me to thank."

West smiled urbanely. "No, I doubt he picked up anything from you. He seems a modest man. I can tell you, though, that he recently risked his life to save one of his comrades. He likely would have done the same for you, though some might wonder why." Shreve stared at West, unsure how to respond to the insults, especially since they were delivered in such a cavalier manner. "I hope you enjoy your evening; I find it a bit warm for claret myself, but then again, we do not really seem to have much in common." He wandered off to look at the garden with a lackadaisical air, leaving Shreve bearing a look of injured pride.

"We have a nice Fiano di Avellino, if you find it too warm for claret," said a musical, feminine voice beside him.

West turned and found himself staring into the face of a very pretty young woman; he thought wryly that this was a great improvement after speaking with Shreve.

"Thank you," he said. His words had been meant as setup to a parting shot, but he did feel the dry red wine was rather unsuited to a hot climate— not like rum, which was good in any weather. Then, too, the voice that had made the offer was soft and lilting. "I have not had Fiano di Avellino since I was in Naples."

"I am not surprised. My father was stationed in Naples for a time, and he became acquainted with it there. Because his fondness for it is well-known, someone from the East India Company will usually re-supply us now." Her eyes were brown and they were twinkling with amusement. Her hair was light brown, and it had a warm glow in the light, but not so warm as her smile when she told him, "I am Violet Taylor." As he looked confused, she added: "The Admiral's daughter."

"Captain Bowman West." If West had been a rake, the girl's identity would have made him nervous. As it was, his attraction to her was nothing that he would not have followed up on in any event, for he was not a man given to casual relationships, and he knew he would not be in Madras long. Besides, she appeared to be only a few years over twenty, too young to have much interest in a battle-scarred sailor with silvering hair.

"It is a pleasure to meet you, Captain West." She lowered her voice. "I could not help but overhear your defence of your officer. I think your loyalty to him is to be commended." She smiled then, and added: "And I am sure that Captain Shreve's pride will survive your assault."

"He struck me as a man whose pride is most resilient."

"It seems so. He arrived last week and he has been a guest here once before, already. He spent a great deal of time on that occasion telling my father about Madras."

"He is a quick study, it seems."

"So he believes." West now understood the twinkle of amusement in her eyes. She had already seen Shreve's type, and therefore, she could appreciate West's loyalty— as well as the humour of the situation.

She poured him a glass of the white wine. "Thank you, Miss Taylor." The wine looked and tasted gold. He thought about Italy.

"Where are you bound for, Captain?"

"The Blue Isles, in the South China Sea. I am on a mission of exploration."

Her face lit up. "How remarkable! I have heard of the Blue Isles, but I know little about them."

"All Europeans know little about them, it seems. I am hoping to change that."

"And your ship—"

"The *Promise*."

Violet looked confused. "I thought it was the *Sea Unicorn*. Everyone heard about the great battle you fought, where you saved Scotland from invasion."

"I was wounded in the battle, and I left the sea for awhile. I have a new ship, now."

"And you sail to the Blue Isles. I have not yet been to the South China Sea." They spoke for a few moments about what West knew of the South China Sea: the reefs, the typhoons, the jungles. Then West asked about what Madras was like.

"You mean you do not already know?" she asked in mock surprise. "It is a fascinating city, at least, so far as I have had the opportunity to see it. My life is rather sheltered here. But I have gone to some of the marketplaces with my father."

"Ah, yes, I want to see the marketplaces."

"You must." She spoke of spice merchants and street musicians and monkeys climbing on the rooftops, and West drank his wine. Then, it was announced that the meal was being served. Violet bid him farewell and joined her father for the entry into the dining hall. West stepped out into the garden. He wanted to see it before he had to leave the reception hall.

It was twilight now— a warm gloaming that made West think of a summer night. There were vibrant flowers, here in the back of the garden as well. And there were fruit trees, bearing their cargoes of mangoes, limes, and oranges. Bees were humming about the blossoms and the branches, performing the necessary work of pollination. West wondered how long human life could survive if the bees were ever gone from the earth. Fortunately, of course, that could never happen.

A moment later, the footman appeared through the curtains. "Captain, dinner is being served," he said, apparently believing West had not heard. West thanked him and re-entered.

As he walked into the dining hall, where the guests were beginning to be seated, West found himself standing near Velazquez. "I have been hoping to introduce myself to you, Captain," Velazquez said. "I am Domingo Velazquez y Torres, the Spanish Ambassador. Please allow me to congratulate you on the success of your career."

"We have met before, your Excellency," said West.

"Ah, yes, I did not expect that you would remember. I was merely a pawn on that occasion."

"And Count Vega was the king, I suppose."

"I believe he would see himself more as a knight— as, I imagine, would you."

West smiled. "Perhaps so. I thank you for your congratulations, your Excellency; it shows great courtesy."

"I need not have applauded your victory, Captain, in order to recognize its brilliance. In any case, our countries are at peace now. It is good that we can meet together like this, under the flag of truce, as it were."

"I agree." West wondered why he sensed an air of menace under the ambassador's genteel manner. Their countries were indeed at peace, at least tentatively; and West's current mission had nothing to do with Spain, in any case. No doubt Vega still harboured rancour, but there was no reason why Velazquez should. He had been merely a pawn. As the ambassador nodded and went to take his place at the table, West dismissed his intuition; he could not find a basis for it.

West himself was seated with a Mrs. Agnes Garrideb, a talkative woman whose husband was with the East India Company, and across from Commander Cosgrove. The result was that he did not need to concern himself with conversation; he would barely have been able to get a word in edgewise. Therefore, he could concentrate on the food. He looked down the table to see where Kenmare had ended up. As it happened, Kenmare had been paired with Violet, and he seemed to be telling her a story, while she looked on with enthusiastic attention.

The dinner began with a Mulligatawny soup, a thick lentil soup seasoned with lemon. Then came several varieties of curry: one made with goat and seasoned with cilantro and green cardamom pods; another of lamb with a spicy sauce of tomato, onion, garlic, and ginger; and another of chicken in a mild, creamy sauce with almonds and raisins. There were also several plain roasted chickens, provided for less adventurous palates. West avoided those but sampled all the curries. Overhearing snatches of conversation, he learned that Admiral Taylor's household included both British and Indian chefs. West was pleased by the opportunity to sample Indian cuisine; he had expected that might have to wait until the next day's trip to the marketplaces. Dessert consisted of Stilton cheese and local fruits; West chose some slices of mango and enjoyed the rich flavour. Then he sat back, comfortably full, sipping at the glass of Fiano di Avellino that had been refilled for him.

Although he had not had too much to drink, he felt somewhat drowsy; perhaps he was being lulled by the conversation of Mrs. Garrideb and Commander Cosgrove. His mind began to wander. He thought about the Blue Isles. He thought about the okapis on the deck of his ship. He thought about what the prevailing winds might be like when the *Promise* set sail.

"You are not paying attention at all, are you, Captain?" said Violet, playfully drumming her fingers on the table next to him to get his attention. She was standing beside his chair, and in fact, nearly everyone else had either left the table or at least stood up.

"My mind was on my voyage, Miss Taylor," said West with a smile, belatedly rising and realizing he had no idea what she had said the moment before. "Have I missed anything of note?"

"Only that it is time for dancing. Oh, Mr. Kenmare told me about the okapis— I think that sounds wonderful! I would love to see them." She flashed a bright smile at him and walked toward the dance floor.

West reluctantly joined the general movement in that direction. West's music was, first folk music, then string quartets, and then symphonies. Waltzes and their ilk he liked least of all. He was capable of dancing, but only with some effort of concentration. He therefore danced two or three rounds with women he did not know and then retired to the edge of the room to look for another glass of wine.

As he stood there and watched the dancing, he was amused to see Kenmare very much in the centre of things. The old sailor danced with skill and evident enjoyment. His partners were all, in varying degrees, much younger than he— everyone was younger than Kenmare— but they all seemed utterly charmed by him. That included Violet, who danced a waltz with him and then strolled off the dance floor on his arm, laughing delightedly. The two of them approached West, and the captain saw that his first lieutenant's face was beaming.

"This fine young lady says it's your turn now, sir," said Kenmare. "I hope you are light on your feet."

"I am certainly not the dancer you are, Mr. Kenmare," said West. "But I will give it a go."

Violet was quite light on her feet, and she soon had to slow down in order to dance with West. "Your first lieutenant is such a dear man," she said.

"Kenmare's a good fellow," West agreed. It was not easy for him to make conversation and dance at the same time, so he returned to the last thing Violet had said. "He told you about the okapis, then?"

"Yes. He said you are bringing them to the Blue Isles as a kind of diplomatic gift."

"That's right."

"What an unusual sight that must be, a pair of exotic animals on the deck of a ship! What are the creatures like?"

"They do look exotic. And they are very gentle; that is why the Chinese value them. Well, actually it is giraffes they value, but transporting giraffes on a ship would be even more of a challenge."

"Why yes, I'm sure it would."

"Catching them was a fine adventure, too; we went out on a safari, with Sir Galen Attenfield, as a matter of fact, and saw all manner of creatures."

"Yes, Mr. Kenmare told me about your experience there. It must have been exciting. He told me about the pirates, too— how you pretended to have the plague."

"Ah, did he?" West could not think of anything else to say in response.

"You are a resourceful man, Captain."

"But perhaps not as light on my feet as I should be." There was an ironic tone to West's words, as he saw the way Violet was looking at him. The music stopped.

"I really must stop here, Miss Taylor," said West. "As you can tell, I do not have Mr. Kenmare's talent for this sort of thing."

"You are doing fine, Captain."

"I appreciate your kindness, Miss Taylor," he said, "but it is getting late anyway. I really must return to my ship. I am afraid I will have to take Mr. Kenmare, as well— if I can convince him to leave the dance floor."

She walked with him toward Kenmare. "Will you be remaining in Madras long, Captain?"

"Not long at all. Only until we can re-supply. Then, we sail for the South China Sea." He paused. "It was a joy to meet you, Miss Taylor."

"I wish you a happy voyage, Captain." They had approached Kenmare now. "And a happy voyage to you, of course, Mr. Kenmare," she said.

"Why thank you, Miss Taylor," Kenmare answered with a smile.

As West and Kenmare prepared to leave, the Admiral approached them. "The day after tomorrow, at noon, on the *Vitruvius*— Captain Buchanan's ship. Three captains will be there, and your Acting-Lieutenant can take his examination."

"Thank you, sir."

At that moment, West's eyes flickered to a spot well behind where Admiral Taylor was standing. There was Velazquez, a glass of white wine in his hand, talking to Commander Cosgrove. Cosgrove seemed as talkative as ever, and Velazquez's face held a look of earnest concentration. But why did that matter? Cosgrove was only the commander of a sloop;

it seemed unlikely that he knew anything of importance when it came to international intrigue. "Thank you, Admiral Taylor," West repeated, and took his leave. And he and Kenmare walked out the door, to where the scent of flowers hung in the warm air of the tropical night.

IX.
The Marketplace

or much of the next day, West was caught up, along with Kenmare, in the issues of re-supplying the *Promise*. There was a new kind of rum brought on board; supply of the usual Royal Navy rum, from Trinidad and Tobago, had run low, and a black rum from Jamaica had been provided instead. "They are both from the West Indies," Kenmare had said. "I am sure it will be good." Nonetheless, he and his captain tried a bit at once.

It was good. West was sure that he had had the same kind in pubs. Whereas Navy rum was light amber in hue, and had an oaky flavour that, by comparison, made it reminiscent of port or sherry, this rum was a deep amber colour and had a taste that carried no hint of oak. The taste did carry the flavour of the sugar cane, but it was not sweet; it was almost like the burnt topping of a crème brulee, (a dish that West felt justified the existence of the French nation). It also had the bracing quality of all good rum, for rum, West knew, should be a drink both sturdy and strengthening.

West expressed his approval of the new rum to Kenmare, who agreed. Then, Kenmare brought up the topic of the okapis. "They seem to be doing right well, sir, and we have plenty of feed coming in for them. I have been thinking that they need to be named."

West smiled. "A fine idea. Let's have a look at them and figure something out." They left the captain's cabin and stepped on to the quarter-deck, from where the okapis could be seen.

"Well, I did have a name in mind for the male," Kenmare said. "The rich brown of his coat— well, part of his coat— make me think of a race-horse I once watched. A fine stallion called Sunday Sunrise."

"Were his motions harmonious? That is why the Chinese admire these kinds of creatures, you know."

"His motions earned me some good ale, sir."

West laughed. "Then Sunday Sunrise he shall be, Mr. Kenmare The female, I suppose, would then be Mrs. Sunrise; but she needs a bit more of a name than that. My housekeeper back in Scotland was a fine old woman named Martha, who made excellent trifle and had as good an idea of breakfast as any Scotchwoman. How about Martha Sunrise?"

"A fine name, sir."

Meanwhile, Acting-Lieutenant Alexander Teal was studying furiously. West had mentioned to him the possibility of taking the examination in Madras not long after the ship had left East Africa, and the young officer had been studying hard ever since. Now that the possibility had become a certainty, and an imminent one at that, he was glued to his manuals of seamanship. West wondered how he would fare when he actually went aboard the *Vitruvius* to take the examination. It was never an easy experience, and even if his knowledge was sufficient, his nerve might fail. West would have to offer some words of encouragement before he left.

West's own thoughts, though, were on the city of Madras. Once the business of the day was well in hand, he told Kenmare that he was going go ashore. "I am sorry I cannot ask you to come with me, my friend, but you seem to be needed here."

"Aye, sir, we have stores coming in at a good clip now. You must take someone, though, just for safety. How about Mr. Lang? He seems as though he would be a good man to have around in case of trouble."

West considered that, but shook his head. "I am sure he would, but I need to speak with Mr. Rede, and this seems as good a time as any. Please give him my compliments, and tell him to prepare himself for a trip ashore."

"Aye, sir."

The sun was sinking low in the sky when West and Rede climbed out of the longboat and on to the docks. The officers at the harbour greeted them and told them, in response to their inquiries, of a fine marketplace not far away called the Peacock Market. West recalled that it was one of the places Violet had mentioned the night before. Having ascertained the directions, the captain and the second lieutenant set off for it.

"I wanted to tell you, Mr. Rede," said West as they walked, "that I encountered an old acquaintance of yours last night."

"Oh? And who was that, sir."

"Captain Shreve."

West saw the look of uncertainty on Rede's face, and waited. Then he said: "I did not see much of him, but I believe I saw enough. I hope you know by now, Mr. Rede, that I run things very differently on my ship. Your service has been exemplary, and I hope you will feel able to speak freely aboard the *Promise*."

The tension seemed to slowly flow out from Rede's face; his hard features relaxed into what was almost a smile. "Thank you, sir," he said, relief evident in his voice. "I believe I understand."

They walked on in silence until they reached the marketplace. There, the narrow street suddenly opened up into a broad public square. The scene before them reminded West of something from an eastern fable. Merchants wearing silk cried out in many languages, hawking their wares. One fruit vendor seemed to be yelling even more raucously than the others, and West soon saw why. The man had a row of barrels laden with fresh mangoes, and a trio of small brown monkeys had just succeeded in helping themselves. The vendor waved his arms and shooed them away, and the monkeys ran off, chattering to themselves, their paws sticky with fruit. West walked over, picked up a mango, and handed the man a few coins, which seemed to have a calming effect on him.

West continued walking through the marketplace, stopping next at a spice vendor. He eyed the rows of small jars that held a rainbow of powders. When he turned away, his eye was caught by a frail old woman, sitting in the dust. She was clad in rags and her hands were held out. West threw several coins her way and walked on; he was amused when, out of the corner of his eye, he saw the woman rise and stride briskly away, apparently having made a suitable profit for the day.

"Are you sure you would not care for a mango, Mr. Rede?" said West, finishing his fruit.

"No thank you, sir. But I must say, this is a fascinating place."

"Have you ever been in India before?"

"No, sir. And you?"

"Only once, and not for long enough. Look at the colours of these carpets!"

The carpets were piled under a canvas tent. At the entrance of the tent stood a Sikh in a white cotton robe and a crimson turban. "Greetings, Captain," he said in English, recognizing West's uniform. "May I show you my wares? I have the finest carpets in the city."

"I would like to look at them."

"Certainly, Captain, certainly." West stepped under the canvas and knelt down to the examine the carpets. There was an oil lamp hanging from the ceiling, giving off a smoky odour and a yellow light. It was not the best light for perceiving colour, but nonetheless, West could see that the hues of the carpets were rich and deep. They were red and gold, burgundy and copper, cobalt blue and iridescent green, and their abstract patterns were both intricate and pleasing to the eye. West bent down and ran his hands across them, and then he was startled by a dull thud and a muted cry from behind him.

He turned quickly and saw that it was Rede who had cried out. The lieutenant had fallen to the ground, and behind him stood a man with a dagger The Sikh stared at the scene for a moment and then ran out of the tent. West looked down at Rede, afraid that his lieutenant was dead; but there was no blood to be seen. Then he remembered the sound. The attacker must have brought the hilt of the dagger down on Rede's head. That was well; it could be hoped that he was only stunned.

West turned his attention to the man before him. He was Indian, and he was wearing trousers and a vest of white cotton. His face was weather-beaten and stony, but his movements, as he advanced upon West, showed a youthful agility. He wore a silk turban of a bold green colour that shimmered in the lamplight, reminding West of a bird's feathers, or, perhaps, a reptile's scales. His dagger was long and faintly curved, and it, too, glittered in the light.

It was a good thing West had worn his sword at his side— the sword of honour that he had been given for saving Scotland from invasion. He drew it now, for the first time on this voyage. "Who are you?" he demanded. "What do you mean by this attack?"

"Does it matter?" the man answered in English. There was a weary expression in his brown eyes, but his movements were quick and graceful, and he lunged at West with the dagger poised to strike.

West's own reactions were equally agile. He stepped to the side and parried the blow with his sword. Then he stepped back and allowed the sword to slip just slightly in his hand. It was a controlled slip, however; when his attacker attempted to seize the opening and lunge forward again, West brought his sword up sharply. The blow would have struck the man on the hand, perhaps ending the fight; but he saw what West was doing and pulled back just in time. Nonetheless, the sword struck the dagger, and the smaller weapon fell to the ground, glittering upon the golden thread of a carpet.

But the fight was not over. The man took several steps back and drew a cutlass from his belt. This time, West did not wait for his enemy to advance. He charged forward himself, and steel rang against steel. Back and forth they went then, parrying each other's blows. West was dimly aware of faces staring at them from outside the tent, but no one dared intervene.

On the ground nearby, Rede stirred and groaned but did not awaken. The timing of his groan was, however, essential to West; it reminded him to be careful not to trip over Rede's body. West dodged the next blow, rather than parrying it, and then lunged forward at his opponent, who dodged in turn. Although the man fought with a curved sword, his style and West's were somewhat similar. West had always used a kind of fencing technique in swordplay; it was a technique born of necessity, since he was too slight of build to overpower an opponent, but he was agile enough to dodge and weave. His attacker, too, used an approach based more on speed than strength. As their swords clashed together again, West found himself idly wondering how long this might go on for.

Then, the idea came to him. West parried the next blow with a sharp sideways motion, forcing his opponent's sword away from him. Next, he made a quick feint at his enemy's head. While the attacker neatly stepped to the side, West jumped up into the air, and with a dull clang, he brought his sword down upon the oil lamp. The lamp swung forward. As the attacker leapt toward West again, he suddenly dropped his sword and cried out in pain at the stream of hot oil that was poured out on his arm. Finally, West brought the hilt of his sword down on the man's head, stunning him just as he had stunned Rede.

The fight was now over, but West suddenly noticed an unwanted consequence of his plan. There was a spark of fire upon one of the carpets; the fabric had been set aflame by the lamp oil. Not wanting it to spread, West seized the carpet, rolled it up, and threw it to the ground. Then he lifted it and threw it down again. The spark was quelled.

At last, he could examine Rede. As he had suspected, the lieutenant had been rendered unconscious by a blow to the head. West was sure that he would be fine. Then he turned his attention to the attacker. The man's pockets were empty and he seemed to have carried nothing on him except his two weapons. There was no clue as to the reason for the assault.

"I am so sorry, Captain! I am so sorry!"

It was the Sikh carpet merchant, looking terrified. "Do you know who this man is?" West asked.

"I have no idea, sir. You have my word!"

"Very well. Can you get a message to my ship for me?"

"Yes, Captain, of course."

"It is the frigate *Promise*. Tell them to send an officer here, along with several marines. And the ship's surgeon to attend to Mr. Rede."

"Yes, sir. And myself, sir? My shop?"

"The men will be coming only to take my attacker into custody. You have nothing to fear."

"Thank you, sir." The merchant ran off to deliver the message. Meanwhile, the attacker stirred and opened his eyes. West stood above him, sword in hand.

"Who are you?"

"I said, it does not matter."

"It does to me. Why did you attack us?"

"Perhaps I was simply trying to steal from you."

"You are too good a swordsman for so simple a goal. I think you are an assassin."

"Very good, Captain. You are a clever man as well as a skilful fighter."

"Tell me who sent you."

"Why? I am bound for the gallows now, anyway."

He had a point. "I admit there seems to be little I can offer you," said West.

"There is something, though. There is this." He reached inside his vest and took out a small book, bound in vellum, that had lain against his breast. "Return this to my father, and I will tell you what you want to know."

West reached out for the book, carefully keeping his sword at the ready. But the assassin only handed it to him and lay still. The book was written in an alphabet unknown to the captain. "What language is this?"

"Sanskrit. The book belonged to my father. He is an old man, in a village not far from here, called Jalapur. I suspect you are a man of honour, Captain. Give me your word that you will bring my father the book, and I will tell you who hired me."

"I will bring him the book. The village is Jalapur. What is his name?"

"His name is Kushar."

"Very well. You have my word."

"Tell my father that I failed the book, and I do regret it deeply."

At that moment, Rede opened his eyes and tried to rise. "Captain—" he murmured.

"Just lie there, Mr. Rede," said West quickly. He looked back at the assassin. "Well?"

"A Spaniard. He is a tall man. He wore a burgundy cravat."

West nodded. "Did he tell you why he wanted me dead?" he asked, though he knew the answer.

"Yes, I will give you that as well. He said you had done a great disservice to an old friend of his, and this old friend would reward him well for having brought about your death."

"As I thought. He told you which ship was mine, you kept a watch on it, and then you followed me to the marketplace to seize your opportunity. Is that it?"

"Yes." Velazquez would have found out the name of West's ship from the talkative Commander Cosgrove. And he had himself seized the opportunity to further secure the favour of Count Vega. It all fit together.

"Thank you. You will be placed under arrest in a few moments, but I will keep my word to you." Something else occurred to West. "You could have killed my lieutenant with that dagger. Why didn't you?"

The man looked almost insulted. "I would never kill without a reason," he said. "I was paid only to assassinate you."

Back aboard the *Promise*, Rede's physical recovery was quick, but his pride was badly damaged. "I feel most negligent in my duties, Captain," he said, standing in West's cabin; he had refused to remain in sickbay. "I do not know what happened."

"I know what happened, Mr. Rede. We were in a crowd, and the man came up behind you, drew his dagger, and hit you in the head before you could do anything."

"Yes, but that left you unprotected. I was the only other officer present. I was responsible for your safety."

"Mr. Rede, the assassin was highly skilled at his profession. There was nothing you could have done. I am only pleased that he had some quirk of conscience— if you can call it that— and therefore let you live. This will in no way reflect badly in your record, and you should not feel ashamed of yourself."

"Thank you, sir." Rede seemed, at best, only partially convinced. "Nonetheless, I want you to know that, if I have the opportunity again, I will defend you with my life."

"I saw you ride in front of an elephant to save a comrade. No one doubts your courage, save you yourself. And you have no need to do so. Now go to your cabin and get some rest— that's an order."

West thought about his second lieutenant. Rede had felt relieved, emotionally unburdened, by West's conversation with him regarding Shreve. Yet, Rede seemed unable to accept himself as worthy, and by blaming himself for not thwarting the assassin's attack, he had latched onto a new reason for guilt. It was as though he had let go of one excuse for self-doubt only to seize upon another, which meant that the self-doubt was there, regardless— an aspect of his personality unrelated to actual success or failure. West felt empathy and a trace of amusement, for he was reminded of his own youth.

Then he took out the book that the assassin had given him and stared at the Sanskrit characters. A moment later, there was a knock on his cabin door, and in response to his call of "enter," Kenmare stepped inside.

"There's a longboat coming out here," he said, sounding somewhat surprised. "And Admiral Taylor's on it."

"Really?" Upon returning to the *Promise*, West had immediately written a report to the Admiral and sent a messenger out to deliver it; but he had hardly expected so prompt, or so personal, a response. The Admiral was clearly a man of energy.

West followed his first lieutenant on deck and stood at attention as the Admiral Taylor was piped over the side. He instructed Kenmare to pass word to his steward, and then led the Admiral to his cabin. As soon as the door was closed behind them, Taylor seemed to begin speaking in a blusterous manner. "This is outrageous, West! I've already spoken to the men who took your attacker into custody, and he did not repeat his story to them. But of course I believe you. That Velazquez should attempt this— the man has no honour at all. To think I had him to my home! Truth to tell, West, I feel personally responsible for this."

"You certainly are not, sir," said West, jumping into the conversation as the Admiral caught his breath. "And there has been no lasting harm. My second lieutenant was only superficially injured, and I am quite well." At that moment, Chang entered. "Ah, here is my steward. May I offer you a glass of port, Admiral?"

"Not now, thank you."

"Very well. You may go then, Mr. Chang." Chang bowed and exited.

"I don't know how you can be so cool about this, West," the Admiral went on. "You handled the situation with great credit— fighting off an assassin in the marketplace— it's not every captain who can say he's done that! But we must deal with this Velazquez. He cannot be allowed to order the assassination of a British officer and get away with it."

"I applaud the sentiment, sir, but there would seem to be grave difficulties. He is an ambassador, and our only evidence against him is the word of an assassin."

"I know." The Admiral sighed and sat down in front of West's desk. His energy suddenly seemed to dissipate. "The truth is, that's what has me in such a choler. I can order the arrest of Velazquez, but frankly, I know I would not be able make it stick."

"Yes, sir."

"The man should hang for this, though."

"That seems unlikely to happen."

Taylor raised an eyebrow. "You're an unusual man, West. You're the one who they tried to kill, and you don't seem upset at all by the fact that we cannot do anything."

"I was pleased to at least be able to find out who was behind it; but once I knew it was the Spanish ambassador, I did not imagine we would be able to bring him to justice. As far as facing death, well, I nearly was killed at Andalusia." West saw Taylor look at him with admiration and realized that his words sounded courageous. That troubled him, because he did not consider himself to be courageous, but he was not sure what else to say. Somehow, his lack of surprise at Velazquez's immunity prevented him from sharing the Admiral's outrage. Furthermore, the incident in the marketplace simply had not provoked fear in him. He had taken the duel one step at a time, looking at it almost as a game; and when it was over, it had immediately been replaced by the challenge of getting the man to talk. West realized that his wits, and not his emotions, had been in play throughout. "I admit I never knew looking at carpets was so dangerous, but then, life is full of surprises."

The Admiral smiled and shook his head, clearly with approval. "You'll be an Admiral yet, West." He rose. "I suppose that concludes my business here, then. But rest assured— if I can ever find a way to bring Velazquez before a court of justice, I shall."

"I have no doubt of it, sir. Thank you."

"Oh, and there's one more thing. You are bound for the South China Sea; obviously you are aware of the navigational hazards."

"Yes, sir."

"I can't help you there, but you must also realize that there is another area of danger that you must sail through first."

West nodded. "The Straits of Malacca." He would have to pass through the narrow channel between the great island of Java Minor and the south-eastern shores of the Asian continent before he could come out into the South China Sea.

"Right. It's treacherous sailing, and it's the domain of pirates. I suggest you try to find a local navigator to help you."

"Sounds like a sensible idea." West had thought of it himself, but he was no point in saying so to the Admiral.

"There's even a man I can recommend," Taylor went on. "If he's still there, that is. Name of James Ardshiel."

"A Scotsman?"

"Yes, formerly of the East India Company. He has a small trading vessel of his own now, called the *Flying Fish*. Knows the Straits like the back of his hand. Brilliant navigator. Bit of an eccentric— never goes anywhere without his bird." He cocked an eye at the cage on West's desk, where Autolycus was perched, half-asleep. "Not that there's anything wrong with that. He has a dwelling in the city of Taijung, on Java Minor. The ruler there is favourable to trade with the English, and there are a few expatriates who live there and manage the trade. Ardshiel is the principal man."

"What sort of goods do we get from Java Minor?"

"Ebony, camphor, abalone shell. I take it you've never been there."

"No."

"Well, you'll probably find it interesting. Taijung is a small city, rather primitive, but Ardshiel seems happy there. The expatriates have a tavern called the Blue Cave— you'll be able to find word of him there. If he's off on a voyage, no doubt another merchant can help you."

"Taijung. The Blue Cave." West repeated the names, not because he thought he would have trouble remembering them, but because he liked them. "Thank you, sir."

"Oh— I let slip something of your adventures tonight in front of my daughter. She was most concerned on your behalf." It was impossible to read anything from the Admiral's tone or expression.

"Please tell her I am fine, and thank her for her good wishes." West kept his own features equally inscrutable.

Admiral Taylor nodded. "Thank you, then. Good night, and best wishes on your voyage."

"Good night." The Admiral left.

A moment later, though, Kenmare entered. "It's Mr. Carrin who wishes to speak to you now, sir."

"Another surprise," said West. "It seems Mr. Carrin seldom wishes to speak to anyone. You may send him in."

The representative of the East India Company walked slowly into the cabin and greeted the captain quietly. "I wanted to tell you that I am pleased you are all right, sir," he said. "The word has gone round the ship that you were attacked in the marketplace."

"Yes. I am fine, thank you."

"Do you know who was behind the attack?"

The question surprised West. "I am not really at liberty to discuss it," he said, raising an eyebrow.

"I understand, sir. It simply occurred to me that a distinguished captain such as yourself might well have distinguished enemies." Carrin's voice remained quiet.

"Meaning what?"

"Meaning only that some of those enemies might be out of reach of the law . . . But not necessarily out of reach of the East India Company." Carrin's eyes suddenly met his, and West could read an expression of undeniable cunning in them.

"How much do you know about what happened tonight?" said West sharply.

"Very little, but I do know your background. If this was a random attack, then all is done; for I have heard that you defeated your attacker. However, if this was a deliberate assassination attempt on you, I can only assume that the Dons are behind it. Any Spanish here in Fort St. George would likely be officials, men who would seem untouchable. But there are other options, and I can assure you that the East India Company would be pleased to assist so noble a captain as yourself."

"I see." West wondered whether Carrin's deductive reasoning was actually that astute, or whether he somehow had access to information about what had happened. Either way, he was clearly a man to be watched. Furthermore, he seemed to be proposing the assassination of Velazquez. West's earlier suspicions of Carrin were being confirmed, and he began to wonder anew about the death of Gilbraith. "However, I have no need of assistance in this matter. The services of the East India Company . . . whatever they might be . . . are not required." He stared at Carrin intently, but the man remained impassive.

"As you wish, sir. I am pleased that all is well." And he left the cabin.

West wondered about Carrin for a few minutes, but again, there was nothing he could do about the man. The conversation had been quite politic on Carrin's part; he had not openly suggested anything criminal. For a moment, West wondered if it would have been useful to try and trick Carrin into being more specific; but he had the feeling it would have been futile. There was nothing to do except continue to watch the man.

West poured himself a glass of rum. He thought about the sword-fight and the oil lamp and the warm smile of Violet Taylor. And then his thoughts turned to Java Minor and the Blue Cave. But no . . . Jalapur was first. He undressed, lay down on his cot, and was soon asleep.

There was a hill outside the village of Jalapur; a dry, sun-baked hill, of sparse grasses and red earth. At its top was a crumbling ruin of red stone. There was a wall, high and thick, but without a gate. Only decaying timbers, laying on the ground, showed that a gate had once existed, but that it had been outlived by the stones of the wall. Within the wall was a structure that had once been a great house; a few walls and part of the roof still stood. There was a dry basin in front that had once been filled with water. But there were signs of growth remaining. A palm tree with a smooth trunk reached upward. Part of the wall was covered with green and brown ivy. And the greenest and most vibrant strand of ivy bore a single purple flower.

West dismounted and led his horse into the ruins. The journey had been easy enough. The officers of the port had told him the way to Jalapur and helped him obtain horses for the journey. West was accompanied, once again, by Rede. The second lieutenant was fully recovered, and the captain knew that if he chose anyone else, Rede would take it as a sign of distrust and exclusion. So they had come together to Jalapur, only a few hours ride inland from Madras, and asked in the village for Kushar. The Indian villagers they spoke with shook their heads sadly and pointed to the ruins on the hill.

Now that they were there, West looked around and called out the man's name. Suddenly, he saw a face staring at him from within the ruined building. The eyes were very keen. A moment later, a man came hobbling out, supported by a gnarled cane— an old man, stoop-shouldered and white-haired, but with eyes of a fierce brightness.

"What do you want of me?" he asked.

"I am Captain Bowman West. I bring a message from your son."

"My son? I have no son."

West suddenly realized that he did not know the name of the assassin. However, he had no reason not to be honest. "I was attacked by a man in a Madras marketplace yesterday. I fought him and won, and in exchange for information that I needed, he asked me to come here and look for you. He said you were his father."

The man nodded silently. He said nothing.

"Are you?"

"Yes," said Kushar. "I had a son who became a criminal. I consider him to be my son no longer. But perhaps it was he who attacked you."

"I am sorry, then, that I must tell you he faces execution."

"I am an honourable man, English Captain. My son died to me long ago. Why did he wish you to seek me out?"

"He wanted me to give you this." West drew forth the book, walked to the old man, and handed it to him. "He wanted me to tell you that he failed the book, and he regrets it deeply."

The man took the book but said nothing.

West's word was now fulfilled, but he could not leave it at that. "Please, sir, can you tell me what the book is? Is it some text of religion or philosophy?"

"No, nothing like that," said Kushar, shaking his head. "We are not all philosophers, you know. This book, that my father gave to me and I gave to my son, is a kind of treasure map. My son failed to find the treasure. That, I understand; the path he chose instead, I do not."

"A treasure map? That comes rather in my line. I do not suppose you would be willing to tell me about it?"

"Why not, English Captain? The book has been handed down for generations in my family, but no one has found the treasure. Why should I not tell you something of it?

"The book was written by an ancestor of mine who travelled far and wide. He recorded many wonders, but the greatest of them was a valley of diamonds. Many in my family have tried to find this valley, including my son. But we have never succeeded. There are those who believe that my ancestor did not speak the truth. I do not know.

"But the story is this: there is a valley, a deep ravine amidst high mountains, the floor of which is covered with precious jewels. Most especially, it is covered with diamonds that sparkle in the sunlight. But the sides of the mountains that surround it are so steep, no one is able to go down them. And the valley is enclosed by the mountains; there is no other way there.

"However, in that country there are great birds of prey. These great birds carry off the mountain goats for their food.

"Therefore, what the people who live there do is this: they kill a goat and cover its hide with sap from pine trees. Then they cast it down into the valley. In time, one of the great birds will seize it in its talons and fly up over the mountains with it. Then the people, who have been keeping watch, shoot arrows at the bird. And if they can bring it down, they find that the hide of the goat is covered with the diamonds.

"My ancestor described many things in his travels, but this is the one to make a man wealthy. So when I was young, I travelled north to the Himalayas to look for the great birds and the valley of the diamonds. But I found there only snow and ice and howling wind. Where my son sought the diamonds I do not know. But I know he did not find them.

And I know that I lost my son long ago. And that is my story, English Captain."

"Please accept my condolences, Kushar. And I thank you for your story."

"I thank you for my book."

West turned and walked away, but then he turned back. "Please, sir, if you will forgive one more question: why do you live here, in these ruins?"

"My ancestors lived here when it was a great house with the most beautiful gardens in all the land. I have no money now to restore the house and the gardens. I never found the diamonds, you see. But should a man leave that which is his, merely because it is old and its glory faded? Should a man cast aside his wife because her hair is grey, or should he turn aside from his parents because their eyes have grown dim and they hobble about when once they took great strides? Here I shall remain."

"I understand. Thank you."

West nodded to Rede, and they turned and walked away down the hill. Then, they mounted their horses once again. And they took the dusty road to the sea.

X.
Taijung

*T*he voyage to Java Minor began with congratulations. Alexander Teal had passed his examination and was now considered a full lieutenant. The young man was excited, of course, and grateful to West for having arranged the opportunity. For his part, West was reminded by the incident of his own examination and subsequent promotion: the end of his time as a signal midshipman hoping to be made lieutenant, and the beginning of his time as a lieutenant hoping to be made commander. The thought made him smile ruefully.

Yet the novelty of the new voyage soon drew him out of any preoccupation with the past. As they left Madras and sailed south and then east, there was much to be seen of the coast of India; dry, red plains, rich, green jungles, and long slow rivers that finally reached the sea. There were the okapis upon deck as well, continuing to give diversion to West and to his crew by their very presence. The gentle creatures continued in good health, seemingly resilient to any pressure that the ocean voyage put upon them. Even when the *Promise* sailed through a fierce rain squall, two days out from Madras, they simply lay down upon the deck and waited for the weather to pass.

After the ship rounded the southern tip of India and passed the island of Ceylon, West arranged for another musical entertainment to keep up the crew's spirits. Although the performances were from the men of the lower decks, Wade Lang could not resist adding his voice to the praises of the Spanish lady, joining in with some of the sailors:

As I went down to Dublin city
As sunset faded into night,
Who should I see but the Spanish lady,
Washing her feet by candle-light?

First she washed 'em, then she dried 'em,
Over a fire of amber coal,
In all my life I ne'er did see
A maid so sweet about the sole.

It was a fine evening, and it seemed strange and wonderful to West to hear the old folk songs of Scotland and Ireland echoing across the waters of the Indian Ocean. Ceylon, the fabled island of rubies, was only a few leagues to port. That, in turn, gave rise to more thoughts. West had read Marco Polo and knew that the twelfth-century explorer had written about Ceylon; he also knew that he had written about a valley of diamonds much like the one Kushar had described. His thoughts turned back to Kushar's story, and in his mind, he compared it with the account of Polo. They certainly were similar; Polo had described the same peculiar method of gathering the precious stones that Kushar had. And there was someplace else where the same story came up— West groped for the memory and found it— an Arabian folktale he had once heard from a fellow seafarer. Of course the last source was presented as quite imaginary, but West believed that some legends, especially those of treasure, had a basis in fact. Finding the story from three very different sources made him wonder if there really was such a valley, somewhere in the mountains of Asia. It was a curious thing to think of.

The fair night of music was followed by another rain squall, this one with especially strong winds; and since they were still near the coast of Ceylon, they anchored to wait it out. When it passed and the sun came through, the men were singing again, this time as they pulled the capstan to raise the anchor. And then they sailed on. They had seen nothing of the Ceylonese people, having had no need to make port on the island. The provisions they had picked up at Madras would last them, if all went well, to the end of their journey. Furthermore, West was uncertain of the disposition of Ceylon's ruler toward Europeans: the island maintained a guarded independence from the British Raj.

The *Promise* sailed almost due east from there, toward the sunrise. In the mornings, West would often have Chang bring him his coffee on the quarterdeck, where he could watch the sun come up in a blaze of colour over the ocean. Later, in his cabin, he would speak with Chang more extensively: West had requested that his steward teach him Mandarin,

CHRIS FASOLINO

and Chang was happy to oblige, showing a kind of amused patience at what quickly became a mental struggle for the captain. Although West considered himself something of a linguist, Mandarin was unique in his experience. There were four distinct tones to remember, as well as a neutral tone that still had to be separated from the others. To have tea, for example, was *pao cha*, with the first syllable in a neutral tone and the second in a rising tone. Getting the tones wrong would change the meaning. West's ability as a musician helped him in his quest, but not as much as he had hoped it would.

Nevertheless, it was an interesting pastime for a long voyage, and it sometimes led to discoveries. "In Chinese," Chang said one day, "the future is behind us." In response to West's puzzled look, he smiled slightly and explained. "In the European languages, the future is described as being ahead of us. However, in the Chinese language, the future is always spoken of as being behind us— and we are said to be falling into the future backwards."

"Falling into the future backwards?" West said. "It sounds a somewhat dizzying concept, Mr. Chang."

"The reason is that we cannot see the future. We can see the past, in the sense that we can remember it; but the future is unknown. Therefore, the future is behind us, and we are falling into it backwards."

West raised an eyebrow. "That will give me much to think about."

The Chinese concept of time would be fully supported by the events on Java Minor. When the lookout finally reported that the coast of the great island was visible on the horizon, West rushed to the quarterdeck and stared through his telescope at the great southern island, with no idea at all of what awaited him there.

The island of Java Minor, or Sumatra as it was also known, was almost entirely jungle. The coast was green and lush, full of great trees and towering ferns lit up by bright yellow sunlight. The chorus of insects was loud and continual. At times, the calling of birds would add to the richness of the sound. As the *Promise* sailed along the coast, West was fascinated to observe places where the jungle stretched right into the sea and hundreds of trees seemed to grow out of the water. These were the mangroves.

The sun began to set, and West brought a glass of rum up to his quarterdeck to enjoy in the sultry tropical evening. The last rays of the sun lit up the green foliage and blue-green waters of the mangrove forests while the sounds of the insects continued unabated. Kenmare joined him and they consulted their charts of the coast. They concluded that they should be nearing the cove of Taijung; and indeed they were, for an inlet was soon sighted, and when the ship drew even with it, they could see a port city on its shores. At West's orders, the ship was turned into the harbour and the anchor lowered.

There were other ships in the harbour as well. There were several brigs and schooners of European design, including a brig bearing the name *Flying Fish* upon its prow. That was good news; James Ardshiel was in Taijung. There were several junks, with sails in the characteristic shape favoured by the Asian ships. Most were small, coasting vessels, but one was quite large— as large as the *Promise*. West looked at it admiringly through his telescope. It was long and sleek, not so tall as the *Promise*, but slightly longer, and with four masts rather than three. The sails were a bold red in colour, and that, along with their shape, gave them a most unusual appearance. The hull was painted black, and the prow ornamented with inlays of deep green stone forming Chinese characters. It looked like jade, but jade was too valuable for such a purpose; perhaps it was malachite. From atop the largest mast— the mainmast, West supposed it could be called, though the existence of a fourth mast on the ship did not quite fit with the European terminology of fore, main, and mizzen— a jade-green banner fluttered in the warm night breezes.

Taijung itself was perhaps the strangest city West had ever seen. The buildings were all made of wood, most of them little more than huts, but some considerably larger. Very few of them, however, were on the ground. As West eyed the shores through his telescope, he was astonished to see that most of the dwellings were in the treetops. They were built upon wooden platforms supported by great branches; and their rooftops were nestled amid the deep green foliage. They were lighted by yellow lamps that hung suspended from some of the smaller branches; as night fell, it looked as if bright stars were glimmering there, in the air yet very close to the earth.

Eager to see this new city, West ordered the jolly boat made ready. Meanwhile, he asked Chang to come up to the quarterdeck to read the characters on the large junk. "The ship is called the *Jade Shark*," Chang said. "Where it is from I do not know. The green banner atop, with no emblem or insignia, is hardly informative."

"I wonder," West said. "Admiral Taylor warned us that the Straits of Malacca are the domain of pirates. Perhaps one of their ships has come to Taijung. The junk does look like it would be a formidable ship in battle, or in a chase."

"Ah, mebbe pirates then, be velly careful." West turned and saw Kenmare approaching; he smiled to himself at the resulting change in Chang's speech.

"Thank you, Mr. Chang," he said.

"Captain, the boat is ready," Kenmare told him.

"Thank you, Mr. Kenmare."

West was rowed to the shore, accompanied this time by Wade Lang. The jolly boat pulled up to a small wooden quay at the edge of the trees. There, a man in a yellow silk robe was waiting. The man was Oriental in appearance but with skin somewhat darker than the Chinese norm. He was accompanied by two guards wearing mail shirts and silver helmets, with swords at their sides. As West and Lang clambered up onto the quay, the man in the silk robe bowed low in greeting. West saw that the yellow silk of the official garment was covered with an elegant pattern of white clouds and blue cranes.

"I bid you welcome on behalf of Lo'yu, the King of Taijung," said the official, speaking English slowly and in a formal manner. "He regrets that an illness prevents him from greeting you personally. I am Javin, Advisor to the King."

"It is a pleasure to meet you, Javin. I am Captain Bowman West, of the frigate *H.M.S. Promise*. Please convey my regards to the King, and I hope that his health returns."

"Yes, Captain. The King looks most favourably upon trade with the English. When our watchmen perceived a Royal Navy ship coming into the harbour, the King sent me at once to bid you greetings."

"Thank you."

"May I ask, please, the purpose of your visit, Captain? Usually the English we see here are merchantmen."

"I am on a mission of exploration to the South China Sea. I am stopping here in Taijung only briefly, in the hopes of finding a navigator to guide me through the Straits of Malacca."

"I see. Of course you are most welcome. The King asked me to tell you that your ship could prove most valuable in this part of the world."

"What do you mean?" Javin's courteous tone was suddenly alarming, and West found himself wondering if King Lo'yu was plotting to capture the *Promise*.

"Only that the city of Taijung faces a problem, and that you and your ship may prove able to help us."

"What problem is that?"

"I cannot speak of it openly, lest I risk bringing ruin upon the royal family." West raised an eyebrow. The King's messenger was becoming more and more mysterious. "However, since you seek a navigator, you doubtless plan to visit your countryman Ardshiel? He is reputed to be the greatest navigator of these waters, foreign though they once were to him."

"Yes, I have come seeking Ardshiel."

"That is most excellent, Captain." Javin seemed almost relieved. "Then the good Ardshiel will explain all to you. And I need only bid you listen to his words. You may find him at the tavern where your countrymen gather, the Blue Cave. Take the path to the right and look for a sign in the treetops that fits with the name. Welcome to Taijung, Captain, and good day."

West gave a polite reply, and Javin and the guards turned and hurried off, back into the city. "What do you make of that, Mr. Lang?"

"Not sure, Captain. But they do seem nervous about something."

"Yes. I wonder if it has something to do with that large junk in the harbour. Well, let's see if we can find the Blue Cave, and then perhaps Ardshiel will be more forthcoming than Javin."

There were two paths that led into the city of Taijung. One went straight inland from the quay, and this was the one that Javin and his guards had taken. The other veered to the right, and West and Lang took this. The path was narrow and unpaved, and it led among the trees. There were huts and houses above them, and the light of the lamps seemed to drift down through the night air to faintly illuminate the path. From time to time, doors opened and people stepped out onto the wooden platforms to look down upon the strangers. At times they would call a greeting in an unknown tongue, and West would raise his hand in reply. The sound of the insects was very loud, the air was warm and humid, and on either side of the path the foliage was lush and green and thick around the trunks of the trees.

Before long, they saw a hut that bore a wooden sign painted blue. There was a stylized representation of a cave upon it, as well as the name, in English and also apparently in Eastern characters. A bamboo ladder led from the base of the tree to the platform upon which the hut rested. West climbed up, with Lang following. Several lamps lit the way. When they reached the top, West stood on the platform for a moment and looked out. The jungle city of Taijung was spread out, not below them, but around them, in the treetops. Some of the platforms, he now saw, had wooden walkways leading between them, through the air. He looked up and into the canopy, and saw a rustling there. Then a monkey sprang through the air and leapt to the branches of another tree. West smiled and walked through the door of the Blue Cave.

The wooden floor was covered with a woven rug with abstract patterns of blue and green. The bar was of a darker, polished wood, and there were several bamboo chairs. A large lamp of blue glass hung from the ceiling and filled the single room with coloured light. There were three men there, two sitting in chairs and one standing behind the bar, drinking and talking. They all appeared to be Europeans, and they all looked up when West came in.

"I am looking for James Ardshiel," said West.

"You have found him," said the man at the bar. "These are my comrades—"

"No need to introduce us," said one of the other men, cutting him off. "We were just leaving." He rose and cast a surly look at West. The man was burly and formidable in appearance, with a bristling brown beard. West looked back at him evenly. He walked to the door and left without a word, followed by his comrade. As the door shut behind them, West heard Ardshiel chuckle.

"Dinna take it to heart, Captain," he said in a Scotch brogue. "Those two gentleman had a bit of a misunderstanding with the Royal Navy some years back, and they're none too eager to meet a man wearing gold epaulettes."

"I am not here to press-gang them," said West, "nor yet to try them for desertion, if that was the nature of the misunderstanding."

"I see you're a man of some perceptive ability. For myself, I was fairly sure ye had nothing of the sort in mind. Taijung is a bit out of the way for press-gang operations, or for the tracking down of old sailors who've taken a lengthy sort of leave."

"Well said," West answered, and studied the man before him. James Ardshiel was small of stature and nearly as thin as West himself. His face was weather-beaten enough to make his age hard to guess; but his eyes were bright and sparkling with humour. He wore white duck trousers and a blue shirt that seemed to be made of silk— an apt choice for the climate of Taijung. Despite the heat, though, a cotton scarf that hung loosely around his neck, bearing the bold red plaid of the Stewart clan, the noble, if controversial, kin of the Ardshiels. He wore both a sword and a pistol at his side; but after having seen what they believed was a pirate ship in the harbour, so did West and Lang.

"So, if I may ask then, Captain, who are ye, and for what is it that ye do come here?" Ardshiel continued. As he spoke, there was a sound of fluttering, and West saw a bird flying loose through the tavern. Ardshiel raised his hand and clucked his tongue, and the bird flew over and perched on his shoulder. "A blue magpie," Ardshiel said, in response to the question in West's eyes. The bird was blue and white, with a black head, and it had a long, plumed tail of vibrant blue.

"A beautiful creature. I am Captain Bowman West, and I am looking to sail to the South China Sea. This is my third lieutenant, Mr. Lang."

"Ah! So ye need my expert guidance through the Straits of Malacca." There was no irony in the tone. Ardshiel clearly considered himself an expert.

"You were recommended to me by Admiral Taylor."

"Admiral Taylor, eh? A good enough fellow, though a bit of a whiteshirt." West had never heard the term before, but he could guess at its meaning. "Sit down and have a drink with me, and we'll talk it over." Ardshiel refilled his own glass and took out glasses for West and Lang. "This is a specialty here in Taijung," he said, as he poured from a dusty old bottle. "It's called *gaoliang.*"

To West, the drink smelled and tasted overpoweringly strong. Always interested in the local traditions, he continued sipping at it, though, trying in vain to pick up a flavour other than alcohol. Finally he said, "I wonder that this doesn't eat through the glass."

Lang had taken a cautious sip as well, but then he downed the rest in a single shot. "That was awful," he said, sliding the glass back to Ardshiel. "Could I have another?"

Ardshiel laughed and refilled the glass. Then he sipped at his own glass. "Ye get used to it," he said. "Truth is, I love everything about Taijung. I first came here with the East India Company, but then I left and struck out on me own. Came back here and made a home, and a good business."

"It is a fascinating place. I do not blame you," said West.

"Aye, that it is, and at my age, I'll take this climate over a winter's day in Edinburgh without a shred of doubt. There is just one thing wrong with the place, as of the past month or so. Tell me, Captain West, what kind of a ship do ye have?"

"A frigate."

"A frigate, aye. A frigate with how many guns?"

"Twenty-eight."

"Well, Captain West, we might be able to help each other."

"How so?"

"Our trouble is with pirates, and it's no secret where they come from. The city of Palembang, on the southern tip of Java Minor, is as infamous for piracy as any grog haven in the West Indies. It has been so for centuries. Often, they attack ships trying to sail through the Straights of Malacca. A ship without a good navigator is easy prey for them in those waters. A navigator who kens the waters as well as I do, and who is as brave and clever as I am, stands a fair chance of slipping away nonetheless." This was said without a trace of embarrassment. "However, one pirate captain has begun to take a different approach. He has anchored his ship in the harbour here at Taijung, and he has not left. Whenever a merchant vessel comes or goes, he demands payment at once, or else attacks the ship. This is a small city, but it's always been a fine one for trade. Soon, I fear, every honest merchant will avoid us."

"I understand that King Lo'yu favours overseas trade. Why has he not stepped in?"

"Why, he's afraid to. King Lo'yu rules only this city, and I suppose, a few miles of surrounding forest. His forces are limited to some fifty trained guardsmen. The pirate junk, on the other hand, has a crew of nearly a hundred. Neither side really wants an open battle."

"I see. I presume this pirate ship is the *Jade Shark*."

"So it is."

"And the captain?"

"Ah, the captain is a clever man. His name is Yushan Ren. He's of Chinese extraction, though most of his crew are Javanese from Palembang."

"The pirates must be causing havoc in the city, if they have been here so long."

"On the contrary, they seem a well-disciplined crew. I think that's the doing of their captain."

"Do you have any idea why he sits at anchor here and collects payment, instead of just sailing the seas and taking merchant ships?"

"I am not entirely sure," said Ardshiel cautiously, "but I do think it shows some wit. What Captain Yushan is doing— Ren is his first name, you see, they're reversed here in the East— what Captain Yushan is doing is virtually without risk. The merchants would rather pay his bribes than risk losing everything; so Yushan collects money without firing a single shot or losing a single man. Since there's no other ship here that can match the *Jade Shark*, he will probably keep it up until he bleeds this city dry. Unless, that is, *ye* can stop him."

West smiled. "And if I do, you will guide my ship through the Straits of Malacca."

"As sure as athol brose is sweet, that I will."

"It's been a long time since I've had athol brose," said West. "But when you mix whiskey and honey, the result is sweet for certain." He took a sip of his drink and grimaced wryly. "Not like *gaoliang*."

"Aye, not like *gaoliang*." Ardshiel refilled his own glass. "*Gaoliang* does grow on ye, though, to be sure. Now, what think ye, Captain West?"

"Thinking is just what I plan to do, but I am sure I will be able to put the *Jade Shark* out of action. Two Scotsmen on Java Minor— we have to help each other out, eh?"

"A Scotsman, are ye? I thought I heard a trace of the Scotland in yer speech."

"I have spent much of my life in the Royal Navy, so I suppose that, alas, it is just a trace."

"Ye have an English name, West."

"My father is half-English and half-Scotch. My mother is full Scotch— her maiden name was Balfour, and that was given to me as a middle name."

"Ah, so ye are a Scotsman, for the most part. I am of the proud family of Ardshiel, kin to the brave and gallant Stewarts."

"So I gathered."

"Well, then, Captain West, do ye think between us we can save Tai-jung from the pirate Yushan Ren?"

"Why not? The first thing is to go back to my ship and discuss this with my other lieutenants. What kind of weapons does the *Jade Shark* have?"

"They have cannons— probably pillaged from other ships. About thirty guns. There are other weapons, too, though, that I'm none too familiar with. I've seen them testing something from their deck that looks as if it casts flames into the air. It might give even a brave man pause, if he be wise and canny. We can do it, Captain— but ye be right enough that it needs planning."

"Clearly," said West with a raised eyebrow. "Why don't you come back to the *Promise* with me, Mr. Ardshiel? You obviously know the most about these pirates. You should be part of our council of war."

"It will be a pleasure." Ardshiel finished his *gaoliang* and looked at West expectantly. "Are ye ready, then?"

West smiled. "That I am." They walked out the door of the Blue Cave, Ardshiel with his magpie flapping along behind him.

No sooner had they stepped out into the warm night, though, then they heard the sound of a pistol being cocked. West drew his own pistol and stepped around the side of the hut, with Lang and Ardshiel close at his side. There, crouched in the darkness on the platform, were four men. They were Javanese, they wore cutlasses at their side, and each one held a pistol in his hand.

"You— English captain— come with us," said their leader, gesturing at West with his pistol.

"And why would I wish to do that?" said West.

"It is you we seek. If you come, your friends will not be harmed."

West's mind began to race, as he considered the situation and tried to plan his next move. Before he could get very far, though, Ardshiel leapt forward and brandished his pistol. "Do ye think an Ardshiel is a coward, then?" he cried, and fired. One of the Javanese fell, injured, but a shot was fired in response. It struck Ardshiel on the shoulder. Another man kept his pistol trained on West but used his left hand to cast a dagger at

Ardshiel. The dagger struck him in the arm. Wounded twice in a matter of seconds, Ardshiel dropped his pistol and staggered back, dangerously close to the edge of the platform. West grabbed him to keep him from falling, but doing so meant lowering his own pistol. Lang stepped bravely in front of his captain, his weapon at the ready. But the firing had ceased. The Javanese simply waited, the numbers still on their side, to see what West and his friends would do.

West took a look at Ardshiel's wounds and knew exactly what he had to do. "Mr. Lang, I will be going with these men. You must see that Ardshiel is treated for his injury. It's the dagger wound I am worried about; there is a peculiar colour to it, and I suspect the weapon was poisonous."

Lang looked at him in disbelief. "Captain, I cannot leave you in the hands of these men."

"You will follow orders, Mr. Lang. Ardshiel may be the only man who can get us through the Straits of Malacca."

"But you're the captain, sir."

"Yes, and my orders are that you keep this man alive."

"Captain West, dinna fret about me. Many an Ardshiel has died in battle."

"And I do not want you to be one of them, at least not today. There is a kind of greenish past on the arm wound. Is that some Javanese poison?"

"It is, they call it telok."

"Is there an antidote?"

"Yes, their apothecary, as it were, would have it. But Captain, ye canna place yer own life in the hands of the pirates."

"Do not argue with me, Ardshiel." He turned to his lieutenant. "Mr. Lang, your duty is to save this man's life. Get the antidote, and then get him back to the *Promise*. Tell Mr. Kenmare what happened." West slid Ardshiel into Lang's burly grasp, and then stepped forward toward the Javanese. They motioned him to climb down the ladder, and the three went with him, leaving their wounded man behind.

"Your friend is alive," West said. "Aren't you going to take him?"

"No," said the leader. "Keep going."

They reached the bottom of the bamboo ladder. West looked up and saw Lang staring after him, almost forlornly, with Ardshiel still in his grasp and the blue magpie perched on a branch nearby. He turned back to the Javanese.

"I presume," said West, "that we are on our way to the *Jade Shark*?"

"That is right. Captain Yushan will want a word with you. This way."

West walked through the night, with a pistol at his back, listening to the strange chatter of the insects in the hot, damp, jungle air.

XI.
The Jade Shark

*T*he pirates had a longboat hidden beneath a tree near the shore, and West was rowed out across the black water to the *Jade Shark*. There was a crescent moon hanging in the sky, and the stars were bright and silver. Soon, they reached the sides of the junk, and the longboat was lifted onto the deck. West got out, amid the chatter of the Javanese pirates on watch. Then the leader of the band that had captured him motioned to a hatchway. He climbed down a ladder and found himself in front of a wooden door. The pirate spoke a few words, the door opened, and they entered the cabin of Captain Yushan.

The cabin was small, with a slanted ceiling, but its decoration was opulent. A thick Middle Eastern carpet covered the floor; its colours were burgundy and gold. Upon one wall there were two great ivory tusks. Mounted near them were several ornate weapons: a cutlass with a pearl-studded hilt; a dirk in a golden scabbard; and a straight, long sword of superior workmanship. On another wall was a tapestry that was clearly of European origin. It showed a stylized grey castle and an armoured knight riding forth. There was a battered old sea-chest against the wall, and upon it was a Chinese ivory carving, showing mountains, villages, and people in exquisite miniature detail. On a third wall was a silk painting showing a trio of blue magpies perched among stalks of bamboo.

There was also a desk carved of elegant rosewood; and behind the desk sat a man. In his hand was a brush; paper and an ink stone were on the desk before him. He was writing calligraphy with great speed, the brush skipping lightly across the parchment. He did not stop when they entered, but a in a few moments he did stop, and he looked up.

Yushan Ren was a young man with an unlined face. He wore a black beard that was long, but clean and neatly trimmed, as if he was an Eastern scholar from centuries past. Looking at his fresh and youthful face,

West surmised that the pirate captain wore the beard in order to appear older than he was. He was clad in a bright red silk robe with a pattern of golden birds and clouds. His brown eyes had a brightness of their own, and when he finally looked up, he spoke as quickly, it seemed, as he had written.

There were a few moments of conversation in what West assumed was either Mandarin or Javanese, and then the underling stepped back and stood against the wall as if at attention. His pistol was at the ready; they were clearly taking no chances with the English captain. Yushan looked at West and spoke in English. "Welcome to the *Jade Shark*. I am Captain Yushan Ren of Palembang."

"I am Bowman West."

"And from your uniform, I know you are the captain of the frigate that sailed into the harbour tonight. I have noticed that you carry a pair of *quilin* on the deck of you ship, and I commend your judgment as far as the beauty of the animals. That does not, however, make your presence here entirely welcome to me. In fact, I had been wondering what to do about your frigate, Captain West. When my men spotted you on the shore, they took the opportunity to bring you to my ship."

"I presume they saw my lieutenant and I at some point while we were on the path in Taijung, and then followed us to the Blue Cave tavern."

"It was simpler than that, Captain. I have had the Blue Cave tavern watched, anticipating it would be a source of trouble. They saw you as you entered, and, of course, took action as you left."

"I see. May I compliment you, Captain Yushan, on your English. It seems considerably more fluent than that of your men."

"It is. I believe I was born with a certain skill in languages. You would be surprised how often that skill is useful on the high seas."

"Actually, I do not think that would surprise me. I see you are a calligrapher, as well."

"Yes, I write in the calligraphic style that my people refer to as 'wild.' I suppose that is appropriate for a pirate. The style is said to be as fast as the rain in the wind. The characters that result are strong and clear, yet not quite so . . . tightly bound as those produced in the other styles. But perhaps this is not of interest to an English captain."

"On the contrary, I am Scottish, and I am quite interested. I am surprised, however, that so intelligent a man has such a limited grasp of tactics."

"How so?"

"You thought my ship might be a source of trouble. By abducting me, you are making sure that it will be."

"I have, however, secured an important hostage. I am sure that will simplify my negotiations with your ship."

West stepped forward and smiled. "Tell me, Captain Yushan, how wide is your experience with the Royal Navy?"

"Why do you ask?"

"Keeping information to yourself, I see. That, at least, is sound strategy. But you needn't answer my question. I can tell you that the rules of the Royal Navy are clear. Once an officer is captured— regardless of his rank— he is considered dead. You may have noticed that I did not introduce myself as captain. My former first lieutenant is now the Captain of the *Promise*— or at least he will be, once the news of my capture reaches the ship."

"Yet he will doubtless wish to save your life."

"Why should he? If he gets me back, he goes back to being to second-in-command."

Yushan looked at West in silence for a moment, and then he laughed. "*Captain* West, you speak to me of tactics. If you are telling me the truth, I have no reason to keep you alive. So your own tactics are most foolish . . . regardless of whether you are speaking the truth."

West took another step closer to the desk. Even while he had been speaking, his thoughts had been moving as quickly as Yushan's brush. "Actually, I am negotiating."

"Negotiating? How?"

West turned around then and walked over to the sea chest. "Can I sit here?" he asked, casually picking up the ivory sculpture. "This is quite nice," he added, and placed it on the carpet. Then he sat down on the sea chest and crossed his legs. "You see, Captain Yushan, I really have no place to go right now. Java Minor seems rather inhospitable. My former first lieutenant will not want me back. I am beginning to think I should make myself at home right here.

"You wanted me as a hostage. That will not help you. But I have been at sea my entire life. I have risen to the rank of captain in the greatest navy on earth. Are you sure you cannot find any other use for a man of my talents?"

Yushan stood up and looked at him. "Captain, I do know something of the Royal Navy. I know that its men are said to prize honour. Do you really expect me to believe that you would betray your traditions and sail aboard a pirate ship?"

West reached down, picked up the ivory miniature again, and looked at it, as if he was lost in thought. "My options are limited," he said with a sigh. He caught himself at that moment— the sigh was just a bit too theatrical. He looked up slowly, trying to be more natural. "What do you suggest I do?"

"If you are being honest with me, you should know that I have not yet offered you anything."

"Why not? Do you not think I would be a valuable addition to your ship?"

"Please put that down." There was a note of irritation in Yushan's voice. "I am sure you would be of value. I simply do not believe you would actually join me."

"Well," said West with a wry smile, "perhaps you're right." And he threw the ivory sculpture straight at the pirate who was standing against the wall.

The man saw the look of panic in Yushan's face, and responded to it immediately, dropping his pistol and catching the sculpture. By the time he had, West was standing atop the sea chest with the long sword in his hand.

The pirate set down the sculpture and reached for his pistol. Yushan cried out, obviously summoning more men, and drew a dagger from his own belt. West leaped across the room and brought the hilt of his sword down on the pirate's head as he reached for the pistol. Yushan took aim and threw his dagger at West. West jumped to the side and the weapon whistled past his head to embed itself in the wall. Outside, the clatter of rushing footsteps could be heard.

"You are still on my ship, Captain West, and you are about to be surrounded by my men. Despite your boldness, you have no way out."

"On the contrary, I think your idea of taking a captain hostage was an excellent one." He picked up the pistol from the cabin floor.

When a group of pirates burst through the door a moment later, West was standing side by side with Yushan, grasping the Chinese captain's arm, the pistol at the ready. "Do you have an ambitious first lieutenant I should know about?" West asked dryly.

"I used to, but he is at the bottom of the Indian Ocean."

"That makes things easier for both of us. Please explain to your men that we will be going on deck now, and they will not interfere with us."

Yushan spoke to his men, and West fervently wished he knew what was being said. However, the pirates lowered their weapons, and they stood aside as West and Yushan walked out the door. The ladder that led to the hatchway and the deck was a more awkward business. West had Yushan walk up first, while he followed closely behind, pistol in hand. When they emerged into the open air, he again grasped Yushan's arm. The pirates on deck stared at them through the darkness for a moment, and leapt into action when they saw that West was carrying a weapon. But when West brandished the pistol and Yushan barked an order, they froze into immobility.

West walked slowly to the rail, with Yushan still at his side. "You are a clever opponent, Captain West, but even if you make your escape now, our duel is not over."

"I imagine not," said West evenly. They approached the railing. West looked up and saw the red sails of the junk, looking black in the silver light of moon and stars. "Actually, Captain Yushan, I must apologize for what you may take as an indignity."

"Being taken hostage in front of my own crew? It is indeed an indignity."

"Actually, I meant this." West pushed Yushan over the side, dropped the pistol, and dived overboard himself.

The water was cool compared to the warm air of the Javanese night. When he came up out of it, West saw Yushan spluttering angrily. At the railing above them, the pirates were looking down at them. Most of them had pistols, but as West had anticipated, they were holding their fire for fear of hitting their captain. For a split second, West considered a verbal parting shot at Yushan, but there was no time for wit. He dove under again and swam away from the *Jade Shark*. When he came up again and looked behind him, he had covered a fair distance. The pirates were lowering a line down to Yushan. West turned his face forward and found the *Promise*, there in the harbour before him. He dove under again and swam for it.

It seemed like a long time until he drew nigh to his ship, but it was probably only a few minutes. As he did, West called out, "Ahoy! *Promise* ahoy!"

Kenmare was on the quarterdeck, and he turned his telescope on West's voice. "Captain!" he called in astonishment. And then: "It's the captain! Someone throw him a line!"

A moment later, West was grasping a rope and being hauled up on to the deck. He landed in a sodden heap but got up as quickly as he could. "Thank you, gentlemen."

"Where did you come from, sir?" Kenmare asked.

"Has Mr. Lang returned yet?"

"The jolly boat is being rowed back now." Kenmare pointed across the dark water. "We thought you'd be in it."

"I took a bit of detour. And I can now say without question that the large junk is indeed a pirate vessel. For now, though, I think I need a change of clothing. Let me know when Mr. Lang's boat has pulled alongside us — or if there is any sign of hostility from the *Jade Shark*." He strode to his cabin, amused by the knowledge that astonished glances were following him.

Soon, West had changed into a dry uniform, and Kenmare was knocking at the door. "Mr. Lang is nearly here, and there's another chap with him."

West followed Kenmare onto the deck, where Rede and Teal were also waiting, to watch Lang and Ardshiel arrive. Their faces were troubled, until they caught sight of the captain standing before them. Lang's words tumbled one over the other. "Captain West, what happened? I was afraid we had lost you— thought I'd never live it down, letting my captain go off with those pirates, even if it was under his orders."

West smiled. "And yet as it happened, I made it back to the *Promise* before you did. How is Mr. Ardshiel?"

Ardshiel's shoulder and arm were bandaged, but his eyes were as bright as ever. "We found the antidote all right— there's a leaf from a great braw tree that grows here in the jungle, and they sell it in Taijung; it's an antidote to *telok* poison and said to be good for the rheumatism as well. I will be fine, Captain. And that's more than I can say for Yushan and his pirates. However did ye get away from them?"

West briefly related his experiences on the pirate ship. His officers looked at him admiringly, and Ardshiel said with a perfectly straight face: "Well, I tell ye the truth, Captain— I could have done nae better meself."

"Thank you, Mr. Ardshiel. Mr. Kenmare, where is my telescope?"

"Right here, sir."

West looked out at the *Jade Shark*. "There seems to be no movement there. I do not think we can expect an immediate attack."

"From all that I know of him," said Ardshiel, "I think Yushan will be planning his next move before he makes it."

"You haven't seen him write calligraphy— but on the whole, I agree. And we will do the same. Mr. Teal, you have the watch. The rest of you gentlemen, please join me in my cabin." His mind was racing now. "Mr Ardshiel is going to provide us with some information about the Straits of Malacca."

Ardshiel smiled. "Why, Captain, dinnae argle-bargle with me now. Our agreement was that we would fight off the *Jade Shark* before I guided ye along on your voyage."

"I think we may be able to do both at once, Mr. Ardshiel. The Straits of Malacca are dangerous waters to navigate, and the pirates of Palembang have always used that to their advantage. But my guess is that it can work both ways."

But West and Ardshiel had both miscalculated when it came to the speed of Yushan's response. They were still pouring over charts in West's cabin when there was a pounding on the door. "Mr. Teal's compliments, sir," said the sailor, "and there are longboats from the pirate ship, headed towards our starboard side."

West and his officers returned to the deck to see the boats gliding slowly over the dark and placid harbour. "I am sorry we did not spot them sooner, sir," said Teal, his voice full of anxiety.

"No need to apologize, Mr. Teal. They are carrying no lights and their men are making every attempt at silence. Mr. Rede, do you think you can fire on them?"

Rede shook his head. "They're too close, sir; we won't be able to lower our guns that far."

"Then rig the boarding netting."

"Aye, sir."

"Mr. Lang, begin handing out weapons to the men."

"Pistols and cutlasses, sir?"

"Yes. And both of you, do so quietly, and keep the men quiet as well."

"Aye, sir."

"Mr. Kenmare, take several men with good eyesight, and keep a lookout to larboard, as well as the bow and the stern. This seems a surprisingly direct strategy for my friend Captain Yushan, and I do not trust it."

"Aye, sir."

Ardshiel stepped forward, his good arm suddenly holding a pistol and gesturing expressively toward the pirates' longboats. "No need to wait for yer men, Captain. I can take a good crack at them now."

"Avast, Mr. Ardshiel. They'll be here soon enough."

Ardshiel looked impatient, but nodded. Rede and Lang went about their business, and the men assembled near the sides, ready to repel the boarders. There were no marines aboard the *Promise*, but West was confident in the fighting abilities of British sailors.

A trace of a breeze came rustling through the night air, and then vanished. The crescent moon and the stars hung in the air far above. The sky was cloudless, and they were very bright. The blue magpie left Ardshiel's shoulder and flew to perch near the helm.

Then there was the thud of steel against wood; and again, and again. Grappling hooks were being cast upon the *Promise*. Still, there was quiet, in keeping with the captain's orders. Then, West stepped forward, drew his sword, and cried out: "Now, gentlemen! Defend your ship!"

The men gave a rousing cheer. Some reached over the netting to cut away the grappling hooks. Others began firing their pistols. Ardshiel charged forward with his own pistol at the ready. There were cries from the pirates too, as they attempted to continue their advance. Then, West heard the sound he had expecting and listening for— the sound of Kenmare's voice from the larboard side. "Captain! There's another boat here!"

Immediately in front of West, where the main attack seemed to be taking place, several pirates had made it up the side. They began fighting man to man with sailors, cutlass ringing upon cutlass. Rede was dueling with a tall, slender Javanese buccaneer who moved with the grace of a tiger, but who kept his eyes locked directly on his opponent. With an air of calm, West walked up behind him and hit him on the head with the hilt of his sword. The man went down, unconscious, and Rede found himself staring at his captain.

"Thank you, sir," he said.

"There is an attack from the larboard. You are in charge here, Mr. Rede."

"Aye, sir."

West hurried to the larboard side, leaving the battle behind him in order to seek another. He was convinced that whatever was happening there was somehow more important. The attack from starboard had come first and apparently with greater force. Yushan's intelligence and strategic ability were, West believed, quite formidable. Therefore, the starboard attack was diversionary. The larboard attack was where the danger lay.

West was soon at the side of his First Lieutenant. "The men are at the ready, as you can see, sir," Kenmare said. "But they could not cut away the grappling hooks. The line is too thick."

"Of course it is." The lines being used for these grappling hooks were thicker and tougher than those being used to starboard. The real attack was indeed here. He went to the side and looked over. There were several Javanese pirates climbing up the sides of the ship from the longboat. The sailors at the rail were firing pistols, and two pirates plunged into the water; but three more kept climbing, covering the last few meters up the side in a rush of energy and agility. Then they were fighting with the sailors— it was the same scene being played out on the starboard side, but on a smaller scale. West wondered what the three remaining pirates could do that was so strategically important. Even if the larboard attack had gone unnoticed, what could five pirates do against a frigate? Perhaps their mission was one of sabotage; perhaps Yushan was seeking to damage the ship in some way. West eyed the battle keenly. Two of the pirates pressed forward, taking the brunt of the battle, while one fell back and seemed to reach behind him. West saw that he was carrying something upon his back; a kind of long tube, almost like a wooden telescope. Then, the pirate reached for the tube, grabbed it, and held it in his hands.

Whatever that device was, it was somehow vital to the success of the attack. West leapt upon the rail at the side of the ship. With a nimble motion that belied his fear of stumbling, he ran forward along the rail, moving above the struggle. The sailors and the pirates continued to clash in the darkness, the pirates rushing forward and then drawing back, as if following a defensive strategy. West raced alongside and above them. Then, he jumped back onto the deck.

CHRIS FASOLINO

Beside West was the pirate who seemed to be taking aim with his tube as if it was a gun. He had been the target of the captain's mad dash along the railing. West brought his sword down on the tube, and it clattered upon the deck. The pirate drew back with an expression of fright. Reading the expression, and remembering the pirate's artilleryman posture, West seized the wooden tube and flung it over the side. Sure enough, there came the sound of an explosion. And when West rushed to the side to look out— strangest of all— there was fire upon the surface of the water, burning brightly and not quenched.

West heard the clatter of feet behind him, and turned. The lone pirate was rushing at him with cutlass drawn. West parried the blow with his sword. A moment later, there was the sound of a pistol shot, and the pirate dropped his cutlass and clutched at his hand. One of the sailors had come to West's aid. The other two pirates had been subdued; this side of the battle was over. And as the sound of English cheers echoed from the starboard side, West knew that Rede had won his battle as well.

The ship was safe, and every man of the pirate boarding party taken prisoner. But the captain's eyes turned back to the strange sight of the flames upon the water. Kenmare was at his side, now, wondering as well. "Whatever can that be, sir?"

West did not answer, because he had no answer to give. They simply watched as the ruddy light flickered on the still waters; until, finally, it began to fade away, and there were only sparks left, yellow sparks upon the black still waters of the Javanese harbour.

XII.
Out from Java Minor

he sparks from the strange weapon had faded to ashes, and there was a trace of the coming dawn in the sky, when the *Promise* weighed anchor. An easterly breeze had arisen, which suited West's plans well enough. The ship sailed out with topgallants alone, bearing north-north-east. She was followed closely by the *Flying Fish*; Ardshiel had returned to his brig in a longboat to prepare his crew for action.

Captain Yushan had made no further move after the defeat of his boarding party. The pirates who had been taken prisoner had said nothing, so West had not been able to learn anything about the mysterious weapon and the fire that it produced. However, he wanted to talk to Chang about it. He remembered what the steward had told him about the lost Chinese treasure fleet. Chang had mentioned weapons that used fire and even poison, weapons since lost to the ages. Perhaps Yushan Ren had somehow re-invented such weapons. It was a sobering thought, and all the more reason to put the *Jade Shark* out of action, as West and Ardshiel planned to do.

As they sailed out of the harbour, West stood upon his quarterdeck with his telescope in his hands. The city of Taijung was beautiful. The lanterns in the trees were glimmering gold, and their light was in the waters as well. As the sun began to come up, the colour of the lantern light was embraced by the sunlight colours that were spread upon the bay, and the specks of golden yellow were in the midst of crimson and peach and lemon and violet. Through it all, the rich blue-green of the waters could be seen as well. The *Promise* and the *Flying Fish* seemed to be carried along by the colours.

West smiled. Then, he turned his attention, and his telescope, on the pirate ship. The junk was soon in motion, following them out of the harbour. It was as West had calculated. Yushan would not look away while a Royal Navy frigate sailed through these eastern waters with course and purpose unknown. The pirate captain was both tactical and aggressive, and he would act to eliminate the possible threat.

West ordered the royals and topgallants to be set as they left the harbour. The men scrambled up into the rigging, and soon the white canvas was unfurling with a rush of sound. The *Flying Fish* was clapping on all sail, as well, and the small, light, trim vessel soon pulled ahead of the frigate.

The sun rose higher and the sky was blue and bright. The *Promise* was following the *Flying Fish* along the course that West and Ardshiel had laid out in the cabin the night before. Behind them, the deep green coastline of Java Minor began to recede; but soon, there was a corresponding green blur to be seen when West turned his telescope in line with the bow. It was the southeast coastline of the Asian continent. Ahead of the *Promise* was the greatest landmass in the world; behind her, the island of Java Minor. Both shores were green with jungle. West suddenly recalled reading of a natural historian who claimed that the ocean and the jungle were the oldest environments on earth.

The waters that they were now sailing through, however, had another significance. They had long been an important trading route connecting civilizations. Called the Straits of Malacca, they had been sailed for centuries by merchants of many lands. For many ships, this was the path to, or from, the Far East. It was also the domain of pirates like Yushan Ren, and of navigational hazards like the fabled coral reefs.

Soon, the great green forests of the Asian shore were more visible. West peered eagerly through his telescope. He could see a curving cape protruding from the shore, and at its point, the forest gave way to an outcropping of rock the colour of terra cotta. This was a landmark Ardshiel had spoken of. West turned around and set his telescope on the pirate ship. It was continuing its pursuit, but there was no immediate sign of a change in Yushan's strategy. That was good; it meant that the next move would, indeed, belong to West and Ardshiel.

The question of Yushan's strategy in combat, though, had to be considered. The *Jade Shark* was longer and more narrow than the *Promise*. It would likely be a highly maneuverable ship; but so was the frigate, and it was hard to see any clear advantage there for either vessel. The junk had gun ports and cannons in the European fashion; the cannons had probably been pillaged. Yet West did not anticipate Yushan drawing up alongside him and exchanging broadsides the way that European ships of war often did. Yushan was the kind of fighter who would prefer to fire from a distance, moving swiftly in and out of range and hoping that a fortunate or skilful shot would cripple his opponent. If West had been planning a traditional battle strategy, he might have found it advantageous to counter Yushan by coming alongside the *Jade Shark* and forcing a close fire fight. However, the tactics that West had planned were considerably more unusual.

Then there was the issue of other weaponry. The bamboo tube that had brought fire to the waters— and nearly set the *Promise* ablaze— might be a token of an arsenal at Yushan's disposal. That brought him back to the question of the lost treasure fleet. Chang claimed that the destruction of the fleet had been ordered, and carried out, by China's own Imperial government. He had attempted to explain why, but West found it impossible to understand, even though he thought of himself as broad-minded. In any case, surely some of the seafarers must have taken their ships and fled. That was what had happened in the Blue Isles, apparently. The Italian explorer's book spoke of Alishan, the Chinese captain who had fled from the Emperor and brought his ship safely to the Blue Isles. If one ship escaped, why not others?

West knew that there was a Chinese diaspora throughout Southeast Asia; Yushan was himself of Chinese extraction, though his base of piracy had been Palembang on Java Minor. Perhaps there were other remnants of the treasure fleet hidden along these islands and coasts. Perhaps Yushan had not re-invented the fire weapon, but rediscovered it.

That led to thoughts of Yushan's long anchorage in Taijung. Was it really a matter of blackmailing merchants— taking profit with little risk— as Ardshiel believed? Or was Yushan a clever young man seeking the treasures of the past? Having met the pirate captain, West believed the latter to be a more likely idea. Yushan's calligraphy was wild and creative. It suggested an imaginative and visionary personality.

If all this was true— and West had to remind himself that he was speculating— then Yushan believed that the remains of the treasure fleet might be found near Taijung. That was well worth knowing. Then West realized something else. Despite his fire weapon, Yushan had probably *not* found what he was looking for. After all, he had been continuing to anchor in Taijung. If he had found the ancient ships, or even their wreckage, he would putting them to use. The fire weapon, then, might be the only artifact he had found; a valuable item, yes, but only a trace of what he sought.

Would it even be possible to find further remnants of the treasure fleet? Did they exist? If West succeeded in the upcoming battle, Yushan would not have the opportunity to continue his search; and that was well for the peace of these waters.

But perhaps, someday, West himself might take up the search. After he had sailed to the Blue Isles . . . If he was able to buy the *Promise*, and his freedom . . . But that was foolishness. Yes, he might, on some future day, return to Taijung and search for treasure. Or he might be swept away in a storm at sea before the week was out. Then again, even that was speculation. He was about to take his ship into battle. He might never again walk into his cabin and see his southern thrush looking at him. He might never again taste rum. At that, he shook himself out of his own thoughts and gave the order to take in the royals and topgallants. He fingered the sword at his side. Then his hand brushed against the tin whistle hanging next to it.

The *Promise* and the *Flying Fish* had sailed past the cape now and into a crescent-shaped bay. The waters were a lighter colour here, and they were distinctly green in hue. Marshy islets dotted the bay, and West knew that it was relatively shallow; he set a man to work with the leads. The man called out the distance to the bottom, in fathoms, at regular intervals as they sailed closer to shore.

The coastline here was mangrove forest, much like those they had seen on the coast of Java Minor. Deep green trees grew out of the pale green ocean. Even the islets bore a few gnarled trees that seemed to reach up from the mud with desperation that seemed almost human. In the midst of the bay, at a safe distance from the islets and from the shore, West ordered the anchor to be lowered. Ardshiel had already done the same with the *Flying Fish*. Now they would wait to see what the *Jade Shark* would do.

The sun was bright and hot; the light had an almost coppery quality, too brash and full of itself to simply be golden. The sky was a deep blue. Near the eastern horizon, though, great grey clouds were forming. West lifted up his telescope again— the brass of the instrument was almost blindingly bright, and hot to the touch— and he looked again at the Chinese junk.

The *Jade Shark* had not followed them around the cape, but rather, had tacked southwards. Yushan had doubtless wished to survey the whole scene and see whether he would be sailing into an ambush. Now he could see that the frigate and the brig were situated in a shallow bay, with only the shore behind them. From his perspective, it would seem an ideal place to launch an attack. The junk could sail into the inlet and fire at the two ships. Then, if necessary, it could slip away but still keep them boxed in, especially if the *Promise* was damaged in the first attack. The brig, of course, might be able to slip away, but it was only the frigate that really threatened him.

So, as West had expected, the *Jade Shark* tacked again and sailed into the bay. The *Promise* began to move eastward across the bay, preceded by the *Flying Fish*. The *Jade Shark* continued to come up from the south. And in a moment, its two bow cannons, thirty-six pounders, were run out and ready for action.

At that, West immediately gave the order to tack into the wind. The *Promise* began to steer a course back towards the pirate ship, as if aiming to come parallel to it. As she turned, a puff of smoke and a crash of sound seemed to leap into the air. A cannonball struck the railing of the quarterdeck where West was standing, smashing the wood and scattering the splinters. From there, it barrelled across the edge of the deck, smashing the rail on the opposite side and then plunging into the water. West stared after it, dimly aware that he had not been hurt. It had been the shot from the pirate ship's starboard bow cannon; the shot from the larboard cannon had gone well to the starboard of the *Promise* and plunged into the bay. On the main deck, West saw the okapis crouch down, frightened. No doubt they were trying to hide, but their actions had the beneficial effect of making them smaller; instinct was leading them to strategy.

"Gentlemen, we are now under fire, so this is all according to plan," said West, speaking with a touch of humour, but loud enough so that his men could hear him. "Bear up and we will soon be able to end this battle with a single broadside." With that, he leapt to the wheel and seized it from the startled helmsman. The captain swung the wheel quickly, changing the ship's course from south-west to south-south-west.

Yushan could be heard shouting orders on the deck of the *Jade Shark*, and the junk made its own course correction to follow the frigate. Then, their bow cannons were primed and loaded. Watching the action through his telescope, West cried out, "Brace yourselves, gentlemen!"

There was another thunderclap, followed by the tearing of canvas. The cannonballs left two holes in the mizzen sail and careened forward, through the mainsail and foresail, and finally plunged onto the deck, breaking through it and plummeting into the forecastle. Fortunately, all hands were on deck; and with the energy of their flight spent, the missiles would never be able to smash the copper sheathing of the ship's hull. It was also fortunate that they had struck the sails and not the mizzenmast, as must have been Yushan's intention.

Now, Yushan had had his chance, and he would not get another. On the larboard side of the *Promise* lay one of the muddy islands; they had come upon it as the junk was firing. They sailed past it as the pirates were priming their guns, and West turned the wheel again, heading towards the shore now and keeping the island to the larboard. He waited. The pirate ship was still in pursuit. It was coming up alongside the island now. West looked at the island, at the trees with their green leaves and gnarled trunks rising from the marshy earth. He looked at the great, four-masted junk with its red sails. "Ready, Mr. Rede?" he said.

"Aye, sir, primed and ready."

West could not help but raise his voice to a shout. "Then *fire!*"

On the main deck, the larboard side gunners sprang into action, lighting the fuses simultaneously. Then came the thundering broadside as every larboard cannon fired.

The broadside struck the southern face of the island, where the *Jade Shark* was coasting. And at the strength of the impact, the marshy earth collapsed upon itself, sliding forward— a great brown wave carrying living trees upon itself like small boats. The pirate ship was drenched by that wave, caught fast in what had moments before been muddy island. The bow was enveloped, and from there to the third mast, the sides of the ship were walled in by earth. There were even a few trees cast upon the deck, some toppled on their sides, but some upright, with their green leaves brushing the red sails. It was as if someone had decided to transplant them upon a pirate ship. The trees seemed to have taken the change calmly enough, but among the men, there was great confusion. Yushan himself seemed overawed for a moment; then, the pirate captain turned and began shouting orders. On the *Promise*, a great cheer came up from the men. Kenmare walked on to the quarterdeck and clapped West on the back, his brown and wrinkled face bearing a broad smile. "Beautifully done, sir."

"Thank you, Mr. Kenmare. Mr. Rede— fine work with the guns. And well done, every man of you." West smiled at his crew. They began cheering again, and in a moment, those cheers were echoed from the deck of the *Flying Fish* as the brig came up alongside. Ardshiel himself was waving his plaid scarf over his head in a peculiar but enthusiastic gesture of triumph. West waved to him and then gave the order to anchor. He was about to ask for a speaking trumpet and demand the pirates' surrender when he saw a sudden flurry of activity. Yushan's men were priming their larboard cannons.

"What do you think they're doing, sir?" Kenmare asked. "They'll be firing right into the island, or what's left of it; and they'll do naught but get themselves mired in deeper."

"Yes. It would only add to what we've done in creating a quagmire for them." West paused. "No, wait— I think I have it. It's very clever, actually. I think Yushan is going to try firing the larboard cannons with powder alone."

Understanding dawned on Kenmare's face. "To try to rock the ship free."

"Yes." The reaction of the cannons themselves might serve to shake the ship loose. It was a slim chance, but probably the last one Yushan had. "Mr. Rede, it seems we may require another broadside. If the junk begins to come free, we will fire into the island again and hope to repeat our success."

"Aye, sir."

West climbed onto his quarterdeck and continued to watch the pirate ship through his telescope. Sure enough, the junk's larboard guns soon fired a broadside with no shot. There was a cloud of smoke, and the junk moved slowly from side to side, but did not come free. Yushan tried again— and again— and again. But it was to no avail. The *Jade Shark* was still bogged down and could not be shaken free.

At last, West called for his speaking trumpet. "Captain Yushan," he called out, "do we have your surrender?"

At first, there was no answer. Then Yushan climbed up near the prow of his ship, clutching a trumpet of his own. "What are your terms, Captain West?"

"May I point out, Captain Yushan, that you are not in an especially good position to negotiate."

"My expectations are limited," replied Yushan with aplomb. "However, I do not really believe you are about to blow my ship to pieces with the men aboard. It would seem uncharacteristic."

"You are a fine judge of character, Captain Yushan. And in fact I do have terms to offer you. They are these: you and your men will be given two hours to abandon your ship for the mainland, bringing with you whatever you choose. That is what you will have to do in any event, since the *Jade Shark* is no good to you now. I have no room for your crew aboard the *Promise* even if I wished to take you all prisoner, so you need not fear that I will be bringing you back to Execution Dock— or whatever it is called on Java Minor."

"It is called Execution Courtyard," said Yushan. "You are wise not to attempt to take us prisoner; that does simplify our negotiations, Captain. However, we will require more than two hours. It will be difficult even to reach the shore from the situation you have placed us in. And we must bring supplies with us if we are to survive in these jungles."

"I am prepared to be reasonable. I certainly do not wish to destroy your ship while your crew is still aboard."

"I appreciate your human-heartedness, Captain, but why should you destroy the *Jade Shark* at all?"

"To be certain that it will never again bring battle and pillage to the coasts of Java Minor."

"Very well, then." Yushan paused. "I will abandon my ship. But not in two hours. Let us say— twice that time."

"So be it." Even that was faster than West had expected; but then again, Yushan himself likely wanted to get his crew moving as quickly as possible. This was the kind of situation where mutinies broke out, and it would not do to give the men time to think.

"You have been a worthy opponent, Captain West. Perhaps I was baiting a tiger when I sent my men to the Blue Cave."

"I do not really think of myself as a tiger, Captain Yushan. But it is not wise to bait a Scotsman either." He smiled. "You, too, have been a worthy opponent."

"Farewell then, Captain West." Yushan's voice was as polished as his words, but when he had finished speaking, he threw the trumpet over the side in a gesture of despair. Then he turned and began to give orders to his crew for the abandonment of the *Jade Shark*.

The pirates spent the next several hours struggling through the mud with their longboats, their supplies, and presumably as much loot as they could carry. West allowed the prisoners from the failed boarding party to return to their comrades; he had no wish to continue carrying them about on his ship. Lieutenant Rede kept a watchful eye on the activities of all the pirates, but there was nothing suspicious for him to report. By the early evening, the pirates had abandoned their boats on the shore and vanished into the jungle.

The *Jade Shark* now lay abandoned, and West was eager to explore it. However, there were several good reasons to wait until morning. There was rain coming, and that would wash away some of the mud and make the ship more accessible. Then, too, there was the possibility that Yushan had left an ambush party aboard, and daylight would make it easier to anticipate such surprises. But in the meantime, West had been invited to dinner on board the *Flying Fish*. As usual, he took Kenmare with him, leaving Rede in command. But no one would feel left out of the celebrations tonight. Aboard the *Promise*, West had ordered liberal rations and, best of all, double rum.

The jolly-boat rowed West and Kenmare to the brig, and Ardshiel was on deck to greet them, his marvellous blue magpie upon his shoulders. "Sorry I could not pipe ye aboard, Captain," he said. "We've nae music aboard the *Flying Fish*, save for my own bagpipes, and they're not precisely what ye would call Navy issue."

"Not to worry, Captain Ardshiel." Aboard his own ship, Ardshiel was rightly addressed as Captain.

"And let me offer me congratulations on the success of yer plan, Captain. It was a strategy worthy of an Ardshiel."

"It was an Ardshiel who provided the necessary geographic knowledge; the plan could not have succeeded without that."

"We've made good comrades, we have. And 'tis eager I am to explore that ship tomorrow. For now, though, come into me cabin, and we'll drink a bumper to our victory. Mr. Kenmare of course will join us. Follow me."

He led them to a small but comfortable cabin. The yellow glow of an oil lamp glimmered on slate blue walls trimmed with burgundy. Upon one wall hung a set of plaid bagpipes; upon another, a silk painting that showed a curious blend of western and eastern styles and portrayed the city and harbour of Taijung. Another silk painting was clearly in the Chinese style and showed a trio of strong, graceful horses. There was a thick Indian carpet upon the floor, with colours of burgundy and blue. Ardshiel gestured for them to sit down around the small dining table, and he poured tankards of a golden ale. "A drop of this with our meal," he said, "afore we get to the stronger drink later on."

The meal came soon enough, brought in by Ardshiel's Javanese steward who, unlike some in his profession, admitted his fluency in English. The food he served was excellent. The main dish was mutton, sliced and roasted on an iron skillet with green onions and garlic. There were dumplings filled with roast pork and black mushrooms, and others filled with fish and crabmeat. There was fresh fruit— plums, mangoes, and papayas. All three men ate with good appetite.

"The mutton is prepared in something of an eastern manner," Ardshiel said, "and a fine food it is. And the fruit is always marvellous in these tropical climes. I see ye favour the papayas, Captain."

"They are delicious. We never had these in Scotland, did we?"

"Nor this," said Ardshiel, getting up and grabbing a bottle of *gaoliang* from his desk. The meal was drawing to a close; the steward removed most of the plates, leaving only the fresh fruit. Ardshiel offered the *gaoliang* or a black rum as after-dinner drinks. "I am not one for port or sherry, truth be told," he said with a smile.

Kenmare tried the *gaoliang*, made a face, and went for the rum. West and Ardshiel both drank the eastern fire-water. As they drank and talked, there was a clattering on the roof above them. The rain had begun, and it sounded as if it was coming in sheets.

"These downpours," Ardshiel said, shaking his head. "From the look of things earlier, this one should be just the rain; but ye must be wary of storms, Captain, especially as ye make yer way into the South China Sea."

"Yes, I've heard of the typhoons."

Ardshiel nodded. "I've been through more than a few typhoons on Java Minor, as well, and I can tell ye that I would nae want to be at sea in one. I have friends on land, though, who claim to have gotten used to typhoons, so prevalent they are in some seasons." He drank some of his *gaoliang* and said, "Though it might seem to be a different topic, Captain, I wanted to ask ye where in Scotland ye be from."

West gave the name of his village by the sea, and Ardshiel said, "And what is it that brought ye from that fair place to this one?"

"My parents are lighthouse-keepers, and I was born and grew up in a lighthouse. I always watched the ships, and I knew that I wanted to be sailing one someday. How about you?"

"For me, it was the East India Company. My reasons were much the same, though, I think— a love of the sea and of far lands and of adventures such as we have had today. I visited many countries before I came to Taijung. And then I decided that this was the place to stay. Not that I will ever settle down— I have my own ship, after all. There is a good trade in these waters, though, when the pirates do not spoil it. The *Flying Fish* is my home and I have my Blue Cave in the city. A long way it is from the hills of Appin, no doubt, but just as long a way from the Appin winters."

"How long were you with the East India Company?"

"Nigh on twenty-five years. The last dozen, I was captain of a fine ship called the *Walmer Castle*. The only trouble with her was that they would not sell her to me."

"I think I understand," said West, hoping he would fare better when it came to the *Promise*. "By the way, did you ever know one Nile Carrin, or one Francis Gilbraith?"

Ardshiel shook his head. "No. They are East India Company men?"

"Yes. Carrin is on my ship now, though I do not expect you have seen him. He keeps very much to himself. An older man, and apparently a most reticent one. Gilbraith we lost early in the voyage— he was killed by pirates at St. Helena."

"And why is it that they came aboard?"

"Supposedly, to assess the potential for trade in the Blue Isles."

"Could ye nae have done that yerself, Captain?"

West smiled. "I have my questions about why they were really assigned to the ship. It was an order from the Admiralty."

"Well, such suspicions seem canny, but I dinnae think I have any information that can help ye. Neither name is familiar to me."

West nodded; he thought about using physical description in case the names were assumed, but Nile Carrin was such a nondescript man that it hardly seemed possible. Instead, he asked, "And do you know anything of the Blue Isles?"

Ardshiel's gaze suddenly seemed far away. "I have heard the Chinese speak of them as if they are Paradise. I have never spoken to anyone who has really been there, though. I hope that we meet again after your voyage. I would like to hear of the Blue Isles from a man who has looked on them with mortal eyes."

"It sounds a bit like the stories of mermaids, in a way," said Kenmare. "You know, how some claim they are no more than myths, while others swear they have seen them."

"Yes, that has always been a grand debate, has it not?" said Ardshiel.

West smiled. "I believe in mermaids, myself, though I have never seen one. Columbus reported seeing them in the West Indies, you know. Many reputable men have told of sightings. Of course, some believe that these are merely marine mammals similar to the poor creatures that Steller discovered; but how likely a mistake is that?"

"Aye, I have heard tales of mermaids from, as ye say, reputable men," said Ardshiel. "Yet until I see one for myself I will nae be sure. How could a creature that is so very like a human, in a way, survive in the ocean?"

"Well, one of the great questions about mermaids is whether they breathe air, or whether they somehow have gills like fish. Some of the sightings have taken place while they are on rocks, leading to the thought that they do require air; however, it is also possible that they simply enjoy the sun. Yet in either case, the pattern of life is there. There are creatures living in the sea that require air, and there are those that do not."

"I suppose so."

"Then, too, think of the beauty of such a life. We sail across the surface of the ocean and find great wonders. Yet there are surely wonders that we sail right over without ever imagining. Mermaids would be able to explore the blue depths of the ocean and find the unknown treasures that it keeps." West finished his *gaoliang*.

"Fascinating. Well, then, Captain, perhaps ye will see mermaids on your voyage. For now, will ye have some more *gaoliang*?"

"No thank you, Captain, I think a little *gaoliang* goes a long way. Let me thank you for all your hospitality, though. It has been a most pleasant evening."

"Well, we had to celebrate our victory, did we not? I look forward to exploring the pirate ship tomorrow."

West and Kenmare made their way back to the *Promise* through a downpour of rain; it had already been going on for an hour, and there seemed no point in waiting for it to pass. And indeed, the rain continued well into the night, and the dawn appeared as a finger of yellow reaching through grey curtains.

West drank his coffee in his cabin, and then prepared to board the pirate ship. He had asked Chang to come with him, in case there was a need for the translation of Chinese writing. He also took an armed boarding party in case of ambush. It was seven men altogether who were rowed over in the jolly-boat, accompanied by another boat from the *Flying Fish* that carried Ardshiel and a few of his men.

The rain had cleared away some of the mud, making the *Jade Shark* more approachable, though the ship was still grounded. The ascent up the sides was made with grappling hooks from the boats, and no one succeeded in reaching the deck with clean clothing. On the deck itself, though, much of the mud had been washed away by the downpour. Most of the trees now lay on their sides. Towering above everything else were the four masts with the great red sails. Near the mainmast, West noted a curious feature that had escaped his attention before: a large bronze gong set in a wooden frame. No doubt this was the Chinese equivalent of a ship's bell.

They looked around for a few moments, and then West found the stairway leading down the Yushan's cabin. All was quiet as they climbed down the stairs and opened the door. And although West half expected to find Yushan and some of his pirates waiting in ambush, the cabin was empty.

He entered, followed by Chang and Ardshiel, and looked about. It was interesting to note what Yushan had taken in his flight, and what he had left behind. The ivory miniature that had proven so useful to West was gone, as was the pearl-studded cutlass. The other treasures remained, though, and Ardshiel immediately seized upon the long sword. "This is fine craftsmanship," he said. "I would be pleased to take it, if ye have no objections, Captain."

"None at all. How about you, Mr. Chang? Anything you fancy?"

"No, sir, thank you sir. I am velly humble man." The presence of Ardshiel resulted in Chang's speaking pidgin.

"I have my eye on that silk painting," said West. He walked to rosewood desk. There was nothing on the surface; and as he opened the draws, he found them empty as well. Yushan must have taken or destroyed his papers. More curiously, West realized that even the calligraphy implements were gone. Perhaps they had some sentimental value to the pirate. As he opened the last drawer, there was the faint rattle of some object inside. It proved to be a small ivory box. West reached for it, eager to take a closer look— and for the moment, thinking of nothing except his curiosity.

"Captain, stop!" shouted Chang. West froze and looked up. So did Ardshiel, who was staring at Chang with a raised eyebrow. "Mebbe trap from pirates, velly velly dangerous," Chang added quickly, realizing that the words spoken in alarm had been clear English. West smiled in spite of himself. The second "velly" was overdoing it a bit.

"You think it is a trap, Mr. Chang?" he asked.

Without a word, Chang walked to where the weapons hung on the wall and took down the dirk with the golden hilt. Then he drew the weapon, approached the box, and reached out, using the blade to open the lid. As the lid opened, a needle slid out, its tip green with poison.

"Thank you, Mr. Chang," murmured West.

"You have just saved your Captain's life," added Ardshiel. "I can't say my steward ever did that for me."

"Yes, indeed. I must reward you somehow, Mr. Chang. Are you sure there is nothing here you would care to have?"

Chang hesitated a moment, and looked at the burgundy and gold carpet on the floor. "Rug mebbe is nice," he said, and smiled.

In the end, Chang took the rosewood chair as well as the carpet; West himself took the silk painting of the blue magpies with the bamboo; and Ardshiel took the weapons, the ivory tusks, and the European tapestry.

That proved to be the extent of the plunder to be had on the pirate vessel. Whatever gold and currency they had had been taken with them. Some of their provisions were left, but after the incident with the ivory box, West had no thought of trusting them.

The ship was completely deserted. The pirates had apparently taken no prisoners, and they themselves had all fled to the mainland. West enjoyed exploring the ship. Its interior was a labyrinth of holds. The sleeping area for the men seemed to be toward the stern, and the centre of the ship was divided into areas for provisions and for plundered cargo. The portion of the interior closest to the stern seemed to have always been left empty; there was nothing there except dust, and no trace of recent activity. The same was true of the interior near the bow. West theorized that, given the narrow design of the junk, leaving those areas empty would serve to increase its speed.

When their exploration was concluded, West, Ardshiel, and their men returned to their ships. "Mr. Kenmare," West said as he strode towards his quarterdeck, "heave anchor and take us parallel to the *Jade Shark*."

"Heave anchor!" shouted Kenmare, setting the men to work at the capstan.

As the men began their work, West caught Chang's eye. The steward joined him on the quarterdeck, and West asked softly, "How did you know about the box?"

"I did not know," Chang answered just as softly, "but it seemed a reasonable guess. There is a Chinese opera where such a device is used as a method of assassination. And this Captain Yushan was clearly an inventive character."

"An inventive character who was making one last attempt on my life, in return for the loss of his ship, no doubt. Thank you, Mr. Chang. I made a grave error in reaching for the box with no thought of the peril. I owe you my life."

Chang smiled modestly. "Pleased to be of help, sir."

"Perhaps I should include you in all the boarding parties from now on."

"I doubt this situation will come up frequently."

The ship had begun to move, and now, Kenmare called out, "we're coming up upon her, sir!"

West nodded to Chang, who walked away. "Mr. Rede, prepare the guns."

"Aye, sir." It seemed only a moment later that he added: "Ready, sir."

"Then fire!"

With a clash of thunder and a cloud of smoke, the cannons fired. The scent of powder was suddenly heavy in the air. The smoke made its way up toward the grey sky. Then came the crashing as the cannon-balls struck the side of the *Jade Shark*. This time, it was the ship itself that was under fire— the abandoned ship— rather than the island. The sides were stove in in several places; trapped in the mud as it was, the *Jade Shark* was higher than the *Promise*, and the shots were striking low.

"Elevate the cannons," West ordered, "and take out the masts."

With the next broadside, the foremast came crashing down, the red sails plunging onto the deck. That was the immediate result; but a moment later, the second mast with its jade green banner came down as well, in a motion that began with a creaking slowness but ended with a swift drop. The sails of the third mast and the mizzenmast were tattered from the blast, and there were gaping holes in their scarlet fabric, but those masts remained upright. "Another broadside," said West.

The last two masts fell both at the same time. The red sails actually filled with air for a moment at the speed of their fall and billowed upwards, but they could not arrest the collapse of the masts, and soon masts and sails were tumbling over the sides of the ship.

It was not over yet, though. One of the cannon-balls must have struck a powder-cask. There was an explosion and a blaze of orange fire, as if a volcano had erupted inside the pirate ship. The prow, where the characters of the ship's name had been written in green letters, was destroyed immediately, as was all of the ship from the foremast forward. And from there, the flames spread quickly to wipe out the rest.

When the blaze finally died down, burning itself out upon the marshy earth and the water, the *Jade Shark* was no more. The chatter of monkeys could be heard from the green forests.

XIII.
The Storm

uring the next few days, the *Flying Fish* guided the *Promise* through the Straits of Malacca. Then, Ardshiel bid farewell and turned his ship towards Java Minor. The *Promise* sailed toward the South China Sea.

For the next few days, the wind was foul, and they made little progress; but West smiled to think that the wind was fair for Ardshiel and was bearing him back to Taijung. Then, there was a time of great calm, where there was no wind at all and the *Promise* seemed to hang suspended upon the blue sea. While they were thus motionless, West beheld a familiar but wondrous sight as he stood upon his quarterdeck. There was a great column of water that climbed from the sea to the sky, and beneath it, a glimpse of a vast shape of deeper blue than the ocean itself. A moment later the tail of the leviathan touched the air and struck the calm water, scattering a rain of droplets that glimmered in the sun like jewels. Then it was seen no more.

In time the wind came again, and the direction now was changed. The white sails of the *Promise* billowed and the ship moved forward on its course to the Blue Isles, a course that was drawing nigh to its close. For soon, the *Promise* was within the fair tropic waters of the South China Sea. Holding to a north-easterly course, she would be approaching her destination, and the southernmost of the Blue Isles might be sighted any day.

West set a man to work continually at the leads. He also ordered the men on watch to apprise him the moment another vessel was sighted. He was hoping to meet seafarers who knew these waters and could assist with navigation. The coral reefs were a danger throughout the South China Sea, and especially in the waters surrounding the Blue Isles. West knew that small fishing boats did sometimes ply their trade here, sailing from the mainland of Asia or from the Isles of the Philippines. Such fishermen would likely have some knowledge of Chinese, and therefore Chang could assist with interpretation. He shared the plan with Kenmare, making certain, of course, that he did not reveal the extent of Chang's knowledge of English. However, the seas remained empty of other vessels; and they had to be content for the time with shortening sail to reduce speed and relying on the leadsmen and lookouts to give them sufficient warning of reefs.

As captain of a vessel of exploration, West also took time to carefully study and update his own charts, verifying the ship's longitude with the marine chronometer that he had brought with them from Bristol. Since the chronometer was a new and somewhat untested model, he used the lunar method of determining longitude as well and found a peculiar beauty in it, staring up into the night sky from his quarterdeck and calculating the position of the moon in relation to the stars.

On one such night, he found himself thinking of the music of the spheres that Shakespeare had written about; the music that was once believed to echo throughout the Universe and down upon the deaf ears of sleeping humanity. The waves lapped peacefully against the hull of the ship. West had gone to his bed smiling that night, his thoughts full of silver light and timeless symphonies.

The next morning, as if called into existence by the captain's musings on Shakespeare, the tempest arose. As he stared through his telescope at the glowering horizon, he thought grimly that the *Promise* was a brave vessel, but that the wild waters would soon be aroar.

The sky above was still clear; but on the horizon, massive clouds of black and sable were pressing against each other and doing battle. They seemed to have come into existence, or at least into sight, with great speed; and in the midst of their own battle, they were also moving, and moving quickly.

"It's coming closer, sir," said Kenmare.

"Yes."

"Do you think it's one of those typhoons Mr. Ardshiel spoke of?"

"Yes, I do. Change course, Mr. Kenmare— south-south-east. Perhaps we can avoid the encounter."

"Aye, sir."

The manoeuvre was futile, however. The storm moved more quickly than any West had ever seen. Furthermore, it seemed to have a circular motion, and the wind that it created was rushing back in upon itself. To try to avoid it, the *Promise* was in effect tacking into the wind no matter which direction she sailed. It was no way to flee a pursuer that was soon covering the horizon and most of the visible sea.

"Take in all sail, Mr. Kenmare. And lower the anchor. Riding out this storm will be dangerous enough. I do not want it to cast us upon a reef."

"True enough, sir. It does seem we will have to ride it out, sir."

"Tell the hands to prepare for the worst."

"Aye, sir."

"Oh, and Mr. Kenmare— we must think of the okapis."

"I already have, sir. There are the fishing nets. The okapis are laying down already, sir; no doubt they feel the heaviness of the air. I could order some of the hands to lay the nets over them and secure them. That might keep the creatures safe."

"Indeed it might, Mr. Kenmare. You are a wise man and a good friend. Make it so."

With the anchor lowered, and the masts bare, the ship seemed suspended in the sea once again. This time, though, the waters were turbulent. Soon the wind was howling and shrieking in the rigging. "Sounds like a banshee," muttered Kenmare. West could well understand why the sounds would remind his first lieutenant of the frightening cries of the creature from Irish folklore. Waves began to crash against the hull. And the black and grey clouds of the storm bore down upon them. West watched it through his telescope, then put the thing away as useless. For the storm was upon them.

The wind and the thunder were like the roar of a waterfall. The force of the wind was unbearably intense, and it was necessary for anyone on deck to hold tight to whatever seemed immovable. There was rain, too, coming down hard and fast. At first, the drops could at least be seen, myriad though they were; but then, it seemed that a wall of water was tumbling upon the *Promise*. The men were working the pumps at full force, Kenmare reported, shouting to the quarterdeck where West clung to the rail. "You should go below, sir!"

"No, Mr. Kenmare. I must see my ship safely through." As he spoke, he noticed the okapis laying beneath Kenmare's fishing nets, apparently safe enough for the moment. He hoped they would remain so; yet he knew that the whole ship was in peril.

The sound of the wind became even louder, impossible though that would have seemed, and the waves roared up. The water was grey now, and the foam of the waves white; at first they seemed like grey horses with white manes and tails, and then, they seemed like a herd of elephants, threatening to trample the ship under. At last the waves breached about the ship like great whales, and the *Promise* was tossed about like a cork.

Then, a mighty wave surged across the deck. West heard a muffled cry, followed by a hard sharp sound, followed by shouting. The rain was blinding and he could not see what was happening. The grey water streamed across the quarterdeck, and it carried with it a prostrate figure in an officer's uniform. He looked down, aghast, but the figure was upside down. He could not see who it was and he could not see if the man was alive.

Risking his own life, he reached out with his right arm, while his left arm still clung to the rail. He touched the arm of the fallen figure. The figure stirred and turned over of his own accord, looking up at his captain. It was Teal. His head was badly wounded, and his uniform was stained with scarlet. *"Tulipa clusiana,"* he murmured, and then he went limp and his eyes stared into space. Tulipa clusiana was a species of tulip. Lieutenant Alexander Teal was dead.

West tried almost desperately to find grief in the middle of the raging storm, for he felt he owed that much to the young officer; but it was impossible to feel anything except the rain and the wind that were beating down upon him. A moment later another wave swept over the quarterdeck. West hung onto the rail with both hands and felt himself borne up upon the water and then released. Teal's body was carried into the sea. Until the time— West thought of the words he had heard so often when canvas-draped bodies were lowered over the side— when the sea gave up those dead in it.

Then another wave came, this one striking full upon the quarterdeck, a great towering mass of grey water. West felt as if his fingers were being torn from his hands. Despite the pain, he clutched desperately at the rail. Then he found that he was being pushed backwards by the waters nonetheless, over the quarterdeck. He must have let go of his hold. But no; his burning fingers still clung tight to the rail. It was the railing itself that had broken off. West nearly laughed, madly, like the southern thrush. And then he felt himself dropping through the air. He had been borne over the side. He heard Kenmare cry out, "Captain!" Then he struck the sea and felt the wind go out of him for a moment. But it was not for more than a moment; for in the midst of the waves he reacted instinctively and began to swim away from the pounding hull.

With all his might, such as it was, he swam and then looked back. Yes. He was far enough from the hull. Now if they would just cast him a line. He saw Rede, standing on the sides of the tossing ship. How he was able to keep standing West did not know; he must be hanging onto something that the captain could not see. But he was holding a rope, and he threw it. West reached out for it, but it slipped through his hands. And then he felt himself being borne up, strangely, into the air.

It was as if he was riding one of the great roc birds of Arabian folklore. He could actually feel the air rushing about him. He was on top of another great wave, and there was a dizzying moment of looking out from the top and seeing his ship actually below him. The wave had risen so high that he was at eye level with the mizzen topmast. Kenmare and Rede were small figures shouting up from the deck. Lang was throwing out a line from the bow to rescue someone else, no doubt some hand who had been washed overboard. At least the other three officers were alive, for now. For how long, though? What would happen to his ship? West tried to swim towards it, now, but the great wave was carrying him away from the *Promise*. It seemed that whatever happened to the *Promise* would be happening without him.

For a dreadful moment he wondered if he would be struck by lightning, as it seemed that he was being carried into the clouds. It was not like a roc at all; it was like the fiery chariot of Elijah. The war chariot of Israel and his horsemen. Then came the crest of the wave, and West dropped blindly into the sea with the foam rushing over him. For a moment, perhaps longer, everything went black.

When he was next aware of the water surrounding him he was certain that he had lost consciousness and then regained it. For how long? His entire body was in an agony for lack of air. He had not felt this way since the coast of Andalusia. He struggled against panic and fought to the surface. Then the certainty came in upon him that he would not make it. The wave had plunged him down too deeply into the sea, and he would suffocate before he could reach the surface. That was what was going to happen. He fought on, but he was absolutely sure that he would not succeed. When his head emerged from the water and he gasped to take in air, he was actually surprised.

There was no sign of any wave so great as the one he had been borne upon; but the sea was nonetheless all turbulence around him, and it was a struggle to stay afloat. Then there was a flash of yellow lightning that illuminated the black sky and the black sea. In the instant of its light, West saw a piece of wood floating only a few paces away from him. He made for it, only to stop frozen at the crash of thunder that followed the lightning. He had suddenly realized how much thunder sounded like cannon-fire; and he did not want to realize it then, not with Andalusia so much in his mind.

He sunk below the surface for a moment, pulled himself up again, pressed on, and reached out. The wood was carried away from him by another wave. He caught a breath and kept going. When he reached out again, he was rewarded by the feel of the sodden but firm surface of the wood. He clutched it desperately. It was the piece of a water-barrel, and it kept him afloat. He could breathe more freely than he had since he had been standing upon the deck of his ship. When had that been? A quarter-hour's lifetime ago, perhaps, when the storm was just beginning and the Universe still made sense.

"You have earned your promotion."

Who was that, and what were they talking about? He had just gone from commanding a frigate to commanding a fragment of one of its barrels, and that was hardly a promotion.

"You have earned your promotion to the rank of post-Captain through endurance, courage, and wit. And to speak personally, you have saved my life and my ship. You have my thanks and my congratulations."

It was a voice of memory, a voice had once belonged to Admiral Gervaise Oakes. West wondered if he was going mad. It would be understandable enough. At any rate, this was a better memory to be lost in than some of the alternatives.

"Of course, you will have to bid farewell to the H. M. S. Valiant; she was a fine sloop for a commander, but now that you have made post, you are entitled to a frigate. I mean to see that you receive the Sea Unicorn."

"The Sea Unicorn? I have heard of her, sir. She was sent to discover the Northwest Passage, was she not?"

"Yes. She was a ship of exploration, once. Now she is more likely to be a ship of battle.

"You are to be assigned to the Mediterranean. The Dons may give you a bit of trouble; but you have proven yourself already in the face of peril. I am an Admiral, West, and your superior officer; but I owe you my life for all that, and I will not forget it."

"I will be going ashore myself, Mr. Jameson."

That was West himself, again, but Oakes' voice was replaced by that of Geoffrey Jameson, the First Lieutenant of the *Sea Unicorn: "Yourself, sir? Into enemy territory?"*

West began to realize that he was stunned, and exhausted. He was drifting in and out of consciousness, and in and out of memories.

"Do not be alarmed, Mr. Jameson. I will be appropriately disguised. Allow me to re-introduce myself to you. I am Don Esteban Zapata y Quijana, or at least, that will be my nombre de guerra."

"Your what? And sir, I must protest."

"Duly noted, Mr. Jameson, duly noted. Take care of my ship until my return. I wouldn't want to lose her."

"Captain, there's a boarding party!" West was not sure who that was, but he had been fairly certain this would be coming sooner or later. *There were the Spaniards rushing toward him across the deck, bold and desperate. One of them was cocking a pistol. Thunder. Not from the pistol— from the cannon-fire, all around. The thundering guns. The fires on the shore were bright, and that was good. The invasion ships were being burned. Scotland was safe from rack and ruin. There was a burning pain in West's side.*

"I hereby pronounce you Sir Bowman Balfour West, a knight of the Most Honorable Order of the Bath." The sword touched his shoulders and the red cloak was placed upon him. He smiled weakly.

Then he was home, as he knew he would be. But what was this? *The sound of a young maiden singing.* She had not been there when he had returned home, wounded. She was on the Continent then. Yet here she was, singing about how the sea was wide and she had no wings to fly. This was the past.

What a foolish thought that was. It was all the past.

Then he was not even a youth, but a child, looking up at the light-house. His parents' lighthouse, that they always kept burning clear and bright for storm-tossed sailors. It was a dark night. The light from the summit was just what was needed. It was warm and pure and beautiful.

And there was a seabird looking in at it. A grey seabird with bright eyes, perched on the sill and staring through the glass. He was not throwing himself at the glass, the way birds sometimes did; he was not even beating his wings. He was just staring. No, gazing. Gazing at the light with a kind of longing that even the wisest old seabird could not possibly feel.

Then West realized the illusion. The seabird was merely resting from a weary flight. The longing was something he had himself placed in the scene. It was West who looked up at the light that way, even as he longed for his own ship to sail the ocean. He smiled faintly as another wave broke over his head and he fell into a kind of sleep.

XIV.
The Mermaid

*H*e heard the music before he opened his eyes. Not the roaring dissonance of the stormy sea or the quiet harmony of the calm sea; but the music of a harp.

Then West opened his eyes. He was lying on his side, in a bed, with a blanket upon him. He was looking at a maiden playing a harp.

For a moment, West thought that he had been rescued by a mermaid. She was beautiful. Her hair was a rich chestnut colour and fell to her shoulders. It glimmered in the real sunlight that was beaming upon her. Her features were refined and strangely English in appearance, as if she was a lady from some aristocratic house; yet her skin was deeply tanned, lending her a more exotic aspect as well. Her eyes were wide and bright and blue-green. Blue-green, like tropic waters, West thought. She was wearing a pale blue dress. Then he lowered his eyes and saw that the dress fell to her feet. Her feet— she was not a mermaid. West felt slightly disappointed.

Where was he, then, and how had he come to be here? Who was this young lady, who kept on calmly scattering order into the air? The harp was larger than she was, made of polished dark wood and elegantly curved. She smiled faintly but still did not see that West was awake; she was immersed in her music. Then, as West began to reach out his arm to lift himself up, their eyes met. She stopped playing and West half expected that when the music stopped the whole of the scene would melt away and he would find himself adrift at sea once again. Yet the music of the harp was immediately replaced by the music of her voice, and thus perhaps the illusion was maintained. The moment hung in the air, and she said, "You are awake."

"So I assume," West murmured.

She smiled. "Father, our guest is awake." A man who had been sitting in a wooden chair reading a book now stood up and walked closer to West. Like the young lady, he had aristocratic features that were deeply tanned. His hair was brown, streaked with white, and his eyes a clear pale green. He wore a silk shirt buttoned to the collar, but with no cravat; the garment had a rather Chinese appearance. It was jade green in colour and contrasted with his white duck trousers.

"Greetings, Captain. It is Captain, is it not?" said the man. "Your uniform was quite sodden when we found you, and Paul and I replaced it with one of my old nightshirts. I hope you will forgive the liberty."

He did not explain who Paul was. West glanced down at himself. He was, in fact, wearing a white nightshirt. He looked around at the room. The walls were made of a pale wood and there was a great open window that let in bright sunlight and warm air. He could see flowers outside the window; the blossoms were yellow, blue, red, and purple. Beyond them was a white sand beach. The sea was blue-green now, and calm. The sound of its waves was consonant.

"Who are you? How did I come to be here?"

"As to how you came to be here, you can best tell us. We found you upon the beach, cast ashore during the typhoon. As to who we are, I am Sir Nigel Cove, once bound for the Forbidden City in Beijing as a British Ambassador."

"And I am Amalya. Sir Nigel is my father."

"Amalya?" There was so much to take in that West focused on an apparently insignificant detail: the unusual name.

"My real name is Amaranthine, but that is a bit unwieldy for daily use."

"Amaranthine? The flower of Paradise, that lives forever."

"Yes," she said.

"*Amaranthine* was once the name of my ship. My ship!" West breathed. "Have you caught any sight of it?"

"We have not seen an English ship here in all the time we have been on these islands," answered Sir Nigel.

"There was a dreadful storm— well, you know about that. I was swept off my quarterdeck. I do not know if my ship survived."

"I have no news for you there, I fear. We can only hope that they endured."

"There is the mountain, father," said Amalya.

"What of the mountain?"

"Perhaps from the topmost peak, with your telescope—"

"Ah, you would scan the horizon, as we did during the early days of our life here. Well, well, perhaps it is worth the attempt."

"Yes," said West eagerly, lifting himself up.

"No," said Sir Nigel. "You are in no fit condition to climb a mountain, Captain. You have barely escaped the storm with your own life. Let me bring you some tea, and then we can think of looking at the horizon."

West was about to protest, but a sudden feeling of vertigo convinced him that there was truth in the old gentleman's words. "Very well," he said reluctantly, and laid back down.

"What is your name, Captain?" asked Amalya.

"Bowman West, of the *Promise*. Where am I? You said this is an island?"

"This is the southernmost of the Blue Isles."

"The Blue Isles! It is for the Blue Isles that I was sailing."

"Then you have found them," said Amalya with a smile.

"Yet if I have found my destination only to lose my ship—"

"Come, Captain, do not think of that. Your mind has only just reawakened. Let it not now be troubled."

"My daughter is right. And tell me, Captain, how did it come about that you were sailing for the Blue Isles? Surely it was not to seek us, after all this time?"

"It was not. Indeed, I know nothing of who you are; and I wondered greatly at finding English faces here."

"Yes. You may not know of us, Captain, but perhaps you recall a ship called the *Dolphin*?"

"I do. Believed to have been lost in the South China Sea, with all hands, some years ago."

"Lost, yes, but not with all hands." Sir Nigel smiled. "Let me get you that tea." He left the room.

"So I was washed up upon the shore?" West asked, looking at Amalya.

"Yes. We found you lying on the beach, unconscious, after the typhoon had passed by."

"There does not seem to have been any damage to your home from the storm."

"The typhoon did not strike the island itself this time. The sea was turbulent, and there was some flooding in places. But yes, our home is fine. Captain, if I may ask, you said that you came seeking the Blue Isles."

"Yes," said West. Though there was no actual question in Amalya's words, he understood what she was asking. "I am an explorer. This archipelago is almost unknown to the English, save for its name and something of its location." He smiled. "To the rest of the English, that is."

"We have learned something of it in the last twelve years," said Amalya, returning his smile.

Her father returned bearing a tray that seemed to be made of a richly-hued wood, but which West later learned was made from thick stalks of bamboo. Upon the tray was a small teapot, a container for water, and three round teacups of the Chinese fashion, all made of terra cotta. Sir Nigel placed the tray on a table near the bed, poured tea into each cup, and then, to West's surprise, poured them out. There was a cavity in the tray that served to catch the discarded tea. "The first wash only begins to release the flavour," he explained, and poured water into the teapot again. He seemed to time the steeping of the tea with great care, but it was only about half a minute before he poured the tea into the cups. This time, he gave a cup to West, and one to his daughter, and took one himself. The tea was fragrant, not in a flowery way, but in an almost vegetal way. West held it in his hand for a moment, feeling the terra cotta and breathing in the tea. Then he drank and found its flavour rich and deep and its warmth restorative.

"The people of the Blue Isles take their tea very seriously," said Amalya, noting his look of approval.

"It is quite unlike anything in England," said Sir Nigel. "The tradition of tea here comes from the Chinese. However, my daughter and I have learned to love this tea, as we have learned to love many things about our home."

"I can understand why," said West, looking out the window again. "You were passengers on the *Dolphin*, then, and you were shipwrecked here?"

"Yes. I was, as I said, bound for an Ambassadorship in Beijing. We took transport aboard an East India Company ship, the *Dolphin*. And we encountered a typhoon at sea— I will keep this part of the story brief so as not to bring up any painful recollections, Captain. The ship was wrecked upon one of the reefs, but we were not far from shore, and many of us made it to safety. We were received most hospitably by the natives. My ability to speak Mandarin undoubtedly helped. The society here is much influenced by the Chinese, and most of the people do speak Mandarin. So my daughter and I served as interpreters."

"You speak Mandarin as well?" West asked Amalya.

"Yes; my father taught me when I was a child. I find it to be a beautiful language."

"Many westerners are challenged by the tonal nature of Mandarin," Sir Nigel said. "However, my daughter and I are both musicians, and I believe that gives us a distinct advantage."

"You would think," said West wryly, recalling his tin whistle and the slow progress of his lessons with Chang. He drank his tea and added, "This is an excellent *pao cha*."

Sir Nigel smiled with delight. "May I compliment your own tonality, Captain, despite the mild error in your phraseology. You know Mandarin?"

"Very little. So you were well received by the natives?"

"Yes. Their king is a most gracious man. Their society is charmingly simple yet rich in cultural refinement. The islands are beautiful and they abound in everything that one might need. We have been happy here, have we not, Amalya?"

"Yes. I was fifteen when we were castaway, and I will never forget the fear of that time. Yet it was all wiped away by the beauty of these islands."

"Are the people Chinese? Or natives? I had heard they were a kind of mixture of the two."

"You heard correctly, Captain. A group of Chinese explorers settled here some centuries ago and intermarried with the natives. The Islanders of today are their descendants, both physically and culturally."

"I see." Sir Nigel poured more tea for him. "So you built homes here, and settled here."

"Yes. There were other survivors from our ship, and they have all settled here. They had no choice, of course, but I believe most of them have been quite happy."

"The islands are cut off from the outside world, then?"

"Yes."

"And you survive upon the produce of nature?"

"Yes. There is of course fruit here in abundance. Paul is on a fishing expedition now, along with an Islander friend of ours named Shi-hsing. The Islanders have small vessels that are well adapted for fishing in the surrounding waters, though not for any long journeys." Sir Nigel shrugged. "We built this house not long after our arrival. Amalya plays the harp and paints for amusement, and I am learning the art of growing and making tea. It is not quite an Ambassadorship, yet perhaps that is just as well."

"You seem remarkably content."

"The Blue Isles have that effect on you," said Amalya. "If you are here long enough, you may discover that."

"And who is Paul? You have mentioned him several times."

"He is my fiancée," said Amalya.

"Paul Elgin, is his name," said Sir Nigel. "He is the son of the man who was to act as my principal aide in Beijing. His father, alas, did not survive the shipwreck. But Paul is a fine young man, and he and Amalya grew up together."

West nodded. "I wonder if he will find my ship. I told my first lieutenant to look for fishing boats, as I hoped that we would find someone to guide us past the reefs."

"Paul and Shih-hsing would certainly be able to. Let us hope that they did encounter your ship."

"Yes. My ship." He paused. "This tea has been excellent, Sir Nigel. Your daughter spoke of a mountain?"

"No, Captain." Sir Nigel smiled but raised a cautionary hand. "You are still far from well. I do not know how long you were unconscious, or how long you were adrift before that—"

"I do not know myself," said West, shuddering at the recollection. It was true; he could form no estimate of the length of time he had been conscious while adrift in the storm-tossed sea.

"However, you are clearly in no condition to ascend a mountain. I suggest you eat and sleep. If there is no sign of your ship by tomorrow, you may consider climbing the mountain then."

West shook his head, threw off the blanket, and stood up. And at that moment he realized that he would never make it to the top of the mountain, or perhaps even to the foot, without losing consciousness again. He lay back upon the bed with a self-mocking smile. "You are right, of course, Sir Nigel."

"Yes. Allow me to bring you some fruit, Captain."

He returned with a fresh mango that West found delicious, as well as some small, round fruit with a fibrous brown shell. "These are lychee nuts. They are a local favourite."

West felt the shell in his hand. "You peel this away?"

"Yes, and you eat the fruit within."

The fruit inside the brown shell was white and moist. The flavour was bittersweet; there was a sugary quality to it, but the tang of bitterness was there at the same time.

"The Islanders say that if you eat too many lychees, they make you feel warm."

"Why?"

"I do not know. Fresh lychees do not taste like any other fruit, so perhaps they do not affect you the same way, either."

"Fascinating." He paused. "Sir Nigel, Amalya, I must thank you for everything. I fear I have been so overwhelmed by events that I failed to do so. Your hospitality has been quite life-saving."

"You are among friends here, Captain, and you can rest here undisturbed," said Amalya. West finished the lychees and felt, not warm, but sleepy.

"Thank you," he said again.

"And now you must sleep again, Captain," said Sir Nigel.

"I will. You must promise to wake me, though, if there is any sign of my ship."

"You have my word upon it."

"Sleep well, Captain," said Amalya. He lay down again, beneath the blanket despite the warmth of the sunlight, and was soon overwhelmed by sleep.

The next morning— for it was the morning of a new day when he awoke— West felt that the strength was returning to his body; but he was in mental distress over his ship. There was no news. Nothing could be seen on the horizon of the sea, and Paul Elgin had not returned. There was another visitor in the home of the Coves, however; a man named

Ch'en Tsu, who was the father of Shih-hsing. He was the first Islander West had met. He looked as if he could have been Chinese, save for a somewhat darker skin tone. He was dressed in a jacket and pants of yellow silk, and he wore a woven hat of the Chinese style upon his head. It was no easy task to guess his age; he was strong and wiry of build, and his hair was jet-black, but there were whispers of many years in his deep brown eyes.

Ch'en Tsu knew no English, but spoke freely to the Coves in Mandarin. Sir Nigel seemed almost to have forgotten that West did not know the language, but Amalya translated while the four of them drank tea.

"He offers you greetings, Captain, and hopes you have returned to health; but he has seen nothing of your ship."

"Please give him my greetings and thanks," said West, attempting to conceal his disappointment.

A few minutes later, Amalya said, "he is concerned about his son, and about Paul. They were not expected to be gone this long."

"I see. You must be worried, as well, then."

"Not so much as he is. You see, I know that my Paul is something of an explorer himself. He is quite capable of taking a long and unexpected route home because some area of the islands, or some sight upon the seas, stirred his curiosity."

"I understand."

"I rather thought you would. Ch'en Tsu is worried because he thinks that his own son, Shih-hsing, is not like that. I do not think he realizes that Paul could talk him into many an adventure that Shih-hsing himself would not consider." She smiled.

"Amalya, yesterday you and your father spoke of a mountain that commands a fine view of the sea. I would like to climb it today. Given his concerns— unfounded though they surely are— perhaps Ch'en Tsu would wish to accompany me."

"I am sure he will. And I will come, as well. I am not worried about Paul, but . . . It will do no harm to look out. Besides, the mountain is very beautiful." She paused, and then began to speak to Ch'en Tsu in Mandarin.

The arrangements for the journey were soon made. After finishing their tea and partaking of a hasty breakfast of fruit, Ch'en Tsu, West, and Amalya set out for the mountain. Sir Nigel bid them a warm farewell and set about tending the extensive tea gardens that surrounded his house.

The mountain could be seen as soon as they stepped out of the door; indeed, it was not far from the dwelling of the Coves. The three companions walked through the gardens and along the beach and soon came to its foot. "It is called the Mountain of the Horizon," said Amalya, "because of the view that it offers." It was a solitary peak near the edge of the sea. On the seaward side, it took the form of a rocky cliff; but on the landward side, the slope was more gradual, and the mountain was covered with lush green vegetation.

They began the upward trek. West realized that, since they had to ascend on the landward side, the sea would be hidden from their view until they reached the top. The ship might well be within sight when they arrived at the summit, not only because of the vantage provided, but simply because of the passage of time. In a way, the future was behind them, as the Chinese said, while also being ahead of them. Or perhaps his thoughts were still muddled.

"So tell me, Captain West, where else has your ship sailed?"

West smiled and spoke of the voyage of the *Promise*: the grey waters of Bristol harbour; the stony slopes of St. Helena; the savannahs and water holes of East Africa; the marketplaces of India; the jungles of Tai-jung. "I have wandered and wondered far," he said with a smile.

Amalya listened eagerly and asked many questions. "I have lived upon these isles since I was fifteen years old," she said at last. "They are wondrously beautiful; yet it is good to hear of distant lands, too."

West smiled. "To me, this is a distant land. Did you spend your childhood in England, then? Your voice is English."

"Yes, I grew up in London, and on an estate in Hampshire. I was educated as— well, as the daughter of Sir Nigel Cove was expected to be. And I have spent most of my life far from the places where Greek and Latin are quoted over black tea and proper British etiquette must be maintained at all times. It is a good thing that my father taught me Li Po as well as Horace." Her voice had a lilting quality, not only by virtue of its sound but because of the trace of humour that caressed each word.

"I have learned some Li Po myself," said West, "and one verse, I think, applies well to the household of the Coves:

Why do I live in the green mountains?
I laugh and answer not.
My soul is serene.

"For it seems to me that, curious though you may be about other lands, you have no thought of being rescued."

"Rescued from our home? When we do find your ship— I do not think my father would wish to leave this island. I know I would not wish to. No doubt some of the castaways will wish to accompany you when you leave. I do not think the Coves will be among them.

"So you are right about your Li Po verse. And I have one for you, as well:

Leaving the Emperor's city crowned with clouds
My skiff has sailed a thousand miles through mountains in a day.
With the monkeys' farewells the riverbanks are loud
And I have left ten thousand mountains far away.

"It is one of Li Po's traveller's songs, you see, and so, I think, a fit song for an explorer."

"I think so too. Is it not a Chinese proverb that teaches us that a good traveller has no fixed destination and is not intent on arriving?"

"You know your Chinese poets, Captain."

"I have friends who know them well."

The climb up the mountain was beautiful. The jungle was a deep green, full of ancient trees, giant ferns, and thick groves of bamboo. There was a trail leading up the mountain; if there had not been, it would have taken forever to get through. Bright copper sunlight shone down upon them whenever there was a break in the foliage. Streams of water were flowing through the jungle as well; once, they crossed a wooden bridge over a rushing brown stream. The chorus of insects was as loud as it had been in Taijung; and the chatter of monkeys from the canopy seemed to echo Amalya's poem.

West was not sure how long it took them to reach the summit; it was hard to keep track of time in such a place, perhaps because it seemed quite useless to do so. The jungle and the ocean were the oldest environments on earth, and the most full of life. Yet reach the summit they did, and they looked out upon the sea. And there it was, beyond denial even to the naked eye: the *Promise*. It was sailing toward the shore.

After a moment of pure joy and relief, West wondered about the coral reefs. But Amalya took out a silver telescope that her father had given her to take on the journey. She stared at the ship and said, "I can see Paul and Shih-hsing on the deck. They will guide your ship safely to shore." She spoke some words of Mandarin to Ch'en Tsu, and for the first time that West had seen, the taciturn man smiled.

As West breathed in deeply of the sweet air, he saw something extraordinary close at hand. The small clearing at the summit, where the stood, had a carpet of long grass; and in among the grass there were tiny flowers. He knelt down to look at them. He looked for a long time. Then he looked up at Amalya.

"What are these?"

She smiled. "They are flowers that grow only here in the Blue Isles."

"The colour—"

"Yes. It is a new colour."

The colour was like nothing West had ever seen, but it was beautiful. He felt like a man blind from birth, suddenly given sight and seeing blue for the first time. This was a discovery worthy of any explorer.

"Do you know," he said, "that when I first awoke after the storm, I had no idea where I was— I imagined that you were a mermaid?" He had no idea why he said it, but it seemed the right thing to say.

It was. She laughed delightedly. "That is wonderful, Captain. When I was a child, I always wished I could be a mermaid and live amid the blue waters."

"When I was a child, looking out from my parents lighthouse, I always wished I could see a mermaid."

"Then let us agree that for a few moments, a mermaid I was."

"It is so agreed." It was a perfect moment: the *Promise* sailing safely upon the waters, the golden laughter and blue-green eyes of the mermaid by his side, and the new colour of the flowers at his feet. West felt his voyage fulfilled.

Yet a voyage fulfilled is not a voyage over. West noticed a blur on the horizon— another ship. He asked Amalya for the telescope.

It was too far away for him to sure, but the second ship looked strangely familiar. It looked like a Spanish galleon from the Age of Exploration. West began to wonder if the *Clouded Leopard* had come to the Blue Isles as well.

XV.
Clarion's Return

*T*here was phosphorescence upon the waters as the boat moved toward the *Promise*. Its bright glow was like a reminder of the sunset that had come and gone. It had taken some time, after all, to return from the mountaintop, and to prepare Ch'en Tsu's boat for departure. As for the frigate, it had anchored offshore while the sun was setting, and remained there; Kenmare was apparently waiting for dawn before sending a landing party into unknown territory.

The boat was a narrow vessel, made of light wood, with a high prow. It held West, Ch'en Tsu, Sir Nigel, and Amalya. As they rowed out to the ship, West paused a moment to dip his hand in the water and move it back and forth, admiring the fiery glow upon the sea. There was a silver crescent moon in the sky, amid thousands upon thousands of stars. Yet it was not so bright as to allow the occupants of the canoe to be seen from the ship, and West was able to enjoy the thought of the surprise he was about to offer the lieutenant on watch.

It proved to be Rede, who shouted: "Who goes there?"

West stood up and called out, "Captain Bowman West, of the *H. M. S. Promise*."

The murmur from the deck echoed across the water, and when West climbed aboard, he was greeted with three loud cheers. Kenmare rushed up to him and shook him warmly by the hand, and Rede and Lang followed suit. "'Tis good to see you again, sir! We thought we had lost you, we did," said Kenmare.

West had a moment to smile at his first lieutenant before the realization hit him: Teal was dead. There had been no way he could think of that while the safety of the entire ship was in question; and once he had seen the *Promise* again, he had been overcome by joy and relief. Now, he remembered Teal's death in the storm, and he felt sad to think of the young, newly-promoted officer.

He murmured as much to Kenmare. The old man shook his head in melancholy agreement. "Aye, Teal was a fine young man. A pity it is, to be sure."

"I see that you, Rede, and Lang are all right. Besides Mr. Teal, were there other casualties?"

Kenmare nodded. "Wheeler, Ellis, and Gardner," he said, giving the names of the hands who had been lost in the storm. "I am sorry to see any man lost. But I am thankful that the ship survived, sir. That was a perilous storm, and no mistake."

"I cannot argue with you there." West looked about him at the three masts that still stood tall with their white canvas shrouds. The okapis were on the deck, as well, safe and sound; and Ch'en Tsu was staring at them with wonder. West smiled. "You seem to have brought the *Promise* through in fine condition, though, Mr. Kenmare."

"Well, our anchor held, and the storm passed us by in due course. We have had some time since then to get shipshape again. But, Captain—" he broke off and clutched West's arm, "it is good to see you! After we found these fishermen, sir, I made course for shore, hoping you might have been washed up upon the islands. Was that what happened, then?"

West raised an eyebrow at the sight of Kenmare, Rede, and Lang gathered around him, eager to hear his story. "Yes, and I was found and cared for by these good people. Let me introduce you to Sir Nigel Cove, his daughter Amalya, and Ch'en Tsu. You doubtless know who they are, since you yourselves encountered Paul Elgin and Ch'en Shih-shing."

"Yes, and they guided us through the reefs to this anchorage," said Kenmare. He introduced a young Islander and a young Englishman; the latter had embraced Amalya and shook hands with Sir Nigel, and now, he shook hands with West. Paul seemed to be in his late twenties, about Amalya's age. His greeting was warm, and he at once seemed to be someone who was friendly and quick to laugh, with an open face and a youthful light in his eyes. West liked him at once and felt a peculiar mixture of relief and melancholy; relief that Amalya seemed to have found a suitable match rather than an unsuitable one, and melancholy in knowing that his own moment with her had come and gone and would not return. Yet for an explorer, perhaps that was just as well.

"Now, Mr. Kenmare, what can you tell me of this ship that seems to be coming towards us?"

"Well, Captain, not very much. We spied it early today, as we came into shore. And it does seem to be following us. It is too far off, though, for us to make out."

"I am sure that was their idea. I observed it from a somewhat higher vantage point today, and I believe I may have recognized the ship. Recognized it as an old enemy— the *Clouded Leopard*."

"The pirate ship from St. Helena?" broke in Rede. "They've certainly come a long way."

"So have we, Mr. Rede."

"Yes, but we're explorers. Why would pirates make such a long journey?"

"You'd think there was something left in the Atlantic to pillage," added Lang.

"You may remember that their captain, James Clarion, seemed an unusual man. I think he's a man to be reckoned with, and I think he has had a scheme in mind ever since St. Helena. He said something to me, then, about our perhaps meeting again."

"What is his purpose here, Captain?" asked Sir Nigel, a note of concern in his voice.

"I am not sure, but I think I can find out. Mr. Kenmare, please make our guests comfortable. Mr. Lang, bring Mr. Carrin of the East India Company to my cabin at once. I will be waiting for him there." He started to stride toward the cabin, then stopped himself and turned around. "I am sorry to be so abrupt," he said, looking at Sir Nigel and Amalya. "I appreciate all your kindness. This may be my way to repay it."

"Captain, the Blue Isles are a place of peace," said Sir Nigel. "If you can protect us from the pirates, we will be in your debt."

"You will never be in my debt. But I will do all I can to protect the Blue Isles, as I once did all I could to protect Scotland."

He resumed his walk to his cabin. Behind him, he heard Sir Nigel ask Kenmare: "What does he mean about protecting Scotland?" The Coves had, of course, been shipwrecked twelve years ago, and would not have known about how West foiled Count Vega's invasion plan.

West entered his cabin and saw Autolycus, who had weathered the storm with no harm at all. Indeed, the bird immediately began laughing, a raucous and joyful sound. The captain smiled. He found his sword of honour and strapped it to his belt. Then, he picked up his tin whistle, which was on the desk; someone must have put it back there after the storm. He held the tin whistle while the bird laughed; and when Autolycus stopped laughing, West began to play.

He had been playing for only a moment, though, when Nile Carrin knocked on the door. "Come in," West said. Carrin entered and looked at him strangely. West put the flute at his belt with an air of unconcern that was entirely genuine. "Mr. Carrin," he said. Then he called out through the doorway, "Mr. Lang!"

Lang had been walking away, and he turned around quickly and said, "Yes, Captain?"

"Please join us, Mr. Lang."

"Aye, sir."

Lang re-entered the cabin and West closed the door behind him. Carrin said: "Captain West, I am pleased to see that you are alive."

"You may find you change your mind about that in a moment. I know enough about you, Mr. Carrin, so that you may as well tell me all."

Carrin's face remained as inscrutable as ever. "I do not understand, Captain."

"I have had my suspicions about you ever since St. Helena. Now that the *Clouded Leopard* has arrived at the Blue Isles, I believe I understand what happened there. It is all rather convoluted— a great deal of plotting and counter-plotting— but it will end with a simple hanging all the same."

"I did not realize that the pirate ship had been seen here. However, I am certain that you will succeed in hanging its captain."

"I was referring to you, Mr. Carrin."

"Surely you are joking."

"Murder is a hanging matter, even for a representative of the East India Company." Even as he spoke the words, West remembered the calluses on Gilbraith's hands. Yes; it was coming together. He repeated: "Even for a representative of the East India Company."

Carrin rubbed his chin. "Captain, I hope you realize the gravity of your accusation."

"I do. You killed Francis Gilbraith at St. Helena, after he betrayed your secret to the pirates." He drew his sword and pointed it at Carrin with a purposely dramatic flourish. "You killed him with a poisoned dagger!"

"I deny it."

"Very well. If you will not tell the story to me, I will tell it to you." West was growing increasingly confident of his deductions, and somewhat excited. He sat down, not on the chair, but on the edge of the desk, and stared at Carrin like a falcon. He kept his sword in his hands, and occasionally swung it in the air as he spoke to provide emphasis.

"First of all, someone at the East India Company— perhaps you yourself— had obtained a book entitled *Voyages in the South China Sea*, written by an Italian explorer who had visited the Blue Isles. The account told of a great treasure that he saw there: the Pearl of Long Ages.

"When I was given this ship and asked leave from the Admiralty to take her on a voyage of exploration, the Blue Isles was one of the suggestions I raised. I did not know of the treasure; but the East India Company did, and insisted on one of their own representatives. The plan was for this representative to keep the existence of the Pearl a secret even from the captain and officers of the ship, if it was possible; and to find some way to . . . shall we say, obtain it . . . for the Company itself.

"The representative chosen for this mission had to be a man of intelligence and cunning. Experience would be useful as well. Perhaps he was the same man who had discovered the book and suggested the mission in the first place. In any event, in order to add another layer of misdirection, and more effectively deceive the captain and his officers, it was decided that this man would pose as a secretary. An accomplice would be obtained to portray an East India Company representative. He would be briefed on the plot, out of necessity, but the idea was that he would play only a minor and diversionary role. The real agent would be the man pretending to be his secretary.

"I trust you recognize the character of Francis Gilbraith, and the character of yourself. Gilbraith was an actor. You are the real East India Company agent."

Carrin smiled without humour. "You are spinning a fine tale, Captain, but you have no proof of it."

"I am a sailor, and easily convinced by circumstantial evidence," said West, with a smile that did show humour but also showed steel. "I know that when the wind grows fierce it is time to reef the topsails.

"When I shook Gilbraith's hand after he first came aboard, I noted that it was callused. Not something I would have expected of someone as wealthy and pretentious as he seemed to be. However, acting requires more physical labour than many people realize. Aside from the celebrated names of Drury Lane, most actors lend a hand in constructing their own sets and then disassembling them when a run is over. Gilbraith's hands were not hard enough for him to be sailor before the mast, but they were not soft enough for him to be the man he claimed to be. The identity of actor fits perfectly. It also fits with the fact that his so-called secretary is obviously a more cunning person than he is.

"I might also point out that Gilbraith's performance had a touch of cliché about it. I think he overplayed the arrogant condescension of the East India Company representative just a bit. Please forgive my digression into theatrical criticism; but you know that I, too, have played a few roles in my time.

"In any case, Gilbraith was curious about the mission. He borrowed or stole the book about the Blue Isles from you. Of the landing party that was sent to St. Helena, you and Gilbraith were the only ones who knew about the Pearl of the Long Ages. You were the only ones who knew that the Blue Isles held a treasure that must surely be one of the greatest in all of history."

West tossed his sword in the air and caught it. "The kind of thing that would interest pirates, don't you think?"

"You have no proof."

"Ah, that refrain again. Then you do not deny it."

"Of course I do."

West reached into his desk drawer. "I wonder if you're making a mistake at last, Mr. Carrin, or if you are continuing to deny it simply because you see no alternative. The fact is, I do have proof." In one hand, he still held the sword; with the other, he picked up the book and held it aloft. "*Voyages in the South China Seas*, by Nazzareno Primo. Would you like me to show you the passage about the Pearl of the Long Ages? It's really rather poetic."

Carrin was silent.

"When the landing party was captured by the pirates, you and Gilbraith were put in a cell together. At some point, Gilbraith shared his knowledge with his captors— probably in an attempt to make a deal with them. You did not approve of that, Mr. Carrin. Not out of morality, which I imagine is an unexplored concept for you. But you are not one to break so easily. Therefore, you killed Gilbraith in attempt to stop him from giving up the information.

"It was too late, though. He had already given them enough: the story of the great pearl in the Blue Isles. I do have some questions as to why the pirates believed him, but I attribute that to Captain Clarion. He seemed an unusual man. When his henchmen told him about the amazing story the East India Company man had told them before he died, there was something about it that caught Clarion's imagination. What it was, I do not know. But it was enough to bring the *Clouded Leopard* here.

"And that, Mr. Nile Carrin, is your story."

"You have the book, Captain West."

"I have the book."

"Yet that only proves knowledge of the Pearl. If knowledge of the Pearl brought the pirates here, that was Gilbraith's fault, as you yourself admit. The only criminal action in your story is the murder of Gilbraith, and the book does not tie me to that. I have told you that he was killed by the pirates. I stand by that. Even with all your deductions, do you really consider that impossible? Or even improbable?

"Captain, I admit that I had some knowledge that I did not share with you. You seem to have remedied that by breaking and entering a passenger's quarters. No matter. You cannot charge me with murder."

West considered that. As certain as he was about his other deductions, he had to admit, it was quite possible that the pirates had killed Gilbraith. He certainly could not prove otherwise.

"Very well, then. We will leave matters at that, for now. Mr. Lang, escort Mr. Carrin back to his cabin, and place a guard at the door." He raised a hand. "For your protection, Mr. Carrin. We would not want the pirates to capture you again."

"Aye, sir," said Lang, who led Carrin away and closed the door behind them.

West considered the situation. In a few moments, he would go back on deck and make sure that the guests were comfortable. He would ask whether they wished to stay on the *Promise* for the night or go back ashore. Either way had some small chance of danger; but West doubted they would see anything of the *Clouded Leopard* until dawn. The galleon would not possibly dare coming in at night. Indeed, how could it dare the reefs at all? If Clarion tried to come closer he would be putting his ship at great risk. Was it possible he did not know about the reefs? That would be a gift; but no, the coral reefs around the Blue Isles were fabled.

There was still something here that he had not been able to discern. Probably several things, and all of them important. He tried to think back to his parley with Clarion, so as to review everything he had learned about the man; but he was too spent. Any further strategic thinking would have to be put off until tomorrow.

When he returned to the deck, he found his business there to be pleasantly brief. The Coves, the Ch'ens, and Paul Elgin accepted his offer of hospitality aboard the ship. "With a pirate galleon in the vicinity, I think we will all feel safer aboard a British frigate," said Sir Nigel. West offered to give up his own cabin for the night, but Kenmare already had everything arranged. He would give up his cabin for Sir Nigel and Amalya; Rede would give up his for Elgin and the Ch'ens. Then Rede would bunk with Lang and Kenmare with West. "I will simply string up a hammock in your cabin, sir; you will not even know I am there. And that way you can sleep in your own bed; you might need to, sir, after all you have been through."

"I slept quite well at the home of the Coves. However, your ideas all sound fine, Mr. Kenmare. See to it." West returned to his cabin and poured himself a glass of rum. By the time Kenmare entered, he was in bed and nearly asleep. The First Lieutenant set up his hammock quietly, assuming his captain to be sleeping soundly. West did not disillusion him; as much as he liked Kenmare, he was too weary, and overwhelmed with experiences, to want conversation with anyone. Before long the illusion became real; and the captain was indeed asleep.

West had given orders that he was to be woken before first light the next morning, and when dawn came, he was standing on his quarterdeck, staring at the galleon through his telescope. For about a quarter of an hour after dawn, the galleon moved slowly closer to shore. Then, it stopped. The reason was not mysterious. There was no longer even a breath of wind.

Meanwhile, a boat was coming towards the *Promise* from the island. It was similar to the vessel which had brought West from the shore to his ship: a coasting craft, small and narrow, made of light wood and characterized by a high prow. There were four men inside. Three were dressed much as Ch'en Tsu and Shih-shing; they took turns rowing, two at a time. The fourth was wearing a silk robe of bright yellow with a pattern of white clouds. Sir Nigel was awake and on deck by this time, and he identified the man for West. "He is an advisor to the King of the Blue Isles. His name is Lin Mun-lee."

"They must have spotted the ships, then."

"Yes. I will introduce you to him, Captain West. The King has always been most gracious to us and I consider him to be a friend. I am sure you will be warmly welcomed. However, I do not know how the King will react to the news that a pirate ship is approaching."

"Sir Nigel, do you know of a treasure known as the Pearl of Long Ages?"

"Of course." Sir Nigel looked surprised. "It is kept at the King's court. It is the greatest treasure of the Blue Isles, believed to have been discovered by Alishan himself— their great Chinese hero. How do you know of it?"

"I know of it from the writings of another explorer. Do not be alarmed; I am here as an explorer, not a thief. However, I do not think the same can be said of the pirates."

"You think they know of the Pearl as well?"

"I believe that is why they are here."

"That is alarming news. You must inform Lin Mun-lee when he comes aboard."

"I will. You will translate for us?"

"Of course."

"Thank you. Mr. Kenmare, the boat is bearing a delegation from the King of Blue Isles. See that they are piped over the side. They may not be familiar with the custom, but perhaps they will recognize that it is our way of showing honour."

"Aye, sir."

As the boat approached, the men within began to show great excitement. They pointed to the deck of the *Promise* and spoke to each other quickly. West smiled. They had seen the okapis.

Standing on the quarterdeck a few moments later, West and Lin exchanged gracious compliments through Sir Nigel. West explained that he was here on a mission of exploration, and that he wished to discuss the possibility of a trading relationship with the King. Lin was not sure how the King would feel about trade, but he was confident that he would welcome West as a guest and friend. Then, Lin asked about the okapis. There was an air of suppressed excitement about the man, as if he had been eagerly awaiting the moment when he could ask the question.

"He says they were amazed to see *quilin* upon the deck of your ship," said Sir Nigel.

West smiled. "I have brought them across the ocean—" here he paused dramatically and hoped Sir Nigel would do the same in translating his words "—as a gift for the King of the Blue Isles."

When this was explained to Lin, his face was filled with wonder. He bowed low. West reached out and touched his hand, bidding him to rise.

"He says that your gift will not only win you great favour from the King, it will be remembered through the ages as a celestial blessing upon the renowned and beautiful Blue Isles."

"Well, then the trip to East Africa was worth it. Do not translate that." West paused. "Tell him that there is something else, as well— a mutual threat we must discuss." West proceeded to explain the presence of the pirate ship on the horizon. "Tell him that I have battled with these pirates before and know their Captain is a dangerous enemy. Tell him that word has gone out from these islands of their great treasure, the Pearl of Long Ages, and that I believe the pirates seek it."

Sir Nigel gravely translated all this, and Lin's expression turned to one of alarm. "The King will never give up the Pearl of Long Ages under the threat of force. It would be a grave dishonour for him to do so. The Pearl of Long Ages is indeed our great treasure, an heirloom of past heroes and a glory of beauty." Sir Nigel had begun translating literally, without the awkward "he saids."

"I know. Yet the threat of force is indeed what will be applied."

"Yet, you have a great ship of your own, Captain. You say that you have fought with these pirates before. Can you not do so again? I hesitate to ask for more from the man who brings us celestial animals. Yet your ship is powerful. And we are a peaceful people, ill-equipped to defend ourselves."

"I will try to help you. However, the pirate ship is larger and stronger than my own. I do not wish to see your great treasure stolen from you. But I can make no assurances. The future is behind us."

"Yes, it is. We must inform the King of all these things. Will you return with us to the royal court?"

"I will." As West spoke, he felt the wind at his back again. It was blowing toward the shore. He turned around and saw the pirate ship beginning to move.

"I believe we will have another addition to our delegation to the royal court. The captain of the pirate ship is likely to speak before he tries to fight. Perhaps it would be best if he came with us, under a flag of truce. We will all go before the king and see where matters stand."

Lin considered that for a moment. "Yes, that would be wise."

"Good." Although he knew that he himself could not suggest it, West wondered if the King might decide to give up the Pearl after all. If he did, it seemed unlikely that Clarion would harm a blade of grass on the islands. West remembered the pirate captain's civilized treatment of the prisoners at St. Helena. However, he could not count on such a peaceful outcome. There were preparations to be made. "If you will excuse me, then, I must take some precautions in case he does decide to attack." He turned away. "Mr. Kenmare, clear the decks for action."

The galleon was soon close upon them, for the wind had strengthened. And it was indeed the *Clouded Leopard*. But there was no sign of attack. Rather, Crimson stood at the bow with a speaking trumpet, announcing across the waters that Captain James Clarion requested parley.

Clarion was as elegant a figure as ever, with his plumed hat and his coat of burgundy velvet. There was still the same courtly air about his manner and language, and the same trace of melancholy in his blue-violet eyes. "Captain West," he said, standing on the quarterdeck of the *Promise* and looking around him. "I doubt you expected to see me again, though I believe I hinted to you, during our previous meeting, that our paths might cross."

"So you did, Captain Clarion, and now I understand why. You have come to these islands for a reason. Tell me what it is."

"If the gentlemen of the East India Company have been as forthcoming with you as one of them was with my men, you know what I seek: the Pearl of Long Ages."

"I know of the Pearl, and when I saw your antiquated ship upon the horizon, I guessed that it was that which brought you here. Tell me, Captain Clarion, was it Gilbraith who told your men of the treasure?"

"I met neither of the Company men, myself. It was the younger one who spoke; the older objected."

"Yes, I thought as much. And when your men told you the tale, why was it that you believed it so readily? Why was it that you sailed from the South Atlantic to the South China Sea?"

"Because, Captain West, the story was so absurd. If the East India Company man was simply trying to save his life, why would he place the treasure so far away that it might not interest me at all? He would have invented a great pearl in South Africa or perhaps Madagascar. Yet, he chose the South China Sea. That convinced me that he spoke the truth.

"I also made certain to agree to your terms for the release of the prisoners, so as to avoid battle with you. I wanted you to arrive here first, Captain West, so that I could see where you anchored. A seafarer of your reputation would surely find a safe anchorage, even amid such perilous coasts as these."

"Thank you. So once you accepted the story of the pearl, that was enough to bring you here?"

"Do you think I enjoy capturing merchantmen, Captain West? I, who spring from the noble house of— well, perhaps it is better not to go into questions of lineage. However, I can assure you that both my antecedents and my education are of the finest. If I am to be a pirate, I want to be a great pirate, and battle for a great treasure. The Pearl of Long Ages is the answer; it is as if I have been seeking it for many years."

"Well, things are becoming clearer now. But the future is still behind us." West disliked repeating the line so soon, but he wanted to say something that would puzzle Clarion, and from the way that pirate's brow furrowed, that seemed to do it.

At that moment, Sir Nigel walked onto the quarterdeck and approached the two captains. "Captain West, Lin Mun-lee is anxious to join you. I can translate if you wish—"

He broke off when he saw the way Clarion was staring at him. For the pirate captain seemed stunned, and almost stricken, by Sir Nigel's appearance. At last Clarion murmured: "Do you not remember me, Sir Nigel Cove?"

"Remember you?" Sir Nigel clearly did not.

"I was a privateer when we knew each other, in Naples many years ago."

"Of course! You served England then."

"And I am still an Englishman, though my life has taken a different turn. As has yours, it seems. What brings you here?"

"I was shipwrecked on these islands, a dozen years ago."

"I see." He paused. "I was sorry to hear of the loss of your wife." The words were not mere rote; there was feeling in them, and the melancholy came to the surface of Clarion's clear eyes.

"That was twenty-five years ago," said Sir Nigel. "My daughter was only two years old. How is it that you remember hearing of it?"

"Twenty-five years ago. Strange how memory and time play tricks with the mind. But a daughter— I never knew there was a child."

"What are you talking about?"

At that moment, Amalya came on deck and approached Sir Nigel. "Father, I wanted to tell you—"

"Amalya, what are you doing? You should be in your cabin."

Clarion stared at Amalya and seemed far more stricken than when he had seen Sir Nigel. He stepped off the quarterdeck and began to walk toward her. She started to back away, and he stopped. West followed Clarion, watching him closely. Sir Nigel looked appalled. "You scurvy pirate," he said. "Stop looking at my daughter."

Clarion turned his gaze upon Sir Nigel, looking deeply insulted. He did not, however, deign to answer. Then he turned back and stared at Amalya again. There was a suspicion dawning in West's mind.

"Amalya is your name?" the pirate said.

She nodded.

"So like your mother," Clarion murmured. "And yet there is a trace of your father in you, too. Those eyes have a touch of blue in them, after all."

"My mother had grey eyes. My father's are green, and mine blue-green," said Amalya, looking understandably disconcerted. "You knew my mother?"

"Yes. Your father's eyes are, perhaps, not green." Clarion turned to Sir Nigel. "You said that she was two years old twenty-five years ago. Were you speaking precisely? She is twenty-seven?" He turned back to Amalya. "You are twenty-seven years old?"

She nodded.

"Then it is true. It *must* be true." He stepped closer to her and his blue-violet eyes were actually glistening with unshed tears. "Amalya, I do not know how to tell you this, but your mother and I loved each other dearly, though we knew each other for far too brief a time. I have often cursed the fate that prevented us from marrying, and the fate of her death at such a young age. Typhus, was it not?"

She nodded once again.

Clarion continued: "Yet it seems that a trace of what we were has remained upon the earth. Amalya, I believe that you are my daughter."

XVI.
The Garden

"**I** do not understand," said Amalya.

"My affair with your mother ended shortly before her marriage to your father— an arranged marriage which she regarded as a matter of family obligation and not emotion." Clarion paused and turned his eyes upon Sir Nigel, who stood pale and silent. Then he turned back to Amalya.

"My mother would never have done such a thing," she said. "Certainly not with a pirate."

"Ah, but I was not a pirate then. I was a privateer, in the service of the Crown. I scoured the Mediterranean in search of the enemies of England. And in Naples, I found a treasure that neither privateer nor pirate could imagine— your beautiful mother."

"Impossible."

"I understand that you are not likely to condone our relationship, as it was rather outside the law, so to speak. But I give you my word of honour that I would have married her had it been possible."

"Word of honour?" exploded Sir Nigel at last. "From a pirate?"

Clarion turned upon him, his face dour. "I am Captain James Clarion, a gentleman of fortune. I do not need a letter of marque to remind me of the need for good form."

"My wife would never have behaved in the way that you claim."

"She was not your wife at the time. And I can tell you that she loved me." He began to advance upon Sir Nigel, slowly, with the soft footsteps and bright eyes of a tiger. West placed his hand upon the hilt of his sword. "She loved me," Clarion continued, "and swore that come what would, she would never forget me. She listened to me play the harpsichord and her grey eyes were like the rain upon the sea. We were joyful for a time, in the golden sunlight of the Bay of Naples." Sir Nigel looked deeply stricken. Suddenly, a strange expression came over Clarion's face, like a pang of guilt. He stopped speaking and turned away. "No, but you had years with her. She would have come to love you— aye, to love you more than ever she loved me. And even to forget that she remembered me." His voice was low and his eyes mournful, and West had the peculiar impression that the pirate captain was punishing himself in some way. And that was confirmed by his next words: "Forgive me, Sir Nigel. I should not have said so much as I did, not to you at any rate. That may not have been good form."

He turned back to look at Amalya, who was staring at them both. Then, she ran off, weeping, to her cabin below deck.

"Even if what you say is true," said Sir Nigel softly, "she is still my daughter. You cannot know that she is yours."

"The truth of that," said Clarion, "is that none of us will ever know. But I want to believe that she is mine, just as deeply as you want to believe she is yours." He turned to West. "Captain, I have delayed our business too long."

"I must go to my daughter," said Sir Nigel, and he turned his back on Clarion and followed Amalya.

"You are right about at least one thing," said West to Clarion. "If what you say is true— and I believe it is— none of you will ever know who Amalya's father really is."

"Yes. But I must speak now of the Pearl." Clarion's face and voice assumed a steely expression that West realized was completely feigned. "I have come for the Pearl of the Long Ages."

West could not help but smile. "Well, you have at least proven that you are an Englishman."

"How so?"

"Because, Captain Clarion, you have a stiff upper lip. Let me make this proposal. There is a man aboard my ship named Lin Mun-lee who is an advisor to the King of the Blue Isles. You and I will accompany him back to the royal court under a flag of truce. You can make your demands of the king, and you will be given assurance of safe conduct."

Clarion considered that and nodded slowly. "That sounds like a civilized approach, Captain West. You surprise me, however. I would have expected you to attack my ship, despite the odds against you."

"To what end?"

Clarion smiled. "To defend these poor natives and prevent the pillaging of their national treasure."

West smiled back. "I have not ruled that out. But it might be as well for all of us if bloodshed could be avoided. And as long as you are away from your ship, I know that battle will at least be delayed. Oh, my officers will be ready to set the guns blazing if necessary, but you and I both know that the *Clouded Leopard* will make no move until you return."

"How is it you and I both know that?"

"Because you would never send your ship into battle with another man in command." Clarion smiled at that, but said nothing. West was certain that he had struck home. Nonetheless, he was taking nothing for granted, and he had other preparations to make. He and Clarion agreed to a meeting on the shore at noon and a journey to the royal court, during which the truce would continue. Then, Clarion left the ship, bidding farewell with elaborate courtesy as if he hoped to cover over the emotions that he had revealed. As soon as he was gone, West summoned Paul Elgin and Ch'en Shih-hsing to his cabin.

When Elgin and Ch'en left, West passed the word for Lang; and when the third lieutenant arrived, he gave him an order that provoked a look of surprise. "Have Mr. Carrin brought to my cabin."

"Aye, sir," said Lang. When he returned with Carrin in tow, he was more surprised still by West's next order.

"You may go now, Mr. Lang."

"Sir?"

"I do not think Mr. Carrin is going to attack me, and if he does, I have my sword at my side. He and I have some things to discuss."

"Aye, sir."

The East India Company man stared at West silently as the door closed and they were left alone.

"We do have things to discuss, do we not, Mr. Carrin?"

"What are you talking about, Captain?"

"I would think that an experienced Company man like yourself would recognize a strong negotiating position when you saw it. Our earlier conversation was, I trust, helpful in this regard. However, I am prepared to admit that I may have been wrong about you." West smiled.

Carrin raised a grey eyebrow. "You are telling me that you wish to negotiate?"

"Precisely."

"Then you want something from me?"

"Again, you are correct."

"What about your lieutenant? You accused me in front of a witness."

"A witness who was carefully chosen. Mr. Lang is a capable officer, but he is not the shrewdest man on the ship. I can convince him that I was wrong to suspect you of murder."

"It would seem," said Carrin with an icy smile, "that the shrewdest man on the ship is in this cabin— one way or another."

"Perhaps. I am not at all certain of it. But that hardly matters now."

"What is it that you want, Captain?"

West sighed. "Tell me, Mr. Carrin, do you remember the beginning of our voyage? How frequently I had my men exercise the guns?"

"Yes, I remember that daily din. What does that have to do with anything?"

"I did so for a very simple reason. You know about my past, I trust? The injuries I sustained during my battle with the Spanish?"

"Of course."

"This is my first voyage since then. I found the sound of the guns to be unsettling." He paused. "It is somewhat difficult to explain. Perhaps you have heard of such things?"

"I have."

"The frequency of the exercise was my attempt to render myself immune, as it were. However, the truth of the matter is, I am weary of warfare. I do not want command a ship of battle."

"Then what do you want?"

"I want to command a ship, but under my own colours. This is a mission of exploration— a mission that I suggested to my friend, Admiral Sir Gervaise Oakes. He suggested in turn that if I really wished to be an explorer, I should consider turning privateer. He told me that it is the only real way for me to be sure I will not be ordered back to war."

"That sounds logical," said Carrin.

"Admiral Oakes even offered to allow me to buy this ship upon our return to England. There is only one obstacle."

"Money, I presume?"

West nodded. "So you see, I have good reasons of my own to be interested in the Pearl of the Long Ages. I also think I know how I can obtain it."

Carrin's eyes lit up. "How?"

"I will come to that in a moment. However, there is the matter of actually selling the Pearl. It is, after all, an astonishing treasure. I am no merchant, Mr. Carrin. I strongly suspect that dividing the spoils with the East India Company— say, fifty-fifty— would prove to be even more profitable than attempting to sell such a treasure on my own."

"Yes, Captain. The East India Company would quietly contact the richest men in England, as well as some of the richest men on the continent. Before long, we would have started a bidding war for the Pearl. The profits, even divided, would be far greater than you could hope to obtain on your own."

"So I thought. Obviously, though, if I am going to involve the Company, I need a man who would see to it that I did, indeed, receive my fair share. A man who would have the incentive to do so . . . for example, the incentive to avoid a murder charge."

"I think we both recognize where we stand, Captain West."

"Excellent."

"You also said you had a method in mind for obtaining the Pearl. You must tell me what it is."

West smiled. "The okapis," he said.

Carrin blinked. "What?"

"Why do you think we stopped in East Africa to capture the okapis? The Chinese— and the people of the Blue Isles— believe that they are a celestial animal. Well, actually they believe that giraffes are a celestial animal. But the okapis will be close enough."

"And?"

"And what? I am bringing them a *pair* of okapis. Do you really think they will refuse to give me the Pearl? They will be eager to reward me."

"Reward you, yes, but Captain— the Pearl of the Long Ages is their greatest treasure. You cannot think they will simply hand it over to you because you have given them a pair of interesting animals."

"I am certain that they will." West smiled with an air of sublime confidence.

"You must consider alternatives, Captain. I do not wish to sound uncivilized, but surely a degree of force will be necessary—"

"Absolutely not." West glared at Carrin. "I am not a pirate. I am not going to steal the Pearl from these people."

"But really, how else—"

"I have explained my plan to you."

"The okapis."

"Yes."

"And you will consider no alternative?"

"No, and I have no need to. The matter is not open for discussion." He paused. "However, there is one thing that I want you to consider."

"And what is that?"

"Our escape from the *Clouded Leopard*. Those pirates will not simply let us sail off with the pearl. We need to find a way to defeat them, or, better still from my point of view, slip past them."

"Surely that is a matter for you and your officers— a matter of naval strategy."

"Yes, and I assure you that we are considering it. However, you are a shrewd man, Mr. Carrin. You may be of more help than you think— and you certainly can do no harm. Take a look at this chart." He gestured to his desk, where a chart of the Blue Isles lay unrolled. "This shows the coastlines of these islands, including the locations of all the reefs that are so dangerous to mariners here in the South China Sea."

"You have a chart? This is a treasure in itself, Captain. How did you obtain it?"

"From Paul Elgin and Ch'en Shih-hsing— two young men who have sailed these coastal waters and know them well. They were just here in my cabin drawing this up. I am convinced that this gives us the advantage we need over the pirates— navigational information that we have and they do not. If we study the chart, we will find a way to slip past them. And of course, it may have value even beyond that. Take it, Mr. Carrin; I had them draw up several copies. I want you to have one— now that we seem to have reached an understanding."

Carrin smiled. "We have indeed, Captain."

"Good. You can return to your cabin now. I will explain to my officers that there was mistaken about you. And when I return, I will have traded a pair of African mammals for a priceless treasure." Carrin looked dubious at the last statement, but he returned to his cabin nonetheless, and West gave orders to his lieutenants that the East India Company's representative was to be watched, but not interfered with.

The journey to the royal court of the Blue Isles took a full day— from noontide to noontide— and it was undeniably strange. First there was the matter of loading the okapis into the longboat and transporting them to shore. From there, West simply had to lead them, with two lines in his hand, one looped around the neck of each okapi.

West and Clarion had agreed that they would each bring one companion. West chose Paul Elgin for his ability to translate Chinese and for his knowledge of the islands and their court; also, he wanted to leave all of his lieutenants on board the *Promise*, in case his assessment of the situation was completely wrong and the pirate galleon did attack. Elgin was reluctant to leave Amalya, but the alternative was to ask Sir Nigel to do so. And neither West nor Elgin wished to separate the Coves.

As for Clarion, he was accompanied by a scrofulous pirate who he introduced as Mahershalalhashbaz. "How appropriate," said West dryly, recognizing the obscure Hebrew name and remembering that it meant 'Hastening to the Spoil.' Mahershalalhashbaz was a burly figure with a grizzled face and a receding hairline. He wore a scimitar at his waist, and his primary expression seemed to be a scowl.

The remainder of the party consisted of Lin Mun-lee and his companions. They had arrived by boat, sailing along the coast from the royal court. However, extensive travel in small boats was impossible for the okapis. Therefore, the entire party had to make the journey on foot. They travelled along green fields and jungle paths, with the sun bright upon them.

Clarion made a brief attempt to ply Elgin and West with questions about the Coves, but ceased when he perceived that it was not effective. Then, West asked Elgin about the royal court. "It is a place called Vailima," said the young man, "and it is very beautiful." He described gardens and pavilions by the sea.

After that, conversation lapsed; and soon the divided and suspicious party of travellers fell silent, and each man strode forward wrapped in his own thoughts. When night fell, they pressed on. In time, they stopped for a few hours to rest. No one slept. They then continued on once again, into the grey dawn and the golden morning. The sun was high in the sky when they mounted a hilltop and saw Vailima.

Vailima looked like a garden rolling down to the sea. It was surrounded by a long wall that was painted red and bore a roof of golden tiles. The wall began and ended at the sea, and along its length, it curved to separate out a half-moon of land that ended where the waves lapped against the shore. Within that stretch of land there were pavilions, streams, bridges, and fountains, along with many beautiful trees and flowers. As they approached, West found his heart beating with eagerness. He glanced at Clarion and was surprised to see the pirate captain's expression set in a kind of fixed excitement.

The entrance in the wall was a great round gate. West remembered Chang telling him about this feature of Chinese architecture, and calling it a moon-gate. They passed through the moon-gate and into the gardens of Vailima, and West looked about him with wonder. Clarion bent down to smell a golden flower and look closely at its petals. West watched him. When he stood up, there was a faint smile on his face. He caught West's eye and asked, "can a pirate not value flowers?"

"It seems that he can."

West looked about him, fascinated and joyful. There were green bushes all around that bore enormous flowers made up of clusters of blossoms; the outer blossoms were coral-pink, the inner blossoms a bright pale yellow. There were small trees that had been cultivated so that their branches seemed to come in layers, one above the other; and they seemed to bear neither leaf nor needle, but rather soft green clouds. Other trees appeared to be ancient and wise, with richly gnarled trunks. There were large rocks with intricately weather-beaten surfaces. There were bushes that seemed to have been painted yellow, every leaf glistening like a buttercup in a meadow. There were tall trees with striated patterns in their bark that looked like rainbows. There were palm trees with straight trunks and rich green fronds.

West breathed in deeply. The air was rich with the fragrance of flowers, and also with something else. For a moment he could not place it, and then he realized that it was camphor. Some of the trees were camphor trees; one of the many treasures of the lands in the South China Sea. The songs of birds and crickets blended together in the air; and along with it came another sound, trilling like the birdsong, but less

CHRIS FASOLINO

golden and more silver. It was musical instrument; somewhere nearby, someone was playing a kind of flute.

There was a stream nearby as well. It ran along the wall, very slowly; the current could barely be seen. But in time, it made its way to a tiny waterfall and trickled with a peaceful sound into an man-made lake of deep water. The waters of the lake seemed to be a clear blue, but those of the stream were almost jade green. There were great fish swimming in the stream, with bold colours of orange and glistening white. And there was a turtle there as well, looking nearly as wise as the most ancient of the trees. Some of the trees leaned over the waters of the stream as though seeking to caress its surface. The sun beamed down upon everything.

The garden was luxuriant in some places, and in others, it seemed more trimmed and controlled, and pavilions sprang up. The pavilions were in the Chinese fashion, with columns of bold red, and beams painted bright turquoise. The tile roofs were of gold, and they sloped down and sprang up again with an elegant sense of motion. Within one of them, West saw the flute player, an islander in a deep blue robe who seemed too absorbed in his music to take any notice of the visitors. West could not blame him; the melody was intricate and lovely, and full of a bittersweet yearning.

Others, of course, did take notice. They were greeted by a man in a bright yellow silk robe much like the one Lin Mun-lee wore. He gazed in astonishment at the okapis. Then, he and Lin conversed for some time in Mandarin, and the man seemed to become agitated. Then, he regained his calm, nodded toward the group as a whole, and began to walk away down a garden path. "We are to follow him," said Elgin. "He will bring us before the King."

Follow him they did, to a pavilion that was larger than the rest, with a chair of dark wood in its centre. A man with silver hair and bright eyes sat in the chair. He was clad in a silk robe in the bright pale blue-green colour called celadon. Next to him stood a younger man, wearing a robe that was very similar in colour, but with deeper hint of green. Several other men stood at attention around them, holding long, heavy staves of dark wood. At the edge of the pavilion sat a beautiful young woman, wearing a robe of deep blue and playing a zither.

The music ceased as they arrived, and the man in the chair stood up. There was a moment of stunned silence as everyone in the pavilion looked upon the okapis. Then, the silver haired man cried out with joy. The young woman began to weep, smiling through her tears. West could make out the words *Quilin! Quilin!*

The outburst of celebration, however, was quickly followed another interlude of conversation in Mandarin. The silver haired man, the young man, Lin Mun-lee, and the other advisor all spoke in turn. Again, the tone became graver and more serious. Then, at last, Lin Mun-lee addressed Elgin, and Elgin addressed the others.

"You are presented to the King of the Blue Isles," said Elgin.

"The gentleman who was seated?" Clarion asked.

"Yes. He wears the celadon robe that marks him as ruler. The Crown Prince is at his side."

The King began to speak, in a clear voice.

"He bids you all welcome to the Blue Isles. He thanks you, Captain West, for your most glorious gift. You have brought the blessing of celestial animals to the Blue Isles. Your name shall be remembered here with rejoicing for all generations to come. You have brought honour to yourself and to your family. And you have earned the gratitude of the King of the Blue Isles and all his people."

"Tell him that I honour him and treasure the opportunity to visit his beautiful isles, and I was pleased to bring the gift with me."

The message was conveyed, and the King looked West in the eye and smiled. Then he fixed a sharper gaze upon Clarion, and spoke again.

"He says that your demand has been explained to him, and asks if you are determined to persist in it."

"I am. His isles shall be laid waste unless the Pearl of the Long Ages is delivered into my hands," Clarion declared.

"This is a place of peace," Elgin continued to translate. "And the arrival of the celestial animals is proof that it must remain so." The King stepped forward and ran his hand along the side of one of the okapis. The creature looked at him with soft brown eyes.

"The celestial animals will not prevent me from attacking this place," said Clarion. "I have no wish to break your peace. Yet to preserve it, you must give me the Pearl. I have sailed around the world in order to obtain it. It is a great treasure, and I will fight for it if I must."

The King turned away from the okapis with an expression of sorrow. He looked Clarion in the face and spoke. "Must you?" Elgin translated.

"I must. I am on a quest," said Clarion. "Perhaps it is not the most noble of quests, but it is the only one I have at the moment."

"And you, Captain West? They tell me you do not know if you can oppose this marauder?"

"That is true, Sire," said West. "I am fully opposed to his intentions, however, I must inform you that his ship is far larger and more powerful than mine. I cannot be certain of success should we enter battle; indeed, the odds will be against me."

"Then I cannot ask you to enter into battle. We have another way here, a custom that may allow us to settle the dispute. Captain Clarion, would you consent to single combat?"

Clarion raised an eyebrow and did not respond.

The King continued: "Long ago, the people of the Blue Isles did fight battles. Then, we grew more civilized. We learned that, when it seemed a battle could not be avoided, it was better for only two to fight. Many lives were spared in this way. Now, it is rare for my people to meet even in single combat. The custom, however, still exists among us. And if you are a man of courage, it will allow us to settle the dispute without the kind of devastation you are threatening to bring."

"You would risk your treasure on the outcome of single combat?" said Clarion.

"I would. Our cause is honourable, and I believe we will prevail. What of you? You do not have honour in your cause. Do you perhaps at least have courage?"

"It is possible that you are trying to trap me by questioning my courage," said Clarion. "And I admit, it is an effective trap. To win the Pearl through a duel would be a fitting end to my quest."

"Then you agree to single combat?"

"Let us say that I would like to agree. First, tell me this: whom would you have me fight, and how?"

When this was translated, the Crown Prince stepped forward. "I will stand fast and defend the treasure of our isles. I will meet the marauder in single combat, staff to staff."

"Staff to staff?" repeated Clarion, a note of suspicion in his voice.

"Yes. The people of the Blue Isles are trained to fight— those who are trained to fight at all— only with staves. It is a weapon of great force, despite its simple appearance."

"And one that no doubt requires great skill to wield."

"Yes."

"In that case, Sire, I must decline."

"Your courage is not sufficient?"

"My skill is not sufficient," said Clarion. "I have never before fought in this way. I am trained and experienced in battle with sword and cutlass and pistol. A staff? No. Any man you choose would have an unacceptable advantage over me."

"The weapons that you name are as unfamiliar to us," said the King. "Swords we once knew, but no longer. To fight with the weapons you speak of . . . No, the unacceptable advantage would then be yours."

"Then we seem to be at an impasse," said Clarion, "and, uncivilized though it may be, I can only return to the threat of my ship and my pirate crew."

"No," said West.

The eyes of all turned to look upon him.

"I will stand for the Blue Isles, if it is acceptable to the King." His voice was soft and clear. "I will fight on their behalf, that the Pearl of Long Ages may not be stolen from them." He realized that his words were rather dramatic, and that pleased him. He had made the decision, and resolved upon it, at once. Having done so, he might as well sound heroic. "I will meet Captain Clarion in single combat, sword to sword."

The King stared at him. "Then I thank you once again, Captain West. My gratitude to you is greater than I can express. I accept your noble offer."

"As do I, Captain West," said Clarion. "Sword to sword. You are a worthy opponent."

"Then it is so decided," said the King of the Blue Isles. "Tonight, we banquet and we sleep, in peace. Tomorrow, the two contestants will meet in the bones of the whale." West and Clarion both stared at him, wondering what the phrase could possibly mean. "Tomorrow, they meet in combat."

XVII.
The Duel of the Captains

The feast that evening was served in the garden. There was roasted mutton, rubbed with cinnamon and served in a sauce made from mangoes. There were steamed dumplings filled with seafood. There were fresh fish prepared with tamarind and the juice of oranges. There was wine made from green plums, fragrant and rich. The King of the Blue Isles was a gracious host, courteous even to Clarion, and warmly grateful to West.

There was music during the feast as well. Men and women in cobalt blue robes played the flute and the zither and instruments that West had never seen or heard before. The music was fascinating, moving quickly from melancholy to joy to a pure beauty of sound without any emotion that West could detect. The sun sank toward the horizon and bathed everything in warmth and gold.

He wondered from time to time whether this was the last day of his life. He would have little to complain of were it so, such was the beauty around him; and yet that beauty also fanned his own desire to live, a desire that was always bright in West. He wanted to survive the duel.

He did not, however, wish to kill Clarion. And it would not be necessary to do so. The pirate captain was no madman; if he were disarmed and held at bay, he would yield, and West would have won. The question was, how could that be accomplished?

West had little doubt that Clarion was an expert swordsman. He would hardly have agreed to a duel with swords if he was not; and besides, his whole bearing as a gentleman suggested it was so. West was himself skilled, but he was not inclined to trust his skill; and still less was he inclined to trust in luck. What remained, presumably, was wit. Yet how was he to outwit an opponent— and a clever opponent at that— in a duel with swords?

It was while West was considering the problem, as the feast began to taper off, that Clarion approached him. West nodded at him and took a sip of plum wine.

"Captain West, I admire your decision to meet me in this duel," said Clarion. "You show good form."

"Why, thank you," said West. "You speak of good form rather often, for a pirate— if you will forgive my saying so."

"I must," said Clarion after a moment's consideration. "For since we are to meet tomorrow regardless, I can hardly take offence at your words now. However, I trust you have seen enough of me to know that I am no common pirate."

"I have indeed," said West, "and that was very much my point. Who are you, Captain James Clarion?"

The pirate raised an eyebrow. "James is indeed my given name," he said. "Clarion is not really the name of my family. I do not think that I should reveal more than that. It is possible that you may survive our encounter and return to England someday. And it is best for the entire country that my identity remain a cipher. I might even say that to reveal my name, even at this late date, would set England ablaze."

West smiled trying to determine how much of what Clarion said was true. "So you are a privateer turned pirate, with noble relations." He thought to himself, 'and a lost love,' but did not say it aloud.

"That is correct," said Clarion. "Tell me, Captain West, since this is perhaps the last night of one of our lives, have you found what you were searching for?"

"How so?"

"You have travelled far to find the Blue Isles. Are they all that you hoped?"

"Yes, they are a place of great beauty. That is why I am willing to fight to protect their peace. And you— what do you seek? The Pearl of Long Ages?"

"I am a pirate now, Captain West. I must seek some treasure. And as I told you, I would wish for it to be a fabled one. Yet I think, like most men, I do not truly know what I seek." The eyes glittered with lavender melancholy. And the next statement surprised West. "Do you believe in fairies, Captain?"

"In fairies?"

"In creatures of flesh and blood, intelligent, happy, sharing this earth with us, yet not human."

"Well, I believe in dolphins." West paused. "And I believe in mermaids."

"Ah, yes. There have been many sightings of mermaids, some made by men whose word must be taken seriously."

West nodded.

"I ask myself sometimes," Clarion went on, "if there are other islands where such creatures do exist; where fairies fly through the sky and mermaids sing in pale lagoons among strange birds. For there are many wonders in the world, and the map is not yet fully drawn."

"Perhaps one of us will find such a place, one day."

"Stranger things have happened upon the seas." Clarion bowed slightly to West and then walked off into the gloaming.

The King of the Blue Isles had declared that the duel would take place "in the bones of the whale." This proved to be literally true. On the seashore near Vailima was the enormous skeleton of a whale that had beached and perished long ago. Paul Elgin explained to West that the Islanders traditionally used this site as the place where single combat duels would be fought. Its significance was not precisely defined; but it was so obviously extraordinary that it served to impress upon all the seriousness of the duel, and, most importantly, the binding nature of the results.

And so it was that when dawn broke, West was awoken, and he and Clarion were led to the beach. Elgin and Mahershalalhashbaz were with them, and the King of the Blue Isles himself accompanied them, along with his own retinue.

During the walk through the early morning light, West had been silent, his mind full of the approaching battle. Yet, when they trod over the grassy dune and gazed down upon the skeleton, his amazement was such that even thoughts of mortal danger were driven from his mind.

Whatever expectations he had had regarding the sheer size of the creature were utterly surpassed. Its length was substantially greater than that of a sloop; it fell only just short of the *Promise*. Only the bones of the creature were left, and they came up in a great arc, peaking at one point along the back. From there, they tapered slightly forward to the head, from which stared vacant eye sockets. Rows of enormous white teeth were visible as well. In the other direction, the arc became gradually smaller until it reached the white flag of the tail, half-buried in the sand. The bones had long been exposed to the wind and the weather, and they had the colour and the beauty of ivory. The sand upon which the skeleton rested was very fine and pure white, markedly lighter in colour than the bones themselves. There was an easterly breeze that came and went, sometimes blowing the sand and casting a cloud of it in to the air, so that some portion of the whale would seem to disappear for a moment and then reappear again.

Despite the prevalence of ivory and of white, the scene was not entirely unrelieved by colour. The searching eye could look beyond the bones to the blue waves of the sea; for the sea was blue here, a clear bright blue. Once, the skeleton had been a living creature, and the sea had been its home. The waves crashed upon the shore. And here and there upon the sand were seashells; some of them were of a bright purple hue, while others sparkled and glittered with the iridescence of abalone.

The King of the Blue Isles led the way forward, his celadon robe rustling in the breeze as he walked across the sands to the mouth of the skeleton. The others followed. Then, the King turned back and began to speak.

"He is announcing the duel that is about to take place," Elgin explained, "and stating the agreed terms. And he is thanking you, Captain West, for defending the Blue Isles in this way."

West bowed and felt the motion was somewhat awkward. He had been roused from his study of the scene with the reminder of what was actually about to happen. This would be a strange place to die, if it came to that. Far stranger than the coast of Andalusia. Nevertheless, of the two, he was grateful that it was here instead. He had been able to see so much in between.

Then, the King of the Blue Isles drew forth a box from a silk pouch at his side. The box was made of a dark wood, perhaps mahogany. He spoke again. "He wishes everyone to see what the two of you are fighting for," said Elgin. "He is going to show you-"

The box was opened.

"The Pearl of the Long Ages," said Elgin in an earnest whisper, and there it was, already revealed before them.

The pearl was large, but it was not its size that made it marvellous. It seemed to be a perfect sphere, but it was not perfection that one sought or even noticed in gazing upon it. It was the sheer beauty of its colours. Vibrant green— the kind of colour that might appear on the wing of a parrot. Deep gold— glittering in the sun and speaking of treasure. These two colours mingled upon the surface of the pearl. West caught his breath and was reminded of the strangely poetic words of the Italian explorer who had come here and seen the pearl. They seemed suddenly fitting:

The way the two colours merge together, shifting and changing in different lights. In the sunlight they are blinding in their vibrancy; the moonlight, like rich tropical seas; the firelight a warm glow and the starlight softly caressing. Of all the wonders I have seen in my travels it is perhaps the grandest.

The sunlight sparkled upon it now, and the green and the gold were very bright. It looked like a masterpiece from an artist's hand, and it had grown inside a shell. And the shell had been inside the ocean. West wondered idly if mermaids found such wonders and valued them, or if they considered them mere baubles that would only amuse the humans who trod the shore.

The King spoke further words that Elgin did not bother to translate. Everyone was gazing upon the pearl. Then he closed the box and put it away. He looked at West and Clarion. They stepped forward.

"He is asking if you each have your weapon," Elgin said, translating the King's next statement.

In answer, West drew forth his sword of honour. Clarion drew a sword as well, an elegant weapon with a long and slender blade; the hilt was wrought of silver and gold. The King nodded and stepped aside, speaking again and gesturing to the skeleton. "You are to step within and face each other."

West stepped between two of the creature's enormous ribs. Their height and their thickness, along with their colour, made him think of ancient marble columns. Their upward curvature was also reminiscent of architecture, but in a different way. As West stood inside the skeleton and looked around, he thought it was almost like being inside a dome that had no base or foundation. The bones formed a kind of circular chamber, partially enclosed, yet also open to the outside through the gaps between the ribs. Then he looked up, and saw patches of blue sky between ivory bars, with an ivory pillar the size of a tree trunk running along the middle. West thought of the artificial, sandstone ribs that the Italian genius had used to complete the first great dome of the Renaissance. Clarion followed him, and they stood facing each other for a moment.

Each had his sword at the ready. Blue-violet eyes locked with blue-grey ones. Then the King spoke in his clear and lyrical voice, and the duel began.

As the crashing of the waves continued in the background, steel clanged against steel. The two swords met again and again, as blow after blow was parried. It was a challenge to keep one's footing in the midst of the rib cage; there were only the spars of bone to step upon, or else sand. West tried to remain upon the whalebones, leaping from one to the other. Clarion did much the same. Indeed, the fighting styles of the two men were strangely similar; both relied upon speed and agility rather than force, fighting as if they were fencing. The result was that sword continued to ring upon sword with neither man breaking through the other's defence. West had begun the duel wondering whether he would survive. As it continued, minute after weary minute, he found himself wondering whether it would ever end. Perhaps this was the real plan— to trap Clarion in single combat until they both grew old together, exchanging harmless blows within the skeleton of a whale. At least the Blue Isles would be spared further trouble.

West leapt again, scrambling to land upon another whalebone. Clarion attempted to use the moment of vulnerability, but West was now too far away from him; the pirate's sword tore at his uniform but did no more. West found his footing and Clarion had to jump, too, in order to continue the battle. He did so flawlessly, and the parrying continued. Next, West changed his footing again and pretended to stumble, hoping to draw the pirate closer and strike at his sword-hand. Clarion smiled and held back, seeing through the ploy.

A gust of wind came upon them then, casting a cloud of sand into the skeleton. Clarion's plumed hat was swept up in the air and then fell to the ground. West was blinded for a moment and began to panic, but he felt nothing from his enemy's sword. Then he realized that Clarion, too, was blinded. The wind fell away, and both men faced each other, blinking, white sand in patches upon their clothes. Then the duel began again.

"She's beautiful," said West at last, as Clarion's sword met his for the thousandth time. The pirate stared at him.

"Amalya," West said. "Your daughter. She's beautiful."

"If you think to distract me, Captain," Clarion breathed, "you will not succeed."

"I speak the truth. Do you know," he paused, not only to parry a blow but because the words that he had planned out in his head were surprisingly painful to speak aloud. "It was she who saved my life, she and her father. I think she cares for me."

"Impossible, Captain West. She is engaged to that young man."

"I know," said West, sidestepping to dodge a blow and balancing precariously. "She's a woman of honour, and I a man of honour. Yet there was a moment there— ah, well, you are right, nothing will come of it."

"A moment of what?" Clarion demanded, pressing forward on the attack.

"A moment when our eyes met." West met Clarion's eyes and looked straight into them. He wanted the pirate to know the truth of what he said. Then, he feinted, giving Clarion an opening— and an opening, not to knock away his sword, but to strike at his body. West held still for a second, not breathing. He knew that he was risking his life on his assessment of Clarion's character.

The pirate's sword hung in the air, motionless. Clarion was now helpless to take advantage of an opportunity to win that might mortally injure his opponent. What was more, he knew it, and he was stunned by it.

And that was the moment West needed. A quick strike at Clarion's hand, and the pirate's sword fell to the ground. An instant later, West's sword was at his throat, threatening the kind of lethal action that neither, now, would take against the other.

"Do you yield?" West asked.

"Yes," said Clarion softly.

West lowered his sword. The duel was over. The Pearl of the Long Ages would remain upon the Blue Isles. And he and Clarion were both alive. The Islanders began to cheer and the King himself bowed low, but West was suddenly too weary to be aware of anything besides the blowing sand and the sound of the waves and the blue sky over it all.

XVIII.
In Search of the Pearl

*T*he duel was followed by a return journey to the ships. West was eager to get back to the *Promise*, and even more eager to see to it that Clarion kept his word and withdrew with the *Clouded Leopard*.

This time, the trip was far faster. For one thing, they were no longer encumbered, as it were, by the okapis. And for another, the King of the Blue Isles gave them horses to ride back, noting that Elgin could return the creatures at his convenience. West was somewhat surprised to find horses upon the islands, but apparently, they had been brought by Alishan and the Chinese seafarers.

They were unaccompanied, this time, by the retinue of Islanders; and the nominal enemies did not ride together. Instead, Clarion and Mahershalalhashbaz departed immediately for the coast, while West and Elgin took refreshment at Vailima and then began their ride.

West was somewhat anxious about how many of his words Paul Elgin had heard; but he had been speaking softly during the duel, and he doubted his voice had carried to anyone other than Clarion. In any case, he had no intention of bringing it up, and Elgin said nothing about it. The young man seemed as friendly as ever, congratulating West upon his victory and praising his courage in the defence of the Islanders.

When they came to the shore, they were surprised to see a longboat just pulling up to the beach. The sides of the longboat were painted light blue, and the oars were light blue; it was from the *Promise*. Amalya was aboard, along with her father and Lieutenant Lang. They climbed onto the shore, and Amalya embraced Elgin and then greeted West warmly. "What happened?" she asked.

"Yes, sir, what happened to Clarion?" chimed in Lang.

"He lost a duel," said West. "Has he returned to his ship?"

Lang shook his head. "We've been keeping a lookout to the shore, but we have not seen him. The young lady here was anxious for Mr.

Elgin, so Lieutenant Kenmare suggested that I accompany her and her father to Vailima."

"There's no need for that now, Mr. Lang, but I am concerned about the absence of Clarion."

"Then you may put your mind at ease, Captain West," said a voice from behind them. Clarion emerged onto the beach from the undergrowth of the jungle, looking somewhat bedraggled. He was followed by his lackey. Lang drew his pistol.

"What happened to you?" demanded West.

"My horse went lame, Captain, and a single horse could not carry us both. Maherhsalalhashbaz is not a small man. Our journey was therefore somewhat delayed."

They walked across the sands, approaching the companions. Sir Nigel looked at the pirate captain intently; Amalya looked down at the sand. Clarion spread his arms wide, as if to indicate that their coming was peaceful. "You can tell your lieutenant he need not be alarmed, Captain. I have no wish to harm any of you. You fought a fine duel, and though you bested me, I would be proud to shake you by the hand." Having finally approached them, he extended his hand to West.

"What are you doing, Clarion?" West asked sharply. He looked at the pale hand and the silver ring that glittered upon it, and did not take it. Mahershalalhashbaz reached for his pistol. Lang saw the motion and stared at the burly pirate, his own pistol cocked and ready. Then, Clarion reached out his hand, and West felt a sting upon his wrist like that of a wasp. He looked down and saw that the silver ring was stained red.

Lang clapped his pistol to Clarion's head.

"If you shoot me," said Clarion, "I will not be able to administer the antidote to your captain."

"A Chinese pirate's trick, eh?" said West, as his surroundings began to blur.

"Actually, a Florentine assassin's," said Clarion with aplomb.

"Captain, what do I do?" asked Lang in a helpless voice. West found himself quite unable to answer, and in the silence that followed, Mahershalalhashbaz drew his pistol and aimed it at Lang.

"We seem to be an impasse," said Clarion. "I suggest you lower your weapon, Lieutenant. Unless, of course, you wish to trade both your own life and that of your captain for the limited recompense of ending mine."

Then the whole scene faded around West, and he saw and heard no more.

Until he awoke, in the Captain's cabin of the *Clouded Leopard*.

It was, as might be expected from Clarion's personality, an elegant place. As he awoke, West took note of a copper oil lamp dangling from the dark wood beams of the ceiling, casting its warm glow. There was a mahogany desk, with a velvet chair behind it, upon which Clarion sat, studying a chart before him. Upon the desk was a Murano glass vase containing a handful of fresh flowers. There was another chair where Amalya sat with a Stoic expression. West himself had been placed, in something of a seated position, upon a similar chair; but his arms were bound in shackles of iron. The cabin was also adorned with a fine harpsichord and, upon the walls, a pair of paintings. One was a portrait of King Charles II. As he looked at it, West realized that there was a strange resemblance between the late Stuart monarch and Captain Clarion. The other was a small but lovely watercolour that appeared to show an estate in the English countryside. The artist's signature in the lower right corner read *Jas. Clarion*.

"Captain, you are awake!" said Amalya, looking at him suddenly.

"Yes," said West, his head beginning to clear.

"Ah, Captain West," said Clarion, looking up from the chart. "I apologize for the necessity of taking you prisoner. I assure you that you have not been harmed. The poison in the ring is one that I discovered in Rio. It is made from a South American flower, and its only affect is temporary unconsciousness."

"Why have you taken me prisoner, Clarion? Our duel was concluded."

"Yes; however, I have no intention of departing these islands without the pearl."

West stared at him. "Then you will break your word?"

Clarion returned the stare. "I certainly will not, Captain. But you must recall what my word actually was."

West was puzzled by that, but decided he could return to it in a moment. "And what of Amalya?"

"She is my daughter, Captain."

"Lang, Sir Nigel, and Elgin?"

"All quite unharmed, I assure you. Lieutenant Lang lowered his pistol out of concern for the preservation of your life; once that was done,

Mahershalalhashbaz disarmed him, and the three of them had little choice but to allow us to return to the *Clouded Leopard*. Sir Nigel and Elgin were unarmed, after all; and the *Promise* could hardly fire upon my longboat with you and Amalya aboard."

West looked at Amalya. "Your father and Paul must have been frantic."

"Yes," she said, "though I think they knew that Clarion would not harm me. Your Lieutenant was fearful for your safety, Captain, and for mine as well."

"He realized, however, that the best way to preserve your safety would be to accede to my demands. Since I told him that the poison required an antidote, he even assumed there was some urgency to the matter," Clarion explained. "Of course, I did stretch a point there; the only antidote needed was time for you to awaken. Since our arrival upon my ship, I have since been receiving all manner of demands and threats from the *Promise* to return the two of you, but I have made my terms quite clear."

"What terms are those?"

"As I told you, Captain, I want the Pearl. But I will not break my oath. Your captivity is the answer to that riddle."

"How so?"

"I swore that if I lost our duel, neither my men nor I would raise a hand against the people of this island. However, I could swear no such oath regarding your men. Therefore, the terms are simple. I will exchange you for the Pearl of the Long Ages."

"You expect my men to attack the Islanders?"

"I doubt it will be necessary. The Islanders are rather in your debt; they may part with the Pearl willingly; and if not, I am sure only a token show of force on the part of your frigate would be needed to make them understand the situation."

"Captain Clarion, my men will never go along with that."

"Not even to save your life? Surely, Captain, you underestimate their affection for you. I have every hope that your men will come through with the pearl. And once they do, I will return you to your ship, and the *Clouded Leopard* will be off to sea." He tapped at the charts upon the desk. "I have another tactical advantage here, Captain, that you do not know of. Accurate charts of the Blue Isles— showing the locations of all the fabled and dangerous coral reefs."

"That's not possible."

"Ah, yet here they are. They were presented to Crimson by a Mr. Carrin of the East India Company, who is also a guest on this ship. Apparently, he decided to change sides and took the opportunity to slip away from the *Promise* during your absence."

"Carrin? He came here with the charts?" West looked crestfallen.

"Yes. He is most eager for a share in the treasure, and he felt that your rather pacific approach to the Islanders was not quite fitting for the South China Sea. Forgive the pun." Clarion smiled insufferably. "In any case, he came here ready to change sides, and to trade the charts for reasonable compensation. Crimson held him here until my return, and I now have the charts."

"I see." West paused. "I should have known not to trust a Company man. And his share of the profits, should you claim the Pearl?"

"He still lives," said Clarion. "He should have known better than to try and negotiate with pirates; but it seems his greed got the better of him."

"And he knew I would never take the pearl by force." West sighed. "What of Amalya?"

Clarion looked at the girl with sorrowful eyes. "I have been trying to convince my daughter to come away with me," he said. "She refuses to do so."

"I will never leave my father," said Amalya simply.

"And you are convinced that your father is Sir Nigel?"

"He raised me, Captain Clarion. He loves me. He is my father. Besides, I would never live aboard a pirate ship."

"I assure you, you would be treated with every courtesy here. I am the captain and I rule with an iron fist. Every man aboard this ship knows that if he insulted you, he would quickly wish that he was dead, and eventually find that wish granted."

"Nevertheless, I will not come."

"And yet think of it, Amalya— what a lifetime we would have! Sailing to the horizon on either side, discovering new lands and new wonders. Think of what I can show you, my daughter."

"No."

"Think of what I can give you, then. No young lady would ever have the riches you would. You could wear the Pearl of the Long Ages around your neck. You could have gold and silver, jewels and corals."

Amalya cast a proud look at him. "Your first effort was better. I certainly shall not accompany you."

Clarion stood upon his feet. His clear light eyes seemed even more melancholy than usual. "As you wish, Amalya," he said. He strode to his harpsichord and began to play, doing so with great artistry; but no sooner had the music begun, then he stopped, walked back to his desk, and picked up the charts. "I must to my quarterdeck," he said, "to observe the actions of the *Promise*. Is there anything that you need, Amalya, before I leave?"

She shook her head.

Clarion looked at West for a moment. "Tell me, Amalya," he said. "When I have been given the pearl and the two of you are released, which of them will you choose? The young man with whom you were shipwrecked? Or the brave Captain here?"

Amalya stared at him.

"They both seem fine men," he said. "I respect Captain West rather more, having fought against him. Yet neither choice would be unwise. I am pleased, in fact, that both my daughter's suitors are gentlemen."

West found himself full of the last emotion he would have expected to feel, as a captive in a pirate's cabin: embarrassment. Clarion noted his expression and Amalya's confusion. "Ah, I apologize," he said. "I see you never spoke of it to each other. Well, you are both English, so I should hardly be surprised."

"I am Scottish, actually," said West, with a somewhat forced smile.

"My daughter is of course English," said Clarion, "whichever man is her father." He paused. "In any case, Amalya, please know that James Clarion wishes you great happiness." His smile, as he walked toward the door, was undeniably sad. When he closed the cabin door behind him, Amalya and West glanced at each other, and then at the floor.

"It was a trick I used in the duel," West said at last. "I guessed that if he thought you cared for me, he would not be able to kill me. He is no ordinary pirate, after all."

"No one who comes to these islands is ordinary." She looked at him and smiled gently, her blue-green eyes now warm. "I do care for you, Captain. It's just that I could never—"

"And I would never ask you to."

She nodded.

"Well, now that that's settled," said West, "let us see if we can find a way out of here."

She stood up and walked to the desk. "I think I can set you free."

West blinked. "How? Surely he was not so foolish as to leave the key?"

"No, he took it with him. But I can pick the lock, if I can find the right sort of— yes, of course." She stopped looking on the desk, reached up, a drew a hairpin from her chestnut hair. Then she bent over the astonished captain and began to work, her hair brushing softly against his arm. A moment later, the lock snapped, and his arms were free.

"Where did you learn to do that?" he asked.

"There was a wooden storage vault that washed up from the *Dolphin*. I used to go down to the beach and fiddle with the lock, until I figured it out. I never thought it would prove so useful." She smiled. "So what do we do now?"

West stood up. "He has a window. Can you swim?"

"Yes."

"Good. Then we've found our way back to the *Promise*." He went over to the desk and removed one of the heavy, mahogany drawers. Inside was a book— the *Collected Works of William Shakespeare*. He put the book on the desk and carried the drawer over to the window, through which sunlight and blue water could be seen. "Stand back," he told Amalya. He threw the drawer, and the window shattered. "Come!" said West. Amalya nodded at him, climbed to the sill, and jumped through. West followed her, landing at her side in the water of the South China Sea.

They began swimming, side by side, toward where the *Promise* lay anchored, closer to shore. West thought his ship looked like a bird nesting upon the surface of the sea. And he thought she looked most welcoming. Behind them, the galleon towered up from the water, solid and vast.

Within moments, there was someone standing near the broken window, calling out to them. The sound of the shattering glass had of course been heard, and soon the ship would be alerted. However, since Clarion would certainly not allow them to be shot at, the options of the pirates were limited. West and Amalya simply swam on. Soon, they spied a longboat rowing out toward them from the *Promise*. Kenmare himself was aboard, not willing to leave the task of rescuing his captain to anyone else.

Suddenly, there was a sound of softly rustling water near them. For a moment West thought that one of the pirates had continued following them, perhaps with a dagger in his teeth. Yet it was nothing of the kind. A green sea turtle had come to the surface, and he was looking at West and Amalya with wise and kindly eyes. Then he dove beneath the water again. West and Amalya looked at each other and smiled. Actually, West very much wanted to laugh at that moment; he was not entirely sure why. They kept swimming, and reached the blue and white longboat, and Kenmare helped them aboard, his sturdy face full of joy.

XIX.
The Charts of the Blue Isles

*A*n unexpected visitor came to the *Promise* several hours later.

West had informed Kenmare of the developments regarding Carrin and the charts, and he had provided some reassurance to Lang, who was plagued with guilt for having been unable, for the second time, to prevent West's capture by pirates. Amalya had been reunited with Sir Nigel and Paul Elgin. Then, finally, West had gotten some much-needed sleep; aside from the loss of consciousness induced by Clarion's ring, it was the first he had had since before the duel.

He was awoken by a knock at his door. "I am sorry, sir," said Lieutenant Rede, "but Mr. Kenmare sends his compliments, and wishes to inform you that there is a longboat from the *Clouded Leopard* on its way here."

"I will be there in a moment," said West, somewhat blearily.

When he arrived on deck, he looked at the approaching longboat with no little surprise. He took out his telescope and confirmed what his first glance had told him. The longboat had only one occupant. Captain James Clarion was alone, and rowing towards them.

Meanwhile, the *Clouded Leopard* was making sail; and by the time the longboat had arrived at the side of the *Promise*, the galleon had already weighed anchor.

Clarion held up a white cloth as a flag of truce, and was helped over the side. He ignored everyone else and approached West on his quarterdeck, breathing two angry words: "It's mutiny."

"I had guessed as much."

"They want the Pearl, despite my oath. When I refused to lead an attack on the Islanders, they turned against me. The mutinous dregs! I was forced to abandon my own ship to them because they would not recognize the word of a gentleman. Captain West, you must help me to defeat them."

"You want me to go into battle against your ship?"

"I would rather see my ship at the bottom of the ocean than in the hands of mutineers."

West smiled. "Well, perhaps that can be arranged. Tell me, Captain Clarion, were you able to retain the charts?"

Clarion shook his head bitterly. "They made certain to take those from me."

"Excellent."

Clarion looked at West quizzically.

"The charts are false. I was fairly certain that Mr. Carrin would turn traitor."

"You wanted him to come to the *Clouded Leopard*?"

"Yes. I was playing him rather carefully in all of my conversations with him. I left strict orders with my First Lieutenant that Carrin's escape was to be monitored but permitted. My only fear was that he would realize how dangerous it is to bargain with pirates; but as you said, his greed must have gotten the best of him. It did seem to be a powerfully motivating force in his personality."

"Then the charts that he brought—"

"Are quite different from the ones I kept in my own cabin. Mr. Carrin's charts happen to show the location of a number of coral reefs that exist only in my imagination, while regrettably omitting several that exist in the real world."

"Then the *Clouded Leopard* is already doomed?"

"Where were they headed?"

"Along the coast to Vailima."

"Then, yes. We should probably pretend to offer pursuit." He called out: "Mr. Kenmare, order the hands to make sail! We will pursue the pirate ship at your leisure."

Kenmare grinned. "Aye, sir. All hands!"

"And is Mr. Chang about? I could use a glass of rum. Can I get you anything, Captain Clarion? Port, perhaps?"

"Not now, thank you." Clarion was looking at him with profound respect. "Well-played, Captain West."

"Why, thank you. You have been a civilized opponent."

West stood upon his quarterdeck, watching the *Clouded Leopard* through his telescope. He remembered that when he had first seen it, he had thought it looked like something from the Age of Exploration. The strong and towering forecastle, the unpainted hull of dark wood, and the huge rudder were all characteristic of an earlier century. Even the elegant copper wheel had an archaic appearance. The square canvas sails were like great clouds against the blue sky; they were far larger than those of the *Promise*. And from the top of the mainmast flew the banner that West had once marvelled over, and that he was now certain had some connection to Clarion's mysterious lineage: the claret field with the silver sword and the golden flower.

The sun was setting in the east, and a strong new wind was coming up from the surface of the sea. The wind was favourable for the galleon's course. The vast sails billowed, and she moved through the water. Her passage was slow compared to what the *Promise* could have made; fortunately, Kenmare knew he had to take his time in making sail, for they certainly did not want to catch up with the *Clouded Leopard*. However, the galleon did convey an impression of great strength as she sailed. It was almost like watching a slow but inevitable change in the tides.

However, the pirate ship was not really like the changing of the tides, for she was not so powerful, nor was so timeless. As West and Clarion watched, disaster overtook the galleon. There was a sound like thunder, and the *Clouded Leopard* came to a halt. Her stern, which was toward the *Promise*, rose up in the air. The bow had struck upon a reef, and its hull was shattered, and water was pouring in. The sails were still vast and full, but the ship could not move. Confusion broke out upon the decks, and there were shouts of alarm and desperation.

West ordered a course set parallel to the *Clouded Leopard*, one that he knew was free of reefs. His intent was to pick up survivors, something that Clarion did not see any necessity for. The *Promise* quickly sailed to the place West had in mind and anchored once again. West could see through his telescope that fighting had broken out upon the decks of the *Clouded Leopard* now. Pirates were turning upon each other with cutlasses and pistols. West simply waited; he would not risk any of his men by sending a boat over until the fighting had ceased. Meanwhile, he could now see the shattered bow and the blue waters of the South China Sea pouring into the ship. Upon the deck, above the water, there was fire. Someone had broken a lantern in the turmoil. The red flames began to spring along the wood and up the rigging. Soon, one of the sails was alight, its canvas blossoming into a scarlet flower.

Then, one of the pirates— from the colour of his jacket, it seemed to be Crimson— emerged from below decks, carrying a barrel over his head. He gestured to some of his mates, toward the starboard cannons and toward the *Promise*. It seemed he wanted to open fire, and, most foolishly, the barrel he was holding was of powder. Against the railing not far away, a group of pirates were brawling furiously. One of them drew a pistol and fired. The shot passed over the heads of his comrades and his enemies, and struck the barrel of powder.

There were two explosions then. The first was caused by the bullet itself; the second, the one that destroyed the pirate ship, came when the barrel fell upon the deck and rolled into the fire. Then, the tawny flames that were already consuming the sails were themselves enveloped by a vast explosion of white and yellow light. And the blue water kept on flowing and the fire died away and the sea claimed what was left. The *Clouded Leopard* was gone. The pirate crew was in Davy Jones' locker.

And the seabirds called to one another above the now still water.

XX.
The Explorer

West and Amalya were on the quarterdeck, with Kenmare, some hours later. Night had fallen, and the stars were very clear and white, and the moon was silver. The waves lapped against the side of the *Promise* as she lay at anchor.

"I am somewhat concerned for Captain Clarion," said Amalya to West, softly.

"I understand," answered West.

"I realize you had no choice but to take him prisoner," she went on. "But I do not wish—"

"You do not wish to see a man who may be your father facing execution. Do not be troubled. I have no desire to see Clarion executed, in any event. I will make certain that he has the opportunity to escape well before we reach England. I was thinking of the Maldive Islands, in the Indian Ocean."

"Thank you. You are really willing to do that? To let a pirate go free?"

"Even though I am in the Royal Navy? I am. Truth to tell, I had hoped this voyage would free me from the Navy."

"How so?"

"I have had enough of warfare, Amalya. Yet I do love the sea." He smiled. "Do you know that these beautiful islands of yours were once known to the English only as a blur on the horizon? That is why they were named the Blue Isles."

"Yes, I know."

"A blur on the horizon, a speck of blue against the blue— and look at everything that turned out to be here." He looked into her eyes for a just a moment. "That is what I want to do, Amalya. I want to be an explorer." He told her about his thoughts of buying the *Promise*, and his Admiral's offer of letters of marque. She looked very thoughtful.

"I hope that you can buy your ship, Captain," she said. "I hope you can be an explorer." Then she left the quarterdeck.

The conversation that night, between West and Amalya, proved to chart the course (or part of it) for James Clarion; for it did indeed happen that the pirate captain escaped, alone in a small boat, in the vicinity of the Maldives. The Captain of the *Promise* opted not to pursue.

Those same moments of conversation also charted the course for Bowman West.

As it happened, the *Promise* sojourned for a happy month in the Blue Isles. And during that time— just a few days after he had given his word to Amalya that Clarion would be allowed to go free— West was given a surprising reward.

It seemed that the King of the Blue Isles had been greatly alarmed by the presence of foreign pirates seeking his people's great treasure. He was concerned— as Sir Nigel later explained to West— that the Blue Isles would no longer be the havens of peace that they had been for so long. For if the world knew of the Pearl of Long Ages, how could the world be kept away?

West could hardly disagree; in fact, he himself had been troubled by the realization that, while Nile Carrin had died in the explosion of the pirate ship, there must be others at the East India Company who knew about the Pearl. They had arranged to place agents aboard the *Promise* in order to steal it; they would hardly forget about the Blue Isles and their treasure simply because the first attempt had been unsuccessful.

It was the King's conclusion, however, that was quite unexpected to West. The ceremony was held at Vailima, in the midst of the gardens. West and Kenmare were there, knowing only that it had been a royal invitation. Kenmare, of course, was looking upon the gardens for the first time; and his blue eyes showed his pleasure in its beauty. The Coves were there as well, and Sir Nigel translated as the King spoke.

The King of the Blue Isles stood in the bright pavilion, wearing his robe of celadon. He spoke of his love for his islands and his people. He spoke of the danger that the Pearl might bring. And he spoke of how, although it would be shameful to have the Pearl stolen, it would be a most honourable act to give it away. To give it to a man who had proven his courage and loyalty in the service of the Blue Isles.

And then the King drew forth the Pearl and held it up glistening golden and green in the warm sunlight, and gave it into the hands of Bowman West.

"With this treasure," said Sir Nigel, of his own accord, "you can buy your ship, and your freedom, as my daughter has told me you wish to do."

West bowed to the King and stammered his thanks. Then he looked at Sir Nigel. Then he looked at Amalya. "Then this is from your hand?"

"It was the will of the King," said Amalya. "But I knew you would be able to put the treasure to good use. There is more," she said, and gave West a cloth banner. West's joy was already pure and untrammelled, yet when he looked at the banner and held it in his hands, he began to realize anew how much wonder there is to be explored in a single moment.

"Your true flying colours, Captain West," she said. The banner had been dyed using the flowers that grew only in the Blue Isles, and it was their colour— the new colour. This would be West's banner, flying from the main topmast of the *Promise*.

He murmured thanks and friendship to the King and the people of the islands, and to Amalya.

"A voyage begun," he said, "and a voyage fulfilled as well."

"You have wandered and wondered far," said Amalya. "I hope, Captain West, that you will have fair winds and following seas, and the heavens smiling upon you, whether you are in the Blue Isles or upon the far side of the world."

West stood in the garden with his friends. He listened to the sound of their voices and the songs of the birds, and the music of the sea that was near. He looked at the blue above and the new colour in his hands.

"If you'll pardon me, Captain," said Kenmare, "I thought this was the far side of the world."

At that, West laughed. It was a gentle laugh, but the sky seemed to ring with it.

The End

CPSIA information can be obtained at www.ICGtesting.com
Printed in the USA
BVOW08s0239270616

453580BV00005B/145/P